EMMA ENSLAVED

By the same author:

EMMA'S SECRET WORLD

EMMA ENSLAVED

Hilary James

This book is a work of fiction.
In real life, make sure you practise safe sex.

First published in 1994 by
Nexus
332 Ladbroke Grove
London W10 5AH

Typeset by TW Typesetting, Plymouth, Devon
Printed and bound by
Cox & Wyman Ltd, Reading, Berks

ISBN 0 352 32922 X

Contents

Introduction

Emma is a pretty and vivacious petite young woman in her late twenties. She is Irish, but is married to a rather dull English scientist who spends a lot of time abroad. They live in the country. She feels that life is passing her by and longs for excitement. Being a natural masochist, she fantasises about being dominated by an older man more commanding and decisive than her husband, John. She finds that Henry satisfies this need, but he is married and lives abroad, only occasionally coming to London.

Emma's Secret World, by the same author, describes how she meets and is seduced by Ursula de Freville, a rich older woman. She is a highly intelligent artist who introduces Emma to a new secret world in which older women enjoy using, dominating and controlling younger ones.

Emma is completely besotted by Ursula and willingly lets herself become her secret slave. Ursula is the most exciting person she has ever met and she is thrilled to be her girl.

However, Ursula demands complete submission. She is livid when Emma defiantly tells her that she has a girlfriend of her own – and even more so when she learns that Emma is still seeing Henry.

Ursula sends Emma to a special school in France to which young women are sent by wealthy women to be taught the art of pleasing their mistresses – and to be frightened off men by their brutal instructors.

She puts Emma into a cleverly designed chastity belt that not only ensures her chastity, but also her purity.

She also takes Emma into her employ, officially as her assistant, but in reality as her servant, so that Emma has no opportunity to be unfaithful to her and has no money of her own.

EMMA ENSLAVED

PART I

ABJECT SUBMISSION AND STRICT CONTROL

1

The golfing weekend – the caddy

Emma was so excited when Ursula suddenly rang her.

It was now six months since Emma had first met Ursula in the health club – a meeting which had completely changed Emma's whole life. Before, she had been a bored young housewife with a dull job, living in the country with a rather boring husband who spent much of the time abroad. Now she was a highly sensuous creature, devoted to Ursula, for whom she now worked and who controlled and dominated her every thought and action – much to her delight.

Ursula had suddenly disappeared off on one of her mysterious visits to her villa in Morocco, from which she would return with a new collection of paintings of beautiful, half-naked women in an oriental setting. She had sent Emma back to her home with instructions to wait for her return. Now she was back!

'I'm spending the weekend with some American friends at a golf course near London,' Ursula announced. 'I shall need a caddy, so I'm taking you with me.'

Emma was thrilled that Ursula needed her again. She would do anything Ursula wanted. But even so, to be a mere caddy!

'But surely, Madam,' said the surprised Emma, 'people don't use caddies these days. I thought they put their clubs on trolleys or take them with them on little buggies and anyway caddies are men, not girls – a golf bag is so heavy.'

'I like a caddy,' replied Ursula in a firm tone of voice. 'And I like my caddy to be a girl and next weekend it's going to be you.'

'Yes, Madam,' said Emma meekly, lowering her eyes. She knew it was a waste of time to argue with Ursula. 'Who are the friends you will be meeting?'

'Never you mind. But make sure you call them Sir or Madam,' answered Ursula angrily.

Emma still knew very little about Ursula's friends. Ursula never told her who they were or how she knew them – she was just kept totally ignorant about them. Was Ursula frightened, she wondered, lest they might try to steal her away?

'Don't expect me to allow you any pleasure,' added Ursula cruelly. 'You're going to need all your strength running along behind me carrying my clubs.'

Pleasure! thought Emma bitterly. Ever since Ursula had made her wear her awful chastity belt almost permanently, pleasure had been replaced by frustration. Indeed purity belt would be a more accurate description, for it was quite impossible for her to give herself pleasure, or to receive any from anyone else, whilst the belt was in place.

And her clever but naïve scientist husband, John, was completely unaware of the belt, for engrossed as he was with his often far-flung oceanographic studies, he had not even queried it when Ursula's lady doctor friend had written to him saying that Emma was still not fit enough for any conjugal relationship. Fit enough! Sometimes Emma wanted to spur him into demanding a fuller explanation – but her fear of Ursula's cane always made her keep silent for, she knew, Ursula insisted on complete faithfulness.

But it was not only fear of the cane that made the masochistic Emma accept the hated chastity belt. It was also the fear of Ursula breaking with her, and that was something she simply couldn't bear to even think about. She was, she knew, besotted with Ursula – for Ursula was the most exciting, and cruel, woman she had ever met . . .

Ever since Emma had been made to wear her belt, all that she ever thought about all day was whether Ursula was going to summon her to London, and if so whether the belt was going to be removed, and if it was, whether she was at last going to be allowed a little pleasure. She could feel herself moist and excited under the belt but was quite unable to do anything about it. It was all so frustrating – and yet desperately exciting.

She also knew that, in turn, Ursula found controlling Emma's sensuality, completely and utterly, to be incredibly exciting as well. The knee chain meant that Emma could not wear trousers or very short skirts, but then, although she herself enjoyed wearing trousers, she certainly did not approve of them for Emma. Nor did she approve of short skirts. She liked to dress Emma in longish skirts, more suitable, she felt, for a servant girl.

So it was that all day, and every day, Emma, wearing a calf-length skirt over her chastity belt, would eagerly listen for the telephone to ring. Now at last it had. Finally Ursula's summons had come, but it did not appear, she had to admit ruefully, as though she was going to be allowed much pleasure!

Arriving on Friday evening at the luxury country hotel, with its own golf course alongside it, Emma, as usual, carried Ursula's luggage up to her suite. She was thrilled when she recognised, hanging from a bracelet on Ursula's wrist, the distinctive little key to her chastity belt. She could scarcely take her eyes off it.

Not knowing whether to be disappointed or thrilled, she found that Ursula had booked a nearby small child's room for her.

Ursula was eager to get on and meet her friends for drinks and dinner and chided Emma constantly as she hurried to bathe and dress her.

'Shall I come down and join you?' asked Emma, greatly daring, her eyes still fixed on the key hanging from Ursula's wrist.

'Join us for dinner! You! Certainly not,' answered Ursula angrily. 'These are intelligent and wealthy people. They won't be interested in a chit of a girl like you. And I am certainly not going to waste an expensive dinner and good wines on you, my girl. Just remember that I've brought you here as my caddy, and nothing else – and certainly not as my companion. You will eat in your room. I'll have some plain biscuits sent up to you and don't you dare go downstairs and try to pick up some men in the bar. Later, I shall send for you to undress me and prepare me for bed.'

Poor Emma felt really put in her place by this tirade. Later on, as she sat in her room listening to the romantic music wafting up from the dining room, and imagining the delicious dinner that Ursula would be eating, she felt even more put down.

Despairingly, and yet strangely excited, Emma lifted up her skirt, under which, in accordance with Ursula's strict orders, she was naked – except for Ursula's damn chastity belt locked round her loins, and for which only she had the key.

It was so frustrating! And yet it was also so exciting having to sublimate her natural sensuality into helpless feelings of longing to serve her Mistress. And then, and only then if she was lucky, having her hated chastity belt removed and then perhaps . . .

Excited at the thought, she looked down at the cleverly designed, heart-shaped, soft plastic artificial beauty lips. Deliberately, they looked more like the pale pink slit-like lips of a little girl than the scarlet pouting lips of a grown woman. But when Ursula held her down under her, wriggling and writhing, they gave Ursula as much pleasure as Emma's own real ones would have.

Moreover, as Ursula would explain to her friends, these artificial lips avoided the nuisance of the girl herself also becoming aroused in the process – for hidden under them was a thin plastic shield, with a long narrow slit, through which her own beauty lips protruded. But these real lips were held hidden and tightly compressed under the perforated plastic shield to which the soft, artificial lips were attached.

She was thus now quite unable to get at herself, even with her little finger or a vibrator. But whilst keeping her completely frustrated, the narrow slit and the perforations in the plastic shield allowed the passage of her liquid wastes. They also allowed her to wash herself and to lead an otherwise normal life.

Angrily, Emma tried to press the artificial lips down onto her beauty bud. But the hard shield under them was cunningly raised over her bud and so, of course, she could feel nothing – nothing at all.

Even more angrily, she tried to get her fingers under the shield but, of course, it pressed tightly against her skin. And anyway her lips, which she was trying to reach, to part, were held tightly compressed in the slit in the plastic shield. Only if she parted her legs wide would she be able, perhaps, to touch herself – but this she knew was also impossible.

Frustrated, Emma looked down at the four little chains that hung down from the belt round her waist: one down the front of each thigh and one down the back. They supported two padded, circular stainless-steel metal rings, each of which went snuggly around each of her lower thighs, just above the knee. The rings did not worry her and indeed she scarcely noticed that they were there. But that was not the point!

Instead, what was so devilishly clever, was that the rings were joined by a short length of light, but very strong chain.

This chain allowed her to walk normally – albeit taking short little steps, like a model wearing very high heels. The chain even allowed her to run after a fashion, again with short little steps – rather like the way a little girl runs.

But what the chain completely prevented her from doing was spreading her legs in the way a girl normally does when pleasing herself – and which she would need to do, to try and touch herself under the chastity belt.

Yes, it was all so devilishly cunning!

Sighing with frustration, Emma looked down at the little padded, stainless steel belt that went round her waist, preventing her from slipping the artificial beauty lips down over her hips. Attached to the front of this was a slightly curved, stainless steel strip which went down over her tummy and which held the curved, plastic strip tight against her body between her legs.

Then, she put her hand behind her and felt the thin, also

curved, stainless steel bar attached to the back of the plastic shield between her legs. The bar ran up tightly between her buttocks, barring access to her other orifice, and on up to the small of her back. Here the top of the bar was locked with a padlock to the two ends of the stainless steel belt that went round her waist. Even if she did ever manage to get hold of the key, it would be almost impossible to get at the padlock and unlock it unaided.

She had learned how to go to the loo despite the bar between her buttocks, and to keep it spotlessly clean and shiny.

Ursula was in a good mood when later she rang for Emma to come and undress her. As Emma took her clothes and carefully hung them up, Ursula, excited by several glasses of vintage champagne, laughingly told her that she expected to bed the prettiest of the American wives before the weekend was out.

Emma felt madly jealous as Ursula described her: 'She's a delightfully naïve young woman – just like you were, Emma, when I first met you. I'm sure she's never been taken by a woman. She's like a little fawn, and obviously bored with her monster of a husband. I'm really going to enjoy taking her. I want you to keep my rubber manhood nicely oiled and slippery, and ready for use, in the drawer of my bedside table. You can start oiling it now.'

Biting back her jealous rage, Emma carefully unpacked the artificial double manhood, Ursula's own private dildo. It was designed for Ursula to strap it around her thighs, so that one of the lengths was inside her, with the padded base rubbing against her own beauty bud, as she thrust into a girl with the other. Below the two stiff imitation erections hung an imitation male sac that could hold quite a large quantity of fluid – usually warm milk.

'You must make sure that, this time, it is loaded with a mixture of warm thick cream and camphor, Emma. I shall want you to be kneeling behind me, pleasing me and I shall want to feel the girl really wriggling under me. Then when the girl and I are both ready, I shall give you the signal to squeeze the sac and shoot the warm, burning mixture into her. I shall want to keep both hands free to hold her down by her wrists, for then she's going to get the surprise of her life, as almost immediately the burning sensation from the camphor will really make her jump about and I shall then have the excitement of holding her down as I ride her! Now are you sure you understand your role? It will be your job to ensure that the mixture really makes her jump when she feels it jetting into her.'

Emma blushed at the thought of being used by Ursula merely to assist her in enjoying another young woman. But she knew that she had no alternative but to do as she was instructed.

Emma helped Ursula into her nightdress and into her bed. She wondered if she would be invited to join her. She could feel herself getting warm and moist under her wretched chastity belt. She was ready to be taken by her Mistress's dildo, and it was extra frustrating knowing that it was not going to be used on her. Her chastity belt was not going to be removed!

'Now go back to your room, Emma, and get undressed,' ordered Ursula, casually picking up a magazine as she lay in bed. 'And come back here quickly. And make certain your belt is spotless. You can sleep on the bedside rug until I want you – or rather your tongue and your deliciously exciting artificial beauty lips . . .'

Repeatedly during that night Ursula reached down sleepily to feel the body of the young woman sleeping on the floor by the side of her bed. Emma did not dare say a word, but each time she raised her hips, offering herself to her Mistress. Finally Ursula snapped her fingers and reached for her whip. This time Emma crawled into her bed, and began to lick her Mistress happily under the chin in a gesture of utter submissiveness.

'Get on your back!' ordered Ursula. 'And put a couple of pillows under your hips.'

Then Ursula mounted the still highly frustrated Emma, gave her a sharp tap with her whip and, ordering her to wriggle, began to excite herself against Emma's artificial body lips. But before long she had moved forward and ordered Emma to bring her well-trained tongue into play.

Soon Ursula reached a highly satisfactory climax. She lay back on her bed, satiated and sleepy, completely indifferent to the fact that Emma was still completely unsatisfied.

'Get back onto the floor, girl,' she ordered.

Next morning saw a still frustrated Emma out on the links with a well-satisfied Ursula and her American friends. There were a couple of married couples and two other unmarried women. Emma wondered if the two unattached women were having an affair and whether it was through them that Ursula had met the others; perhaps on one of her trips to New York to sell pictures.

One of the married women seemed much younger than her husband and was very innocent looking. This girl, a Mrs Guggenheim, must be the girl Ursula planned to seduce, Emma decided. Judging by the way she kept looking at Ursula in an openly admiring way, the task would not be all that difficult, Emma thought jealously. Clearly Ursula had made good use of her time at drinks and dinner last night. She wondered if Ursula had danced with the beautiful Mrs Guggenheim, just as she had danced with her that weekend at the health club, when she had first been seduced by Ursula.

She could see that Mrs Guggenheim with her pretty figure, her expensive clothes, her big innocent eyes and her nonchalant husband, would certainly be a prime target for Ursula.

Ursula did not, of course, introduce Emma to her friends. They merely took her for granted as Ursula's girl caddy.

'Such a good idea,' said the luscious Mrs Guggenheim in her Texas drawl. 'Why, in the States we hardly ever have caddies – and never girls.'

'Give her your clubs, my dear,' said Ursula smiling. 'She can carry yours as well as mine.'

'Are you sure they won't be too heavy for her?' asked Mrs Guggenheim anxiously, as Emma struggled to put both straps round her shoulders.

'Oh no,' laughed Ursula. 'She's a strong girl and anyway that's what she's paid for. Now hurry up, Emma, I don't want to be kept waiting by my caddy.'

Ursula and Mrs Guggenheim strode off towards the first tee, whilst poor Emma ran along behind them, struggling under the weight of two sets of clubs. The knee chain of her chastity belt, hidden under her long skirt, made her run, much to Ursula's delight, with awkward little steps.

It was a long and tiring morning for Emma, as she trotted along behind the two women, weighed down by their golf bags. Not knowing much about golf, she seemed to do everything wrong: handing them the wrong clubs, getting in the way and failing to spot where each ball had landed.

'She's not very good,' she heard Ursula say to the beautiful Mrs Guggenheim as she squeezed the American woman's hand. Then with a knowing smile she added: 'But she does have her uses, my dear.'

As Ursula and Mrs Guggenheim expertly drove their way around the course, Emma could see that they were laughing together in an increasingly intimate way. Clearly they were hatching a secret little plot.

'As we are all going to the theatre in London tonight,' Emma heard Ursula say to the American woman, 'why don't we let the others play by themselves this afternoon whilst we, officially anyway, have a rest and get ready. Then you can come and see me in my suite, to ask my opinion about what to wear . . . We'll have a little fun together!'

'Oh Ursula! You think of everything,' came the whispered reply.

'Very well, darling, I shall expect you as soon as the men have gone out to resume play after lunch. I can't wait!'

'Nor can I,' said the blushing Mrs Guggenheim.

But to Ursula's secret anger it was not to be. Mr Guggenheim proposed that after buffet lunch in the club house, they should all return to the hotel. He turned to his beautiful young wife. 'Then we can have a rest and a little relaxation before getting ready to go to London!'

Emma caught her breath. Ursula would be furious at the

thought of her prey, her target, the glamorous Mrs Guggenheim, being taken to bed by a man instead of by her, even if he was her husband. Indeed she saw Ursula flush with anger.

'But I want to show Ursula my new dresses this afternoon,' wailed Mrs Guggenheim, flashing her big eyes at her husband.

'Oh, you'll be able to do that tomorrow afternoon,' he replied. He pointed to the other man in the party. 'Jack and I have arranged to take a private lesson with the club's professional after lunch tomorrow. So you'll have all the time in the world then to do as you like.'

'Oh good,' cried Mrs Guggenheim with a meaningful look at Ursula. It would be all the more exciting, she thought, to have to wait twenty-four hours before being able to surrender her body to Ursula. But Ursula, temporarily thwarted, was livid.

That afternoon Ursula sent Emma scurrying back to the hotel to run her bath. Quickly she changed into the short little maid's uniform, with its flared skirt, that she knew Ursula would expect to find her wearing, and underneath which she was naked, except for her chastity belt.

But after Emma had run the bath, got it to just the right temperature, added Ursula's favourite bath salts, laid out the bath towels, and gone back into Ursula's room to announce that all was prepared, she saw that Ursula was standing in the middle of the room, stripped to the waist. She was still wearing her long wide pleated golfing skirt and in her hand was her cane.

Emma's heart jumped. Clearly, frustrated at not being able to enjoy herself with the beautiful Mrs Guggenheim that afternoon, Ursula was feeling in need of a little light relief. Emma was only too happy to oblige. Anything rather than being displaced by that rich young American woman!

Emma sank to her knees in front of Ursula. She thrust her head under Ursula's skirt. Ursula was, of course, now naked under it. Silently Emma applied her tongue. She felt the cane tap her buttocks and worked her tongue even more diligently. Perhaps, she was thinking, if she tried hard to please her Mistress, then she might relent, take off the horrid chastity belt and . . .

Suddenly there was a knock on the door. Emma heard the voice of one of the unmarried women asking to come in. Emma froze. She was about to rise to her feet, when she felt Ursula's hands holding her still. She felt a sharp tap of the cane, making Ursula's implied order even clearer. She reapplied her tongue.

'Come in, Elizabeth!' called Ursula.

Emma was desperately embarrassed. She could see nothing from the darkness under Ursula's all-enveloping skirt. But she knew that the American woman would see her naked little bottom poking out from under Ursula's long skirt – and would see the humiliating chastity belt too.

'Oh! I'm sorry, I didn't know . . .' Emma heard the woman's embarrassed voice.

'Don't worry about my girl,' she heard Ursula reply with a laugh. 'She's just doing the job I use her for. Pay no attention to her! What can I do for you?'

'Well,' came the American voice, 'I just wanted to look in to ask you what sort of dress I should wear to the theatre tonight. A cocktail dress?'

'Yes, that'll do fine,' replied Ursula, one hand still pressing Emma's head, under her loose skirt, to her thighs, the other tapping her bottom with the cane. It was a sight that clearly fascinated the American woman. 'Would you like to borrow my girl before you get dressed this evening? Perhaps your friend Betsy might like to use her as well? I'll send her to your room in half an hour's time, shall I?'

'Well, that sure would be a fine gesture,' came the reply. 'I think we'd like that very much.'

'I've had her very expensively trained,' Emma heard Ursula say. 'As you can see she's an obedient little creature, but you need to have a whip in your hand to get the best out of her, as you can tell.'

Emma felt even more embarrassed at being talked about in the third person in this casual and denigrating way.

'And you like to keep her . . . chaste?' laughed the American woman.

'Yes indeed!' replied Ursula. 'Emma! Part your legs a little and thrust back with your bottom to show off your chastity belt better! Now, Elizabeth, you can see better. See those artificial beauty lips? They can give as much pleasure to a woman as a girl's real ones – provided you keep the girl wriggling with your whip – and without the bother of having to take off the belt.'

'Well that's certainly very clever! But actually it was her tongue that I was thinking about more really. Is she any good at . . . performing from behind?'

'Oh yes, I've often made her do that whilst I've been pleasuring myself in other ways. Here take the cane! She's very scared of it and so you'll find it very useful.'

'Why, thank you, Ursula. Thank you very much. You're a real lady! We'll be expecting her in half an hour's time, then.'

Emma heard the door close. Her pleasure and excitement at pleasing her Mistress were replaced by her resentment at her services being offered, without her being given any chance to refuse, to these two American women. She simply wouldn't go, she decided, and if she had to, then she certainly wouldn't make much of an effort to please them. Then she remembered the cane.

'Yes,' she heard Ursula say, as if she was reading her thoughts, 'I shall be discreetly asking my friends, during the intervals at the theatre, whether or not you pleased them. And if you didn't then when I get back you'll get a dozen strokes. I'm not going to be made a fool of! Do you understand?

From under the thick skirt, Emma gave a faint sigh of assent.

'And just to make sure, since they obviously want you to perform from behind whilst they are caressing each other, I think we had better have a little rehearsal. Go and fetch my vibrator!'

A minute later, Emma was kneeling again under Ursula's long golfing skirt, but this time she was kneeling behind her. Ursula was standing with her legs astride. Her skirt was held raised in the front by one hand, whilst with the other she was gently moving the humming vibrator.

'Tongue, Emma, tongue! I want to feel it – and so will they! Just remember those twelve strokes! They're going to be applied nice and slowly and really hard! And all the time we are driving up to London, all the time we are at the theatre, dining out and then driving back here, you're going to be chained to the leg of my bed! You'll be lying there, helpless, praying and praying that I wasn't given a poor report on your performance. You'll be eyeing the cane all the time, terrified lest it is going to be applied to your rear when I get back. So just make sure that you won't be cursing yourself for not having tried harder . . . Now! Try harder now! This instant! Use your tongue, you slut! Now!'

With a cry of deep delight, Ursula fell forward onto the bed. She lay there motionless for several minutes, then her eyes opened. She looked at the still kneeling Emma. 'Just make sure you give them both pleasure like that,' she warned. 'Now take me to my bath . . .'

Half-an-hour later a very nervous little Emma, dressed in just her abbreviated maid's uniform, knocked on the door of the bedroom shared by the unmarried American women.

'Come in, and lock the door behind you.' It was the same American voice as before. She entered, locked the door and stepped into the large bedroom. There, standing and kissing each other, were the two American women, each also wearing only a long wide golfing skirt, just like Ursula. Their lips and their naked breasts were touching as they clasped each other. They were moaning with delight.

For a moment Emma toyed with the idea of pretending that she did not understand what she was meant to do. Then she remembered Ursula's threat. Hastily, and in silence, she knelt down behind one of the women. She put her head under the long skirt . . . A few moments later she crawled round and repeated the process with the other woman, and then back again to the first one.

Not a word was said. The women remained embracing

each other. Nonplussed, Emma thought desperately of Ursula's cane. Quickly she brought her fingers into play to supplement her tongue. She was rewarded by deeper and deeper moans, and then by little cries of ecstasy.

Suddenly, the first American woman turned, grabbed Emma by the hair, and pointed to the door. 'Out!' she said, and resumed her embrace of her companion.

Emma crawled to the door, and out into the corridor. Had she been dismissed because she had not pleased them enough, or simply because they did not wish her to participate in their subsequent lovemaking?

It was a question that she anxiously asked herself over and over again as she lay for all those long hours, naked on the floor of Ursula's bedroom, with her wrists handcuffed round a leg of the bed, unable to sleep because of her anxiety. She could not take her eyes off the menacing cane that hung over the edge of the bed, just out of reach.

'I'm leaving my little dog with three small bowls,' Ursula had said. One contained a little drinking water, one a handful of dog biscuits, and the other was empty. 'In case you can't hold out,' Ursula had explained with a cruel smile. 'I wouldn't want you wetting the carpet!'

The long hours passed slowly. Emma sipped the water, lowering her face into the bowl which her handcuffs stopped her from reaching with her hands. Feeling hungry, she grabbed with her teeth first one, and then another, of the dog biscuits. Finally, very carefully, she positioned herself over the third bowl . . .

2

The golfing weekend continues – the seduction of Mrs Guggenheim

Suddenly the door was flung open. Ursula and Mrs Guggenheim came into the room, arm in arm, laughing and whispering.

Overcome with shame, but also feeling very jealous, Emma heard the young American woman whisper to Ursula.

'Oh darling, if only I could stay here all night. But I must get back to Guggenheim. Even that stupid slob will begin to suspect something if I don't.'

'Waiting will make tomorrow afternoon all the more exciting,' replied Ursula.

'Oh look, Ursula, look at your little caddy!' cried Mrs Guggenheim as she turned for the door. 'Why, I do declare she's wearing a sort of chastity belt! I'm glad we're off back to the States in a couple of days. I wouldn't like to become one of your girls!'

'Oh no,' laughed Ursula, 'I'm planning something quite different for you!'

'Keep it a surprise,' laughed Mrs Guggenheim as she walked to the door.

'Don't worry, darling,' smiled Ursula innocently, 'I will.'

No one would have suspected, when Ursula and the gorgeous Mrs Guggenheim met outside the clubhouse the following morning to play against the other two unmarried American women, that they were planning to become lovers that afternoon.

Emma, however, jealously recognised the signs of

Ursula's rising excitement. Her temper was short, her mood unpredictable and her eyes glinted cruelly as the women climbed on board the electric buggy that they had hired to drive around the course.

'Get off,' screamed Ursula as Emma sat down on one of the seats. 'How dare you, you little slut. Don't you dare sit down with your Mistress and her friends. You just run behind us. And make sure you keep up. And you can carry these.' She threw her golf bag to Emma, who was trembling at Ursula's outburst. 'And think yourself lucky you don't have to carry all our golf bags!'

The other women laughed at Emma's discomfiture.

'You certainly believe in treating a girl tough,' laughed one of the unmarried women.

'It's the only way to get discipline and obedience out of them,' said Ursula as she drove the buggy off.

Emma sadly passed the strap of Ursula's golf clubs over her shoulder, and began to run behind them, the hidden knee chain of her chastity belt keeping her from running with long strides. How heavy the clubs seemed already! How much heavier, she told herself, it would seem by the time they had all got round the course.

However, it was not only the physical weight of Ursula's golf clubs that Emma had to put up with during the morning. She also had the emotional anguish of having to watch Ursula and Mrs Guggenheim secretly kissing and fondling each other as they took advantage of the absence of the men. The sight of Ursula flirting with such a lovely creature – far more lovely than herself, she thought – made her mad with jealousy, especially since she knew it was all a build up to the younger woman's seduction that afternoon.

Emma was indeed glad when the women all went into the clubhouse for drinks and an early lunch, though she was again pointedly left outside.

She was very hungry again. She had not had a proper meal for two days. On the Friday night she had been sent biscuits and on Saturday she had just the lunch-time leftovers, and that night, just those awful dog biscuits. Ursula believed in keeping her girls half starved. It made them keener to please, she used to say.

Now Emma could see Ursula and the others enjoying a delicious lunch of fresh salmon. They were pointing and laughing at her. It was very humiliating.

When they went off to have coffee, however, Emma could not resist the temptation to steal into the clubhouse. She surreptitiously made her way to where the delicious buffet was laid out. Hastily she grabbed a handful of liqueur chocolates. She gobbled one – it had been weeks since she had dared to even nibble chocolate – and stuffed the remainder down her blouse.

'I'm sure your Mistress never gave you permission to eat those!'

Startled, Emma jumped round. It was Mrs Guggenheim. She was looking very pleased with herself at having caught Emma red-handed. 'You'd better come and explain yourself.'

Desperately ashamed, Emma followed Mrs Guggenheim to the spacious lounge where the women were enjoying coffee and liqueurs.

'What's she doing here?' demanded Ursula angrily. 'She had orders to wait outside while her elders and betters had lunch.'

'Well, I don't know about that, but I sure found her stuffing herself with chocolate at the buffet,' said Mrs Guggenheim with a laugh. 'I guess you'll find plenty more stuffed down into her blouse.'

'What!' screamed Ursula. 'How dare you come into the clubhouse without my permission. How dare you eat chocolates! Lift up your blouse. At once!'

A dozen expensive liqueur chocolates tumbled to the ground. Ursula went red in the face. She looked as if she was going to have a heart attack. This insolent chit of a girl not only had the audacity to help herself to forbidden chocolates, but by this act of indiscipline she had also made her Mistress look a complete fool in front of her friends. To make it worse, they had just been congratulating her on the way she controlled Emma – and now this had happened!

'You'll pay for this, my girl,' she said. 'And as it was Mrs Guggenheim who found you out, it is she who will punish you.'

Ursula turned to the young American woman. 'I shall expect you as soon as you have taken a shower after we get back to the hotel, darling. And as a reward for catching Emma, you will be allowed to punish her. And as for you, Emma, go to my room at once and wait for me. You know what to do. Now go!'

As she ran back to the hotel, Emma was cursing herself for being so greedy.

She should have known that she would not get away with stealing food from the buffet. It was bad enough to have to suffer the acute jealousy of having to prepare both Ursula and Mrs Guggenheim for their mutual lovemaking. Lovemaking from which, she knew she was to be excluded. And yet she was to be present and play a vital, if utterly frustrating role. Now, thanks to her greed, she was also going to be thrashed by Mrs Guggenheim as a way of arousing herself before she entered Ursula's bed.

Once in Ursula's bedroom, she quickly heated the thick cream and camphor. She loaded the mixture into Ursula's dildo. She tested the little rubber buds on the inside of the base which would rest against Ursula's beauty bud. Then she put Ursula's cane by the side of her bed, undressed, took a quick shower and, wrapping a towel round herself, knelt by the door, naked except for her chastity belt, to await Ursula.

Ursula paid no attention to Emma as she swept into the room. She undressed and went into the bathroom. Emma was feeling so ashamed of herself. Then suddenly she heard Ursula's voice, 'Come here, Emma. And crawl!'

Delighted at being able to attend upon her Mistress, Emma happily crawled to the bathroom, where Ursula was standing under the running shower.

'Little girls who steal, lie and deceive their elders and betters have their mouths washed out with soap, don't they Emma?' she asked archly.

Emma gave a little gasp. 'Yes, Madam,' she murmured contritely.

'Well you're going to hold the bar of soap tightly between your teeth whilst you please me with it, and get me ready for my lover-girl.'

She bent down and thrust the soap into Emma's mouth as she knelt at her feet, then pulled her towards her slightly parted legs.

'Now think of what fun I shall soon be having with my lovely young friend,' Ursula said as the slippery bar of soap slid up and down. 'Think of how much more beautiful she is than you, how much more attractive, amusing and intelligent. Think how inferior you are to her, not only physically and mentally but also socially and financially.'

Emma gave a little sob from behind the bar of soap. It was all so true. Mrs Guggenheim was vastly superior to her. She was a lady, and she was rich and free. She herself, however, was outwardly merely Ursula's maid servant – and dependent on her. She could not help feeling madly jealous.

As if reading Emma's thoughts, Ursula added: 'Instead of feeling jealous, you should be pleased and excited that your Mistress is going to bed with such a delightful creature. And you should be honoured that someone so far above you, is shortly going to cane you in front of me.'

These remarks were greeted by another little sob from behind the busy bar of soap. It was again all so true, Emma felt. She really should be pleased that her beloved Mistress was going to take such a lovely woman. She should be honoured that she was going to be beaten by such a superior person.

Ursula looked down at Emma's busily nodding head. The bar of soap was proving both exciting and tantalising, but it was not merely the physical touch of the slippery soap that was arousing Ursula so much. It was also the sight of the kneeling Emma working to get her ready for another woman. Another woman who would shortly be thrashing Emma. She pushed Emma's head away and switched off the shower.

'Dry me and fetch my satin negligée,' she ordered, 'and keep the soap clasped between your teeth.'

A few minutes later Mrs Guggenheim entered the room. She too was dressed in a satin negligée. She saw Emma's naked bottom facing her, bent over the back of a chair. The soap had at last been removed, but the taste of it was still in Emma's mouth.

Emma heard Ursula and Mrs Guggenheim embrace tenderly. Their hands ran inside their negligées. Mrs Guggenheim cried out: 'At last, darling, at last!'

After a few moments Ursula drew away. 'Before we get too involved, don't forget there's a little job for you to do!' She handed the cane to the American woman. 'Six!' she said with a smile.

Mrs Guggenheim took the cane wonderingly. 'I've never done this before,' Emma heard her say, and did not know whether to be pleased or scared.

'Have a couple of practice strokes on the cushion,' advised Ursula. Emma jumped as the American brought the cane down hard onto the cushion.

'But I think we'd better first take off the little slut's chastity belt,' laughed Ursula. She bent down, unlocked the padlock and drew the belt off the blushing Emma.

Mrs Guggenheim came up behind Emma. 'Oh look! She's quite hairless – just like a little girl. How pretty!'

'Yes,' replied Ursula. 'I like my little girls to look like little girls.'

'Oh, Ursula, you really are thorough!' laughed Mrs Guggenheim. Then she applied the first stroke to Emma's buttocks. To Emma's great relief it was quite gentle.

'Darling, I'm sure you can do better than that,' Emma heard Ursula say. 'It'll be much more exciting for us both if you make the girl really jump and cry out.'

The next stroke was only a little harder than the first, but the next four were hell for Emma, who cried and begged for mercy, falling at Mrs Guggenheim's feet in an abject picture of submissiveness. But this, much to Ursula's delight, only served to make the young American woman more determined. She even threw off her negligée for the last stroke so as to make it really sting.

Then, whilst Emma was still bent over the chair weeping

little tears of pain and shame, Mrs Guggenheim flung herself into Ursula's arms.

'Oh, darling, that was exciting,' she cried. 'But can I put the belt back on the girl?'

'Yes, darling,' Emma heard Ursula say with a laugh. 'You'll find that the beating has made the slut wet. And we certainly don't want her having any fun, do we?'

Astonished, Mrs Guggenheim put her hand down between Emma legs. Ursula was right! Despite the pain of the beating, the little slut was wet.

Oh, how the embarrassed Emma now hated Mrs Guggenheim, as giggling she drew the belt firmly up between Emma's legs and locked it behind her back. 'That'll teach her!' she heard the American woman say. Emma gave a sob of despair.

Ursula now led Mrs Guggenheim over to the bed. Emma heard Ursula beginning her seduction of the American. She felt utterly miserable. She did not dare move or say a word.

After what seemed to be hours, Emma heard the noise of fingers being snapped. She looked up. Ursula, standing naked by the bed, was beckoning her. She ran over. The American's ankles were fastened to the bedposts, and her thighs had been raised by a couple of pillows under her hips. She was blindfolded. She was also moaning with excitement and raising her hips lasciviously. The soft blonde hair on her mound was glistening.

Silently, Ursula pointed to the drawer containing the dildo. Emma quietly pulled it out, inserted one of the manhoods into Ursula and strapped it round her thighs. Ursula put her hand down and felt the heavy full artificial testicles. She felt its well-oiled tip. She nodded at Emma and gestured to her to get behind her. Then she mounted the bed between Mrs Guggenheim's outstretched thighs. Emma knelt behind her, her tongue busy. She could hear the two women kissing and whispering.

Suddenly there was a cry from Mrs Guggenheim. 'Oh, that's exciting, what is it, what is it?'

But there was no reply from Ursula. Then there was a scream of protest from Mrs Guggenheim. 'No! What are you doing? Oh! Oh! No! No!'

Emma could feel Ursula's hips pressing down and in and out as she rode the struggling and wriggling Mrs Guggenheim. Clearly the more she struggled and the more she wriggled, the greater was Ursula's pleasure. Anxious not to be left out of it all, and to give Ursula even more pleasure, Emma applied her tongue more diligently.

Soon Ursula was crying out with the double delight of her dildo, and Emma's tongue. Soon after, Mrs Guggenheim was also crying out in ecstasy.

Only poor Emma, locked into her chastity belt again, was not experiencing any pleasure – though she had to admit that pleasing her Mistress in this way was very exciting in itself, as well as frustrating. She had often imagined herself being used in this way by a strong and dominant man as he thrust into a rival girl. Indeed Henry had threatened to use her like this one day. But she had never imagined finding herself having to do it to an equally strong and dominant woman.

'Now, Emma, now!' shouted Ursula after several minutes. Emma squeezed the rubber scrotum. The warm thick mixture shot up into Mrs Guggenheim, who gave a shriek of pleasure and a violent shake that resulted in Ursula too giving a sudden cry.

But more was to follow. As Mrs Guggenheim slowly relaxed, Ursula kept her dildo firmly in place. Mrs Guggenheim suddenly gave a little cry of pain as the stinging camphor in the mixture reached her tenderest membranes. As the burning sensation increased, she began to wriggle madly, struggling to free her hands and to close her legs, but Ursula was gripping her wrists and holding her down as she pressed her body down onto the slight American woman. With her lips, Ursula sealed the American woman's screams.

'Oh, that's wonderful, wonderful!' cried Ursula, holding her down, and thrusting into her. 'Just go on wriggling like that. Wriggle with the pain, as I hold you down, and ride you! Go on! That's wonderful! Now Emma! Use your little tongue, you damn slut! Properly, Emma, or you'll be thrashed again . . . That's better . . . Go on, the two of you! Go on! Oh! Oh!'

A few moments later Ursula finally collapsed onto the sweating body of the delicious Mrs Guggenheim, within whom the burning pain had eased, to be replaced by ecstasy. But there was no such ecstasy for the still aroused Emma.

That night, Mrs Guggenheim slipped out of her husband's bed, tiptoed along the corridor and slipped silently into Ursula's bed again. Ursula was thrilled. She had been enjoying herself with Emma and was even considering allowing the poor girl a little pleasure, when Mrs Guggenheim arrived. As she pressed her beauty lips against Emma's artificial ones, she had been wondering whether to take off the belt and to use the slut as she had used the lovely Mrs Guggenheim. But not now!

Emma was kicked out of the bed. As she lay frustrated on the floor by the heaving bed, she thought how unfair life was. Ursula had just been about to take off the belt and allow her to climax. But she would not bother, Emma realised despairingly, now that she had the glamorous Mrs Guggenheim in her bed.

Indeed, when Emma returned home the following morning she was as pure as she had been when she had left it three days before. But how exciting it had all been, she thought. What a fantastically exciting woman Ursula was. She might enjoy keeping Emma frustrated as a punishment for all her naughty escapades with Henry, but even so she was still a wonderful Mistress – her Mistress, whose humble servant she was.

3

Under her mistress' thumb – and off to Ireland

Emma was rushed off her feet. She never knew when she was going to be summoned by Ursula to come to London. But when she was summoned she had to drop everything and rush. She never knew whether she was being summoned because Ursula genuinely needed her physically, or, as she often suspected, had been satisfying herself with other girls and was merely enjoying stamping her authority on Emma.

Sometimes, for instance, she would be met at the door with eager voluptuous kisses and immediately taken off to bed.

On other occasions, however, she was met by the sour faced maid, Rafaela, and told to undress. Her chastity belt would be removed and the depilatory cream rubbed into her mound and down her beauty lips. Then smooth and hairless as a little girl again, the belt would be replaced.

Sometimes she would then be told to put on her maid's uniform, sometimes she would be left naked. Either way, she would then be locked in the bare, maid's bedroom, to wait frustrated under her belt until her Mistress needed her. Ursula would call her on the intercom and press the button by her bed that electrically unlocked the door of the maid's room.

Often Emma would be left disconsolate and alone for hours on end, occasionally rattling impotently on the lock of the door or lying equally impotently on the hard little bed, unable to touch herself because of her chastity belt.

Oh how she hated the wretched belt!

It was so damned clever with its soft, perfect imitation, plastic beauty lips, that covered the hard plastic shield with its long, but very narrow, slit. The slit fitted perfectly over her own hairless, secret lips and allowed her to spend a penny, but it was far too narrow, frustratingly, to allow even her little finger to pass through it.

Even more infuriating, the shield was raised over her own bud, so that she felt nothing if she tried to rub herself, whilst the short chain connecting the two high rings prevented her from parting her legs sufficiently to get even a little finger under it.

Only Ursula and Rafaela had the key to unlock the padlock that held the securing chains of the shield fastened firmly in the small of Emma's back.

It was all very ingenious. Not only did it make it impossible for a lover, like Henry, to penetrate her, even from behind, but it also kept her completely frustrated; whilst enabling Ursula to take great physical pleasure from the knowledge that, as she enjoyed the girl's body, Emma would be having no pleasure at all, and that the slut was only wriggling from fear of her cane.

This cruel contrivance had changed Emma's whole life.

Sometimes Rafaela, apparently acting on Ursula's orders, had, to Emma's initial delight, taken off the belt before locking Emma, now naked under her maid's uniform, into the maid's room. But this was equally frustrating for her as the internal television camera was constantly watching her. She was being monitored, she knew, if not by Ursula upstairs in her bedroom, then by Rafaela in her kitchen, and she still did not dare touch herself.

She would just have to lie there, jealousy driving her mad, as she imagined Ursula pleasing herself with another girl upstairs.

Twice she had been let out of the maid's room after several hours incarceration, only to be told to get dressed and go home again – without even seeing Ursula. Only the way that the remotely controlled television camera had frequently zoomed in onto her, made her guess that Ursula, busy amusing herself with another girl, had used her simply as an erotic image on her screen to increase her own arousal. Emma's jealousy and frustration had known no bounds.

Alternatively, even more embarrassingly, she would be taken into the nursery. There she would be put into a clean set of rompers, with her hands tied helplessly in special gloves that made it impossible for her to use her fingers.

Then, with a dummy strapped into her mouth to keep her quiet, she would be put into a little baby's crawling cage by Rafaela, to await the arrival of her Mistress. To Emma's great embarrassment, Ursula would then often enjoy showing her off to some of her women friends, before having her put to bed in the little child's cot in her dressing room. Later she might be summoned to her Mistress's bed with instructions to snuggle up to her like a little girl.

It all served to make Emma realise the extent to which she was now completely under Ursula's control – and just how exciting that was. But, oh, if only she did not have to wear that chastity belt!

But she had to admit that since she had deceived Ursula not once, but twice, with Henry, and had tried to deceive her with Sonia, that Ursula was now quite justified in ensuring both her purity and her chastity.

Ursula was also, she had to admit, justified in generally treating her so harshly. She realised that it would be some time before Ursula could both trust and forgive her completely. She would have to work hard to get back into Ursula's good books. And of course, Ursula wanted her money's worth from the amount she had spent having Emma properly trained. She would have to show complete submissiveness and humility. But it would all be so worthwhile.

Ursula was the most wonderful and exciting woman she had ever met. Being under her complete control was the most exciting thing that had happened to her – far more exciting than being married to dull old John, and often even more exciting than having an affair with Henry . . .

Despite her determination to submit to Ursula's will, and to do whatever Ursula wanted, on one occasion she had been driven into a fury of jealousy. She had found that Ursula had the beautiful young Mrs Guggenheim staying with her. Emma had been terribly jealous of the wealthy young American socialite when Ursula had taken her on a golfing weekend, and now here she was back again!

Ursula did not, of course, treat the haughty Mrs Guggenheim as one of her girls, but rather as her equal. She ordered Emma to attend on the American just as she attended on her – using her simply to help the juices of love flow freely inside them both.

Emma, prettily dressed as a ladies' maid, had to open the door when the gorgeous Mrs Guggenheim arrived, carry her luggage upstairs and unpack her things in Ursula's room. Then she had to serve the two women tea and then, humiliatingly, accompany Mrs Guggenheim to the loo.

Later she had to undress both of them and then bathe them, using all the skills she had learnt at the school in France to make it an unforgettable experience for the still relatively innocent American woman.

Then, whilst the two women writhed in ecstasy on Ursula's large bed, poor little Emma, her chastity belt still firmly fastened round her loins, had to lie listening to it all from the cot in the adjacent dressing room. Periodically she would be imperiously summoned to give pleasure to one or both of them.

Indeed, several times in the course of the night which followed, she was summoned to find Ursula lying back, relaxed like a Turkish Pasha, whilst the American woman, like a favourite wife, knelt alongside her, stroking her and parting her beauty lips, under the carefully shaped surrounding hair; hair the very existence of which, marked her and Mrs Guggenheim's vastly superior position to that of Emma, whose own beauty lips were carefully kept smooth and hairless to give her the look of a subservient little girl.

Emma's role would be simply to increase Ursula's pleasure by inserting the tip of her tongue between the American woman's outstretched fingers, whilse Ursula controlled her activities with her cane.

It was indeed a most humiliating way of having to give

pleasure to Ursula. Moreover, it was one in which she received no recognition for all her efforts to please her Mistress. As Ursula became more and more aroused, she would cry out her appreciation to the lovely American, and flinging her arms around her neck, would pull her down into a long embrace until, stimulated by Emma's tongue, she would reach her climax, murmuring little endearments to the American, whilst merely kicking Emma out of her bed with orders to crawl back into her bunk.

Emma was indeed delighted when after two days of almost non-stop love, Mrs Guggenheim had to leave to rejoin her husband, and Ursula started to take an interest in her again.

Ursula, of course, took great care to ensure that she was constantly in Emma's thoughts, even when the latter was back at her home in the country.

Not only was the chastity belt a constant reminder of Ursula's power over her, but so also were the thrice daily reports she had to make to Ursula on what she had eaten and her bodily functions. Reports that in Ursula's absence had to be made, more embarrassingly, to Rafaela.

Emma had been terrified lest her husband, John, should ask her about the strange belt that she had to wear. But nothing was said, for Ursula's friendly lady doctor had told him that his wife was not in a fit state to receive his husbandly embraces. In any case, he was kept so busy, as usual, going on short trips abroad to attend various professional meetings, that Ursula had a very free rein to enjoy Emma whenever she wished.

Indeed John admired Ursula and suspected nothing untoward in her friendship with Emma. Thus, to Emma's disquiet, Ursula even took to driving down to enjoy Emma in her own house, or if John was there, taking Emma out for what she described as a walk in the country.

Ursula also kept going off to her villa in Morocco for a week or so. Emma had asked several times if she could come too. It sounded such an exciting country.

'No, little girl,' Ursula would respond with a laugh. 'Not

this time. But when I go out for several months fairly soon, then I might take you with me.'

It all sounded rather mysterious.

However what was a more immediate concern was Ursula's intention to take Emma with her for a weekend in Ireland, where she had been invited to stay by a rather grand friend of hers.

Emma, of course, was excited by the idea of going back to her native land – not that she had been consulted by Ursula in any way. Indeed now that she was a paid employee of Ursula's, their relationship had changed in a subtle but significant way.

Ursula still occasionally enjoyed locking Emma into the nursery and making her play the role of a little girl. On these occasions it amused Ursula to invite her women friends to bring round their own girls to romp in the playpen with Emma, or to enjoy a children's tea party. However, more and more she was enjoying making Emma assume the role of a hired servant girl, a parlour maid or her own ladies' maid. But now, however, Emma was no longer a free agent playing at being Ursula's maid. She was now just her paid maid and nothing more – even if her husband thought she was being kindly employed by Ursula as her 'Artistic Assistant'.

Ursula had made the position quite clear when the American woman was staying with her. Not only had she herself pointedly treated Emma as a mere servant in front of the American, but she had encouraged the latter to also treat Emma as a servant girl.

Humiliated, and yet secretly thrilled by the way that Ursula was treating her, Emma was delighted to see the way her bank balance was increasing, even though she could not touch the money without Ursula's agreement. The money helped to make up, she thought, for many of the slights she had to put up with from her moody and often bad-tempered Mistress.

The fact that she was now being paid by Ursula was also, she found, rather exciting. Not only did it make her feel more than ever in Ursula's power, but also it seemed in some strange way to make her feel like a whore. The rich American woman, for instance, had given her a substantial tip. Sadly she had had to hand the money over to Ursula to be paid into her bank account, for Ursula did not allow her to have control of any cash. But clearly she was being paid for her services! That too, she found, was a rather exciting idea.

However, her delight at the thought of travelling alone to Ireland with her beloved Mistress was rather dashed when she learnt that Helga was also coming. Helga was the fat, and very frightening, German woman whom she had first met at a health farm with Ursula.

Emma had learnt that Ursula had invested in Helga's dress shop. It was in this shop that Helga had tricked her girl, Belinda, into letting herself be televised, on a video, taking some money from the till. Belinda had thought it was a joke, but Helga had used it to blackmail Belinda into obeying her every whim, threatening to give the video to the police and have Belinda sent to prison, if she ever disobeyed her.

Emma had thought her a dreadful and terrifying woman when she had Belinda beaten by the Physical Training instructress, Miss Perkins, for 'impertinence' at the health farm. Emma had been even more shocked and terrified when, later, Ursula had allowed Helga to use Emma for her private pleasure at a dinner party at which Emma had to act as a waitress.

Helga had hardly been able to keep her hands off Emma since she had returned from the school in Paris. In particular she had been fascinated with the simple, yet highly effective way in which Ursula's chastity belt ensured not only Emma's chastity, but also her complete purity. She had even asked Ursula to get her a similar belt for her Belinda.

And now this awful woman was coming with them to Ireland for the weekend – and without Belinda to keep her satisfied. Officially Ursula wanted Helga to take the opportunity to visit some local Irish weavers whom she felt might be able to supply the shop with some unique material. But Emma was still very nervous.

* * *

After they had taken off from Luton airport, Emma dressed in her outdoor maid's uniform and went to join Ursula in the nearby empty first class cabin. But Ursula glared at her angrily.

'What do you want?' she demanded. And when Emma hesitated, she added cruelly: 'I don't want you here, get back into the economy class where you belong.'

From her hard seat in economy class, Emma could catch occasional glimpses of her Mistress in first class, sprawled out comfortably over two seats and eating some delicious-looking fresh salmon. Taking up the two seats opposite her was the fat Helga, the dreaded Helga.

Emma began to feel madly jealous of Helga. What gave her the right, she asked herself, to sit next to Ursula? Indeed why should she sit with Ursula in first class at all? After all she was little more than one of Ursula's employees – just like herself – for all the airs she gave herself.

Snubbed by Ursula, Emma became more and more angry and resentful. The whole of the journey was taken up with jealous thoughts. She even tried to think up ways in which she might punish Ursula for showing more favour to that horrible bitch Helga.

She would, she decided, like to destroy fat Helga. But how? And anyway, she asked herself, why should she worry about such a horrible creature as Helga? How could such a cow have any real influence on such an intelligent woman as Ursula? Helga might be a partner in the dress shop, but that did not mean that she had any real influence on Ursula – on the contrary, Emma finally decided as they came in to land at the airport in the west of Ireland.

They were met by Willie, one their host's grooms, sent to meet them with the Land Rover. Emma was told to get into the Land Rover alongside him, whilst her Mistress and Helga sat behind.

They drove for an hour across wild country before arriving at the drive that led them to the big house. In fact, they were staying at the former gate house, now converted into a guest wing. Built in the days of Cromwell, it consisted of two towers joined by a long corridor, forming a bridge over the drive. Downstairs the towes had been modernised with central heating, modern bathrooms and large windows, but the upper floors retained their original narrow slit windows without any glass.

It all looked wonderful from the outside. The sight even made her forget her jealousy of Helga. She was delighted to find that she had been given the top room in one of the towers – immediately above Ursula. As she plodded up the winding staircase, she consoled herself with the thought that the view would be wonderful and the room comfortable and modernised like Ursula's down below.

The reality was quite different. She found herself in a tiny, bare bunk-like room with not even a window. High up on the stone wall was one of the slits she had seen from the outside – a long, narrow, and very draughty slit – for there was no glass.

She called down to Ursula to protest that the room was quite unsuitable, hoping that Ursula would invite her to share her room. But there was no reply.

Then she heard the key being turned in the lock of the door at the foot of the stairs. Emma dashed down and threw herself against the door. It was locked. She heard Helga's laugh from the other side. She cried out, but there was no reply. She heard Helga's footsteps going away.

Poor Emma was left sobbing on the hard little bunk bed for two hours. Then she heard the key being turned again in the lock. It was Ursula – a smiling, radiant Ursula. Emma was so pleased. She forgot all her hatred and resentment and was ready and eager to be Ursula's little slave again!

'We are going off to inspect the stables,' smiled Ursula. 'Come down to my room, I've brought you some riding clothes.'

Ursula's room was on the first floor of the tower. Although not huge, it was most unusual as it was round – just like the tower itself. Big windows had been put in on all sides making it feel as light and airy as Emma's little room seemed dark and dank.

It had a small connecting dressing room and up a little

flight of steps was a big round bathroom. It all seemed rather like a doll's house and Emma gazed about her in awe.

Ursula watched Emma's face in some amusement. She always began to get hot for her little maid servant when she was looking astonished and amazed.

'Now, little Emma,' she said, 'I want you to be my little niece today . . . Now what do you say?'

'Yes, Aunt Ursula,' murmured the embarrassed Emma.

'Well go and plait your hair in the bathroom and put on your bows – and don't forget to put on the riding costume that I have left out for you!' Then her mood changed. She tapped Emma angrily twice with her riding whip. 'Well hurry up girl, don't just stand there. You've got three minutes!'

Emma dashed upstairs to the bathroom. She stood in front of the big mirror. Quickly she twisted her hair into two little plaits, each with a pretty blue bow at the end. Then, as she reached for the jodhpurs, Ursula came in. Emma saw that she held the key to the chastity belt in her hand.

'I think we had better have that belt off you. Come here!'

Moments later Emma was enjoying the extraordinary feeling of freedom – freedom for her body – that always came with the removal of her chastity belt. She could feel her beauty lips opening like a flower. But the stretch material of the jodhpurs was almost like tights. Looking in the mirror, Emma could hardly believe it. Every little line of her small soft bottom was disclosed. The jodhpurs were so tight that she could not have worn pants – even if Ursula had permitted it.

On top she wore a pale yellow, skintight jersey with a new uplift bra that Ursula had produced.

Emma knew that she looked stunning: size eight and not a day over sixteen – but a rather grown-up sixteen with a little rouge and lipstick. Indeed Emma had never seen herself looking so voluptuous without really meaning to do so.

She glanced up at Ursula, seeking approval. She saw that Ursula was licking her lips with anticipation.

'Right, Emma, I'll see you in the stables,' she called over her shoulder as she strode off.

Before Emma had time to think, the dreaded fat Helga walked in. Confirmed lesbian that she was, she relished what she saw. Hmm, she was clearly thinking, I shall certainly try to have some fun with this little filly over the weekend! She gloated over the sight of Emma's little rump under the very tight jodhpurs.

Helga was tempted, in Ursula's absence, to take Emma there and then. But she was frightened lest Ursula might take her money out of the shop – and she needed the money!

Helga knew that Ursula despised her. But she also knew that Ursula was often dependent on her – particularly for keeping an eye on a girl when she was away. It was very convenient for Ursula to be able to send a girl to Helga to be employed – nominally anyway, in the shop, knowing that Helga would train and supervise the girl until she returned.

It had been a matter of regret to Helga that Ursula had not found it necessary, so far, to send Emma to her for a period of close supervision. The girl deserved to be pulled down a peg or two – and having to work as a model in her shop would certainly do that! A thrashing for every time a customer failed to buy the dress a girl was modelling had a very marked effect on a girl's attitude!

However she instinctively knew that if she took this particular little bitch without Ursula's approval, then Ursula would throw her out. She would have to be careful. Ursula was much more emotionally involved with Emma than she let on. It was all very frustrating thought Helga. Meanwhile, she showed her frustration by angrily dragging poor Emma by her plaits downstairs and into a car.

'Get in, you little whore,' she muttered, 'and keep quiet.'

They drove to the stables. Emma was looking forward to riding again. She used to ride quite a lot as a girl in Ireland. When they arrived she saw Ursula and Willie, the rustic Irish groom. Ursula looked Emma up and down. Evidently she was again pleased by the very tight stretch jodhpurs. She turned to Willie.

'Put her up on Phoenix,' she ordered. Phoenix was a huge half-bred hunter: a cross between an Irish draught mare and a thoroughbred stallion.

Willie led Phoenix and Emma into a small paddock. Ursula held the horse on a long lunging rein with her left hand. In her right hand she held a long lunging whip.

For the next half hour Ursula proceeded to give Emma a riding lesson. She was made to walk and trot round sometimes with her stirrups and sometimes without. Emma could feel her breasts bouncing strangely under the yellow, skintight jersey. Now she understood the purpose of the uplift bra that Ursula had made her wear. She could also feel herself being poured tighter and tighter into the tight Jodhpurs. She could hear Ursula and Helga discussing her body – a body that was now well displayed. She heard the muscular groom laugh.

She was made to sit up, keeping her shoulders back and her head raised, with her body lips pressed against the front of the saddle. The slightest sign of slouching was rewarded by a slash across her back or breasts from Ursula's long whip.

Clearly Ursula was enjoying making Emma do what she was told and even had her going over little jumps – with the long lunging rein still attached to Phoenix's bridle.

The constant use of the lunging whip, Emma's little whimpering cries and the feeling of power that all this gave to Ursula, soon had its effect. Ursula was feeling very excited. She would, she knew, have to take Emma soon.

Abruptly, Ursula ended the lesson. Emma dismounted. She was still whimpering from the pain of the long lunging whip.

'Come now, little Emma,' Ursula smiled. 'Aunt Ursula is very pleased with you. You did very well.'

Emma looked up at her tall Mistress with a look of surprised gratitude. Praise from Ursula was praise indeed. Her eyes filled with tears.

'There, there, little one, don't cry,' comforted Ursula in an unusually maternal voice. 'Look what I've got you. A little piece of chocolate! You see how your aunt loves you!'

Gratefully Emma took the chocolate and brushed away her tears. Her Mistress loved her! And the chocolate was delicious. It was the first chocolate she had dared to eat for three weeks, since Ursula had caught her helping herself from a huge box of chocolates that she had been sent by an admirer of her paintings. That had cost Emma a very painful dozen strokes of Ursula's cane. She had not dared to touch another sweet since – not even at her home, for fear that Ursula would beat the truth out of her and then really thrash her . . .

Ursula put her arms around Emma as they walked back to the stables. Emma was licking the chocolate, anxious to spin out the pleasure. She knew that it would be a long time before Ursula allowed her another – not only to assert her authority over the young woman, but also because she wanted her to keep her girlish size eight figure. Shyly, like a real little girl, she put her hand into Ursula's.

Emma heard Ursula sending off the others so as to be alone with Emma.

'Helga, go and give Willie a hand to see to Phoenix,' she called.

But Helga was raging in fury. She knew that Ursula would be enjoying little Emma. She was determined to be in on the fun!

4

Strange scenes of domination in Ireland

Back in the stable there was beautiful fresh straw and hay in the empty loose box. The smell made Ursula feel good. She led Emma into the box with its high wooden walls topped by bars. She shut the door carefully behind her. The stables were just the place, she thought, to bring a little slut like Emma. Ursula loved making Emma perform like a little animal.

'Now, Emma,' she said, 'don't wet your nice clean straw. Use this bowl.'

Ursula toyed with the idea of calling the groom to take the girl whilst she watched, or even of letting the fat Helga have her. But Emma was looking just too inviting as she slipped down her jodhpurs to squat over the bowl.

'Take off your jersey and bra,' she ordered hoarsely. She was becoming more and aroused. 'And be quick about it.'

The sight of the red marks of the long lunging whip across Emma's breasts and back drove Ursula even wilder. Before Emma could move, Ursula had pushed her down on her back in the straw, lifted up her own wide skirt and was on top of her, holding her down with her knees pressing on her arms.

Emma was quite helpless, and with Ursula's skirt over her face she was in the dark. She felt Ursula's wet body lips pressing down onto her mouth. She heard Ursula screaming orders and obscenities. But she knew what she had to do and she knew that failure to give maximum pleasure with Ursula in her present state could result in almost anything. She remembered the awful lunging whip. She applied herself to her task.

Ursula kept her busy in the darkness under her skirt for what seemed to Emma to be ages, as she spun out her pleasure.

Suddenly she heard voices and the now satiated Ursula jumped up off her. She blinked in the sudden bright light. To her horror she saw the groom, Willie, standing over her, his trousers unfastened. Behind him stood a grinning Helga.

'Hold her down, Helga,' she heard Ursula say, 'but let her see him. It will be more amusing like that. I'm going to enjoy watching this!'

Emma started to get up, but was immediately seized and held down by the huge, strong Helga. She saw that the rustic lad was smiling more than ever as he looked down on her naked, hairless body. He held his erect manhood in his hand. It looked as though his seed was about to spurt out all over her body.

'No . . . nooooo . . .' screamed Emma.

'Stop!' shouted Ursula. There was a sudden silence. The boy's hand fell to his side. 'Animals should be covered on all fours.'

She looked round and pointed at a couple of bales of straw.

'Helga! Bring those over here and put the girl on all fours kneeling over one of them.' She pointed to a line of leather straps hanging on the wall outside the loose box. 'Use those to help you hold her down properly. We don't want the reluctant little filly kicking out at the stallion, do we?'

Moments later Emma was strapped, kneeling down over one of the bales, on her hands and knees. The straps held her bent legs wider apart, whilst Helga held her wrists tight. Ursula was sitting on the other bale in front of her, an eager smile of anticipation on her face. Alarmed, she looked round. Behind her she saw the groom slip out of his trousers and kneel down on the straw behind her.

'That's better,' laughed Ursula. 'Now, Willie, grip her hips with your hands. Pretend you're a dog mounting a bitch on heat. That's it! Pull her towards you and now thrust in. Go on! Thrust, boy, thrust!'

Emma gave a cry as she was penetrated. She looked up piteously at Ursula, but saw to her dismay that Ursula now held the lunging whip in her hands.

'Now I want to hear both little dogs barking. Go on. Bark! Bark, Willie, bark.'

Willie gave a hoarse series of barks, as he now jerked to and fro.

'That's a good dog, Willie,' said Ursula encouragingly as she tapped his naked bottom with her long whip. 'Now, Emma, I want to hear you bark in unison with the other dog, every time he thrusts forward. Go on, Emma, bark!'

She brought the whip down several times across Emma's back. Soon the stables reverberated to their combined little barks.

'Well, little Emma, what's it like to have to offer yourself to a dog on all fours?'

The little barks were becoming more frenzied as the young man began to thrust faster and faster.

'Quick Helga, pull him off her. I don't want her conceiving a litter of peasants!'

Helga kicked the boy backwards just as he was about to explode inside Emma. His seed shot harmlessly up Emma's back, leaving the girl gasping with shame and shock.

The rustic boy pulled up his trousers, nodded his thanks to Ursula and left.

'You can do what you like with her now, Helga,' smiled Ursula. 'Shut her up in her room for the night and give her a few scraps to eat. I don't want to see or hear her again until tomorrow morning. Tonight you and I are both invited to dinner at the castle. Just make certain that she's well washed out when you've finished with her, and then lock her back into the chastity belt. Here's the key!'

Ursula tossed the key to Helga and strode out of the loose box. Emma heard the noise of her car driving off.

'Now my girl, you are all mine,' grinned Helga. 'You're going to work like you've never worked before! I want to see what you really learnt to do in Paris.'

She picked up the lunging whip that Ursula had thrust aside as she left.

'And just remember that this is waiting for you at the slightest sign of hesitation or reluctance. You've been spoilt by Ursula. She's too kind hearted. But I'm not, and you are going to do things for me that you've never done for anyone before!'

She brought the whip down across the still kneeling Emma's buttocks.

'Do you understand, girl?'

'Yes, Madam,' stuttered Emma. 'Yes.'

Several hours later, Emma lay on the hard little bunk of her room at the top of the tower. Her chastity belt was locked back onto her. With no glass in the slit high up the wall that served as a window, the room was cold. Emma lay huddled up under several of the old horse blankets she had found piled in a corner of the room. She wondered who had used them last.

She had heard Ursula leave to go out to dinner and, several hours later, had heard her return. She had heard her laughing with Helga – that awful fat slob who had made her do such dreadful things in the stable.

Emma had hoped that perhaps Ursula would unlock the door and call her down. But nothing had happened and she had been left all alone with the bowl of cold rice and scraps of meat that Helga had left her with earlier on.

At first she could hardly bear to look at the food. But now she was feeling hungry and with her hands she eagerly scooped the congealed lumps of rice and strips of boiled meat into her mouth.

How awful it had been when the groom had taken her for Ursula's amusement. How unbelievably cruel her Mistress could be. She would never allow her to have sex with a normal man – but to be taken by a rustic lad was apparently quite different. The awful and shameful thing was that she had been unable to prevent herself getting excited as the boy repeatedly thrust into her with a bark. Under the awful infuence of Ursula's whip she had to respond with another bark, but she had also found herself thrusting back to meet the boy's thrusts.

How dreadful that had been, she thought. And to think that Ursula and Helga had been watching – and laughing at her as she could not stop herself from becoming aroused. It was all too ghastly to think about, she decided, as she fell asleep, her chastity belt once again ensuring her purity.

The following day, Saturday, Helga went off to look at local materials for her dress shop. Ursula told Emma to prepare a picnic. They were going off to an island in a lake owned by their host.

Emma could hardly bear to look Ursula in the face after the way she had had her taken the day before. But Ursula made no mention of the event and instead was a charming and amusing companion – whilst also making it quite clear just who was in charge.

Ursula relaxed in the back of the boat whilst Emma rowed her around the lake, and then they explored the little island and later lay in the warm sunshine in the long grass.

Emma, of course, was instructed to please Ursula, and for a brief moment thought that the chastity belt was going to be removed. She had had no relief the day before, nor indeed for several days before that. She was longing for her Mistress's hand to give her some satisfaction as she applied herself to satisfying her demands. But she did not dare raise the matter. Instead she concentrated on giving Ursula the most exquisite pleasure, hoping that Ursula's conscience would eventually persuade her that it would only be fair to allow Emma to yield to her. But as Emma rowed the now satiated Ursula back to their car, her chastity belt was still firmly in place and her desperate feelings of frustration were unassuaged.

That evening there was to be a dinner party in the Gate House. Several other women who lived locally and shared Ursula's tastes would be coming and so too would their host – the only man. Emma had yet to meet him and assumed that Ursula felt she had to invite him, especially since the dinner was to be cooked by his servants from the castle.

Emma had to bathe Ursula and dress her in one of her most glamorous evening dresses. For once Ursula allowed Emma not only to put on one of her own pretty cast-off dresses, but also to wear some of her most glamorous cast-off underclothes.

The two of them made a striking pair as they went down to the big drawing room to join Helga and await their guests.

Two other pairs of attactive women arrived. Emma was interested to see that whereas one pair were women of the same age and neither of them seemed to be dominant, the other pair consisted of an older woman with a much younger woman who was very much at the beck and call of her older friend. Indeed, Ursula made a point of introducing the other blushing young woman to Emma.

'Emma, this is Juliette, the little girlfriend of my friend Mrs Pankhurst. She's just like you and I want you to look after her. She will help you with the drinks.'

Indeed Juliette turned out to have been very well trained by her Mistress, of whom she was clearly in great awe.

Emma longed for a chance to speak to Juliette – to compare notes as it were. But she knew that Ursula and her friend did not like their little girls to gossip about their Mistresses behind their backs and sadly she had no chance to do so. She thought that perhaps the two of them might be allowed to go off together to spend a penny, but it was Mrs Pankhurst who firmly took Juliette out to the bathroom.

When their host arrived, Emma was surprised to find that he was a highly intelligent man of about fifty, accompanied by a strikingly beautiful youth of about eighteen. Their host was wearing a well-cut dinner jacket, but the youth was dressed more like a nineteenth-century artist with velvet trousers, a white silk frilly shirt and a flowing black cravat. The cravat was not the only thing that flowed, Emma noticed, for the youth's blond hair flowed down prettily over his shoulders. His eyes had been painted, his cheeks rouged and his fingernails painted like a girl's.

'This is Cyril,' said their host, as if that was sufficient explanation for the youth's appearance. 'Bring me a drink,

Cyril,' he added, clearly establishing the boy's status as being comparable to that of Emma and Juliette.

Emma looked at the young man, as he brought their host, his Master, a drink. His clothes and demeanour really made him look more like a girl, as he brought the glass and then humbly offered it. He was tall and slim with an almost girlishly soft skin. He seemed scared of their host who, once he had taken his drink, ignored the boy and turned to talk to Ursula about pictures, art and the theatre.

Emma, Juliette and the boy, Cyril, were left standing smiling awkwardly at each other in the corner of the room, whilst the others sat down to enjoy a protracted and erudite conversation.

At dinner the three of them were seated together at the end of the table, where they listened silently to the animated conversation of their elders and betters.

When the dinner was over, and the maids had left to return to the castle, their host proposed a game of strip poker. The ladies looked somewhat shocked and Ursula was positively bridling.

'No, no, ladies, please don't misunderstand me,' laughed their host. 'It is not we who will take off our clothes, it is our little friends.'

He pointed to the other end of the table where Emma, Juliette and Cyril were sitting. 'They will be stripping on our behalf! Of course those of us who have not got someone to strip for us will have to watch, but I think they will find it all very enjoyable too!'

Soon Emma found herself standing shyly on a low table in front of the card table around which Ursula and her guests were seated. Juliette and Cyril were standing, equally awkwardly and shyly, on other low tables.

'The rules are that each owner can bet one or more articles of clothing from their . . . shall we agree to call them our slaves? When a slave is naked then the owner can continue to play by betting one or more strokes of the cane – to be given by the winner to the slave. Otherwise normal poker rules apply but with articles of clothing and strokes of cane replacing chips or money. Is that all acceptable?'

The others all laughed and nodded eagerly. Emma was horrified by what she had heard and so, she saw, were Juliette and Cyril. She was even more horrified when their host ordered Cyril to run off to his car and bring back his cane which, he said, was in the boot. It turned out to be an exceptionally long and whippy one.

Ursula, Mrs Pankhurst and their host started to play, whilst Helga and the other women looked on eagerly, commenting on the other's hands.

'Stop cheating, Helga,' laughed Ursula. 'This is a serious game, as Emma's little bottom will soon discover if you go on giving away my hand!'

Before long the two girls and the boy were all standing naked on their little tables, in front of a pile of their discarded clothes. Emma saw that Juliette's body hair had been carefully removed – just like her own – as had that of Cyril.

She also saw, however, that Cyril's manhood had been imprisoned in a little copper tube that was curved downwards. It was, she realised, the male equivalent of her own chastity belt. A little padlock behind his testicles kept the tube firmly in place, thereby ensuring that his manhood remained soft and inoffensive, despite the near presence of two very attractive naked girls. It would also, she thought, ensure that he remained quite pure – just as her own belt ensured that she could not give herself relief.

Indeed her own chastity belt caused great interest. Both their host and the visiting women all insisted on interrupting the game to inspect it, and to test that it really did prevent her from receiving any pleasure from the normal source of a girl's physical gratification.

'If you want me to take it off,' laughed Ursula, producing the key and the little bottle of solvent from her bag, 'then you'll have to agree that it counts as five articles of clothing.'

'Done!' cried their host.

Thus it was that a few minutes later, after Ursula had lost a fiercely contested round, Emma now stood with her bare little bald mound and real pouting lips prettily on display.

With no more clothes to play for, the players were now gambling on their charges being beaten with their host's cane. The first one to receive the cane was indeed the boy, who received three stinging strokes from Ursula, after she had tricked the other two players into thinking that she was only bluffing when in fact she really did have a strong hand.

Emma recognised the look on Ursula's face as she wielded the cane on the boy's bare buttocks, making him bend over and touch his toes for each stroke.

It was of course only a matter of minutes before Emma was beaten. The first three strokes came from Mrs Pankhurst, but a few minutes later she had to bend over to be beaten by the host – a far more painful process. She had rarely been beaten by a man, except of course by Henry and by the instructors at the school in France. It was a humiliating experience, but also an exciting one, she realised, as she felt herself becoming moist with arousal.

'Enough! Enough!' Emma suddenly heard Helga shout. 'It is time we non-players also had a little fun. Let's have a competition.'

'A competition?' asked one of the visitors. 'What do you mean?'

'There are three of us,' explained Helga, 'and three slaves. We'll draw for which slave we can beat. Four strokes and the one who makes her slave cry out the most is the winner!'

Eagerly they tossed for which slave should be allocated to whom. Helga, to her delight, got the boy. 'I'll really make him scream,' she announced. Juliette fell to one of the other visiting women and Emma to the other.

'Now, Emma,' called out Ursula. 'I don't want you letting me down. I don't want to hear a squeal out of you.'

Emma and Juliette were beaten first.

Juliette proved to be very brave. She took her four strokes with hardly a whimper. Emma however, couldn't help crying out after the third and fourth strokes, much to Ursula's disgust. But Helga had the boy yelling after her second stroke – a clear winner!

After such an arousing evening it was not surprising that Ursula needed more than a little relief that night. She kept Emma in her bed all night and did not bother to put her chastity belt back on her.

'If you really work hard, little slut,' she promised to Emma as she knelt over her, 'then I'll let you have a little fun for once.'

How happy Emma was that her Mistress had taken off the awful chastity belt and allowed her to yield herself to her. Life seemed wonderful. She was even more pleased to learn that Helga had left to fly back to London to see about getting the materials she had chosen sent over to London. At last, thought Emma, a whole day alone with Ursula.

It was therefore a nasty shock to find that the American woman, the beautiful Mrs Guggenheim, who was supposed to have returned to New York, turned up in time for lunch.

'Just passing through,' she announced, kissing Ursula passionately on the mouth. 'And it sure seemed such a pity not to stop off for a day to join you here – especially as you've got little Emma with you!'

Emma's heart fell. How dare that bitch return and spoil her day. Her forebodings were proved right when, that afternoon, Ursula banished her back to her bare attic at the top of the tower with the orders to write out a hundred times the phrase: 'I must be happy when my Mistress enjoys herself with another women. I must not be jealous. I am only Mistress's little slut. I am not worthy to sleep in her bed. I must be very happy that my Mistress is enjoying herself with a more attractive and intelligent woman than me.'

For what seemed hours, Emma slaved over her lines. She knew that each one had to be beautifully and carefully written. And yet how could she concentrate on her task when she knew that her Mistress was enjoying herself with that awful American woman downstairs?

The wording of the lines, slowly sank into her conciousness. She was indeed a slut. She was indeed not worthy to sleep in her Mistress's bed. But she was just as attractive and intelligent as that American bitch. And she just couldn't make herself feel happy at the thought of what was going on only a few feet away, down the stairs and on the other side of the locked door.

Suddenly she heard the noise of the door being unlocked.

'Emma! Have you finished your lines?'

'Nearly, Madam,' Emma lied. She had been so upset that she had found it difficult to write, and many of the lines she had written had been spoiled by her tears.

'You should have finished by now,' came Ursula's angry voice. 'You're a disobedient little girl. Now bring down what lines you have written at once, and show them to my American friend.'

Feeling very frightened, Emma came down the stairs and entered Ursula's bedroom. Ursula and Mrs Guggenheim were lying naked and sprawled on the big bed. Shyly, Emma curtsied and handed the lines to the American woman who looked at Emma as though she were dirt. She flicked through the pages.

'The slut certainly doesn't seem to have been working very hard,' she finally announced to Ursula. 'If I didn't know she was wearing that chastity belt, I'd say she'd been playing around with herself instead of writing her lines whilst we were down here. And quite a lot of them have been spoilt by drops of water. A very poor effort, I'd say.'

Angrily Ursula snatched the lines out of the American woman's hands, glanced at them and tossed them away.

'Darling, you are absolutely right. Would you find my slipper and give her a sound slippering – and then we'll really make her work on us both in bed.'

To be beaten by another woman in front of Ursula was bad enough, but to be beaten by a woman who had just been making love to Ursula was doubly degrading – and to be slippered like a naughty little girl made it even worse . . .

It was indeed a very contrite little Emma who, a few minutes later, applied herself, under the sheets, to pleasing both Ursula and her American friend as they lay back on their bed exchanging kisses.

Ursula, however, seemed pleased the following day when they arrived back at Luton airport.

'I'm very pleased with you, on the whole, Emma. You can go back home for a couple of days rest. I'll ring you when I want you. And don't forget meanwhile to make your regular reports three times a day.'

Emma blushed with pleasure like a little schoolgirl praised by her teacher. Ursula was pleased with her! Somehow that made it all so worthwhile.

5

The farewell party

Ursula was planning to spend the winter in Morocco, where, she said, the climate was mild and she could paint in peace. Looking back, Emma was surprised by just how much time Ursula had spent in Morocco since they had first met.

What was there in Morocco which so attracted Ursula, Emma wondered, especially since she was so well established in London with her friends and her house?

It all seemed very mysterious, especially as every time she went there she returned with more of those drawings and paintings of half-naked women in oriental settings that sold so well . . .

Emma's husband now announced that he was about to go off on an oceanographic survey in a remote part of the Pacific. He would be gone for over four months.

As soon as Emma told Ursula this, she had telephoned Emma's husband and suggested that Emma should come and work for her in Morocco whilst he was away. Not only, she said, would Emma be paid a good salary and see an interesting part of the world, but she would also be kept busy and out of temptation, she added with a laugh.

Ursula had, of course, not thought of consulting Emma about this – Emma merely did as she was told. She was astonished and embarrassed to hear Ursula speaking to her husband and discussing her as if she were just a child that needed looking after. At the time she was kneeling at Ursula's feet, painting her toenails. Humiliated though she was to hear herself being discussed, she did not dare interrupt. Indeed, she found it exciting to have her future decided for her by her Mistress.

John, not surprisingly, was delighted for Emma to go off with Ursula whilst he was away, and be looked after by her. He would not now have to worry about her whilst he was away in the Pacific; about how she was or what she was doing. She would now be in the care of her intelligent and well-to-do employer.

Ursula put the phone down with a contented smile.

'Well, little Emma, that's all settled then. You're mine for four months in Morocco.' She gave the still kneeling girl a hug. 'Aren't you excited, little girl!'

'Oh yes, Madam,' replied the delighted Emma, looking up at her Mistress with fervent admiration. Quite apart from the prospect of being with Ursula for so long, she was also thrilled at the thought of seeing Morocco; the land of veiled women and secret harems, a land so very different from dull old England.

'Well I shall have to give a farewell dinner party for my women friends here before we go. And you, Emma, will be serving the dinner.'

On the day of Ursula's big party, Emma arrived up in London to find that Ursula had borrowed three other girls from her women friends to help her serve at table. There would be a total of sixteen guests, she learnt, at four tables with one girl looking after each table.

'And woe-betide any girl who doesn't look after her table properly,' said Ursula. 'You, Emma, will be looking after my table and I shall expect a very high standard of service from you after all the money I have spent having you properly trained in Paris, as a serving wench.'

'Yes, Madam,' replied Emma enthusiastically. She was quite looking forward to showing off her newly acquired skills.

During the afternoon two girls were brought round by their Mistresses. To a casual observer it would simply have looked like a young woman out for a walk with an older woman. But Emma was struck by the truth – these girls were simply not allowed out by themselves, even though one of them was in her thirties.

The third girl, dressed as a little girl, with a dummy in her mouth, arrived in a beautifully yellow-painted pram, pushed by a nanny in uniform. The dummy was tied round her neck by a pretty red ribbon, just like that of many real little girls. The girl wore a leather harness, also just like that often worn by real children in prams to prevent them for trying to climb out. But close inspection would have shown that the fingers and thumbs of the gloves had been firmly sewn together to prevent her using her hands to unfasten the harness or dummy. She was indeed quite helpless and unable to make more than gurgling noises.

The girl's body was covered with a pretty little blanket. Once again, to the casual observer she looked merely like a rather large little girl being taken out for an airing.

There were tears of frustration in the girl's eyes as she looked around wildly as if pleading to be untied. However, it was not until the pram had been pushed into the hall, and the front door closed behind them, that the nanny started to unfasten the girl.

Ursula was clearly fascinated by the sight of a grown girl being taken out in a pram.

'Do you often take her out in the street like this?' she asked.

'Oh yes,' replied the nanny. 'Madam likes her little girl to have a little fresh air every day. I take her into Kensington Gardens. She's a good little girl and loves her outings. It makes a change from being kept in the nursery playpen all day.'

Emma saw that Ursula's eyes were glinting. She ran her hand over the beautifully made pram with its big wheels and bright yellow and black colours. It seemed only slightly bigger than a normal pram, but was cleverly designed to take a grown girl. She wrote down the name of the shop where it had been bought.

'It's lucky for you, Emma, that we are off to Morocco, or I'd get a pram like this for you. I'd enjoy the thought of you, strapped into a pram and being pushed round Kensington Gardens every afternoon!'

The girl's nanny now lifted her out of the pram. She untied the dummy in the girl's mouth. She pushed back the girl's little baby cap. Her long hair tumbled out. Emma was astonished now to recognise the girl as Belinda, whom she had last seen as the fat Helga's cowed and much bullied girl at the health farm.

'And are you happy with your new Mistress?' Ursula asked her with a smile. 'She certainly paid Helga enough for you! It must make a change being treated like a little girl with a real nanny to look after you.'

Belinda blushed. 'Oh yes, Madam, it's very different!'

Emma saw that the scared look in Belinda's eyes, which had been there when she had been the cruel and awful Helga's girl, had gone. She was now looking like a happy and relaxed little girl. Clearly her new life suited her well.

Ursula clapped her hands for attention.

'Now girls, your Mistresses have kindly lent you to me to help serve at my dinner party. You will all be dressed up as parlour maids and your outfits are hanging up in Emma's little maid's room. Now run along with her and get changed. Emma will show you how I expect you to be dressed and made up. And then in half-an-hour I shall inspect you all and we will have a little practise at serving. Emma has been specially trained and I want you to watch and copy her. I shall expect you to serve silently and submissively. I'm sure none of you want me to make a bad report to your Mistresses! Now off you go and get ready.'

In Emma's room there were four, tiny black maid's outfits. The skirts were so short that they hardly came down to the tops of the girls' thighs. They were embarrassingly cut away in the front and flared behind so that the girls' little bottoms were displayed at every moment. The top of each dress was open down the front to their navels, disclosing the girls' breasts and allowing them to hang prettily when they bent over to serve. A tiny little white apron was fastened round the waist and hung down over the cutaway at the front of the tiny skirt, partly to hide the girls' exposed body lips – for no underclothes were to be worn under the uniform. White gloves, black stockings and shoes and a white maid's cap completed the revealing and erotic outfits.

The girls were excited by the idea of dressing up, especially Belinda who said it was the first time she had been out of little girls' clothes since her new Mistress had bought her from Helga.

Emma also showed the girls how Ursula would expect them to paint their lips, nipples and sex lips the same colour. She herself was still wearing her chastity belt, which Ursula always knew fascinated her friends, and so it was her plastic artificial lips which received attention.

Finally, the girls were all ready and lined up for Ursula's inspection, following endless practising of serving drinks and various kinds of food as the girls all struggled to follow Emma. Then each girl had to lay her table ready for the party and arrange the flowers in the centre. Emma was detailed to open the front door as the guests arrived, Belinda to take their wraps and the other two girls, including the older one, to serve drinks before dinner. Ursula gave them a final briefing.

'Now I don't want to hear any protesting or giggling if any of the guests should take a closer look at you during the meal. You are to go on serving, as if nothing was happening,' she said.

The dinner had gone very well. The food, cooked by Rafaela, had been delicious and each girl had served her table properly. The girls' outfits had been greatly admired and even Belinda's new owner, an older woman who really enjoyed treating Belinda as her little girl, had to admit that she found Belinda even more entrancing dressed as a maid than as a child. The provocative flair to the tiny skirts and the cutaway fronts, together with the open tops of the dresses, had inevitably resulted in several of the women intimately caressing the girl serving them. It was a situation made all the more piquant by the way the girls pretended to ignore what was going on, despite their inability to prevent themselves becoming aroused by the touch of so many hands.

In the case of Emma, of course, her chastity belt was a source of great interest with the guests at the other tables as well, all wanting to check for themselves that it really was impossible for Emma to receive any pleasure whilst wearing it.

Then, when the coffee was served, Ursula removed Emma's belt and invited her friends to see for themselves what a passionate little creature Emma was – once her restraining chastity belt had been removed. Indeed, her sensuality having been greatly increased during her training period and then cruelly suppressed by having constantly to wear Ursula's chastity belt, Emma was now a virtual time bomb of restrained passion. When the belt was removed she only required the slightest touch to make her display the most uninhibited sensuousness.

'Now,' ordered Ursula to the four girls, 'push back the tables and chairs against the wall. It's time for a little game of Blind Man's Buff but with a slight difference. Emma, go and fetch my cane from the bedroom.'

The guests arranged themselves into a large circle. The four girls were put into the circle and one guest was blindfolded.

'Now she has to try and catch one of the girls before the time runs out,' Ursula explained. 'If she catches a girl before the two minutes are up then she can give the girl three strokes of the cane. If not, then she has to hand the blindfold over to another of us.'

'And you girls,' Ursula added, 'had better do your best not to be caught if you want to avoid a thrashing!'

Emma now found herself with the other three girls in the circle. The guests locked hands to stop the girls from escaping. The blindfolded woman started to grope her way around, listening for the frightened breathing of the girls and their footsteps as they desperately tried to get away from her. Meanwhile, the laughing and excited guests called out encouragement and misleading instructions to their blindfolded friend.

Emma scarcely knew whether to remain quite still and hope to avoid being caught or to run round the circle so as to keep away from the blindfolded woman. The excited women soon started to push the girls into the path of their blindfolded friend, as she groped her way forward, or tripped up girls that were trying to run away from her.

Suddenly Belinda was tripped and fell at the woman's feet. The woman eagerly seized her and pulled off the blindfold. Ursula handed her the cane.

A chair was brought into the middle of the circle. Belinda was made to bend over it and the other girls were told to hold her tight.

'Up on your toes,' ordered the guest with the cane, 'and thrust back for the cane. I want you really taut. Go on! I want you even tauter. That's better. Now hold her like that.'

She stood and raised the cane. Emma, gripping one of Belinda's wrists, heard the woman catch her breath. She herself found it exciting to watch Belinda being prepared for her caning, but was also terrified at the thought that she might be in the same position in a few minutes' time.

'Lift up her skirt,' ordered the woman. 'She's going to get this on her bare bottom.'

Obediently one of the girls raised the tiny little skirt. Belinda gave a little moan of fear. Her new Mistress only smacked her with her hand when she had been a naughty girl. Not since Helga had sold her had she been properly caned.

There was a sudden whistling nose and a scream of pain from Belinda. Emma had to hold Belinda's wrist very tightly to prevent her from breaking her position.

'Keep her down,' warned the woman menacingly, 'or I'll thrash the lot of you! Now, little girl, you're going to count to ten, nice and slowly, and when you say "ten" I shall give you the next stroke.'

'One . . . Two . . . Three . . ." Belinda started to count in a sobbing voice.

'No, that's no good,' the woman interrupted. 'Get back on your toes and thrust back again . . . That's better. Now start counting again.'

The woman was really enjoying dragging out her role as executioner.

A few moments later another of Ursula's guests was in the ring blindfolded, whilst the terrified girls did their best to avoid being caught. Indeed, having witnessed one thrashing, they were now pushing each other towards the woman to avoid being caught and thrashed themselves. Suddenly the older of the girls pushed Emma towards the woman, who grabbed her.

'So I shall have the pleasure of beating our hostess's little girl! she cried, taking off the blindfold. She looked at Ursula. 'I hope you don't really mind, my dear. Would you rather cane her yourself?'

Ursula laughed. 'Not at all. I shall enjoy watching you give her a well-earned beating.'

Dumbly Emma went towards the chair, her heart pounding.

'Oh no, that's too boring,' said the woman who had caught Emma. 'I'm going to beat you lying on your back. Now lie down. Raise your legs straight in the air. You two girls each grab an ankle and hold her legs apart and over her head. Get her bottom right off the floor. That's better! Now you, Belinda, hold her arms down on the floor behind her head. Now keep her bottom nicely up and presented for the cane.'

Now that her chastity belt had been removed, Emma could feel herself blushing at the thought of the degrading sight she must be making to the watching guests. But still the woman was not satisfied.

'No! You must get your bottom higher up off the floor. Just remember that it will be much less painful to be caned on your bottom than on the back of the thighs.' She tapped the soft skin above Emma's knees and Emma found herself straining to raise her bottom – raising it to be thrashed.

The first stroke was administered. Emma could not help sobbing. But to her horror she felt a little spurt of wetness invading her body lips – somthing that did not escape the eagle eye of the woman who was thrashing her. She drew the tip of the cane along the moist and gleaming open lips.

'Well!' she laughed. 'We have a passionate little girl here.

One stroke and she's dripping. That chastity belt was certainly effective all right! Now let's see what she's like after another stroke.'

Emma, torn between trying to hide her shame and trying to prepare herself for the next stroke, could not help noticing how the women's eyes were fixed on her body lips. She saw the woman raising the cane again. The girls lifted her up slightly and held her tight. She felt the line of fire across her bottom. She heard herself scream. Then she felt another little pulse of wetness between her legs and heard the cries of delight from the watching women.

'Again,' they cried. 'Give her the next stroke quickly!'

It was indeed a red-faced Emma who struggled to her feet to take her place again in Ursula's devilish game.

For another twenty minutes they continued the same game. None of the girls had escaped a beating. Emma could not help noticing how the older girl seemed to be able to stand up to a beating much better than herself and the younger girls. Would she still be able to do the same when she was thirty-five? Would she still be Ursula's slave then? Or would Ursula with her love of fresh young women have sold her to someone else? Sold her! She had indeed been shocked at the casual way in which Ursula had referred to Belinda's new Mistress paying Helga a high price for her. Having paid to have her expensively trained, did Ursula now regard her as a valuable investment which she could get rid of at a good profit when the time came? It was all too awful to bear thinking about.

'Ladies! Now another little game. Girls, put the chairs in a big circle . . . Now we'll blindfold all the girls and put them in the middle of the circle of chairs . . . Now sit down ladies. I shall call the girls one at a time to crawl on all fours until they find one of us. Then the girl has to put her head under our dresses and identify us. If she gets it right, then she's let off. But, and this is the whole point of the game, if she gets it wrong then the woman she has insulted by not recognising her, can give the girl three strokes of the cane. But this time it must not be on the bottom, nor on the back of the girl's thighs – anywhere else but not there!

So, let's start. Let's have Belinda first . . . Now, spin her round and let's see if she can recognise the first Mistress she crawls to – and if it's her own Mistress and she doesn't recognise her, then it will be double the number of strokes!'

Emma, blindfolded like the other girls, listened in silence as poor Belinda started to crawl round the circle. At last she found herself at the feet of a woman. She put her head under her dress and a minute later she called out 'Mistress Ursula!'

But she was wrong. It was the woman who had earlier thrashed Emma.

'On the hands,' she cried, 'like a naughty schoolgirl.'

Shortly afterwards Emma heard the swishing noise of the cane coming down across the palm of Belinda's hand, and Belinda's gasp of pain.

Then it was Emma's turn to guess the identity of one of the guests. There was something familiar about the woman's scent, but Emma also guessed wrong and got three strokes across her bare back for her pains. She was surprised at how excited the women became at the sight of the marks of the cane across her shoulders.

But she was delighted not to have fallen into the hands of the next woman who beat one of the girls. She insisted on the old Turkish bastinado – the application of a cane across the soles of the feet.

'This is how the eunuchs kept the girls in order in the harems of the wealthy beys and pashas,' she explained. 'It had a very salutary effect on a young woman! Now, let's get this creature's feet up in the air and ready for the cane.'

It was the thirty-five-year-old woman who had pushed Emma in the previous game, who was going to receive the bastinado. After the way she had behaved Emma found it hard to be sorry for her, even though she was one of the girls who had to hold up the older girl's tied ankles ready for the cane across the bare soles of her feet. The same girl had stood up to being beaten on the buttocks very well, but the application of the cane to the soles of her feet had her writhing in no time.

It was now getting late. Those of the aroused and excited

women whose girls had been waiting at table, and taking part in the games, could hardly wait to get them home and into their beds. Emma saw that Ursula's eyes were also shining. She made little attempt to persuade her guests to stay on and Emma could well imagine what sort of night was in store for her. At least, she thought, as she showed the last of the guests to the door, she was not wearing the chastity belt and there was every likelihood that Ursula would not put it on her again before making Emma give her relief in bed.

Indeed, aroused by the beatings, Ursula did not even wait to get Emma into bed with her. She held Emma between her knees as she sat relaxing on the sofa, her cane in her hands to stimulate Emma into even greater efforts whilst receiving no relief herself. Finally satiated and exhausted, she ordered Emma to stand up in front of her.

'Now you little slut, lift up the front of your apron and let's see you perform to my orders.'

It was half an hour before Emma was finally allowed to yield. Half an hour of hell as she was constantly allowed to bring herself to the brink and then would have to stand to attention with her hands at her sides, breathing heavily, her cheeks and breasts discoloured with the telltale blotches and her eyes glazed. Only the constant tapping of Ursula's cane prevented her from clutching herself with her hands in desperate attempts to seek the relief that she had so nearly been allowed to reach.

Then she had to undress and wash Ursula and then help her into bed, before being allowed as a special treat to curl up on the mat by Ursula's bedside – instead of being banished to her little bunk in the dressing room.

'You'll be nearer later on when I will want you again,' Ursula said.

She could not be bothered to fasten the chastity belt onto Emma again, but instead strapped her wrists to a special leather belt that she fastened round the girl's waist.

'That will stop you touching yourself while I'm sleeping,' she said as she turned off the bedside light.

A few moments later Emma felt her Mistress's hand

absentmindedly stroking her hair as she lay like a dog alongside Ursula's bed.

'Oh yes, little Emma, I'm going to enjoy having you in my power in Morocco. You'll just never guess what's in store for you there!'

PART II

A SLAVEGIRL IN MOROCCO

6

Arrival in Morocco

Emma was surprised how short the journey was. No wonder Ursula had so often thought nothing of dashing off to Morocco for a few days. But once seated in the Air Morocco plane she felt that she was entering a new world with a different culture.

Ursula had produced Emma's passport at London airport and shown her the special visa she had obtained for her – not a mere tourist visa, she had explained, but one that would enable Emma to go on working for her as a maidservant. Indeed Ursula had insisted that Emma should travel in her maid's outdoor uniform so that there would be no doubt about their status. To Emma's embarrassment Ursula had also insisted that she should be naked under her long dress – except of course for her chastity belt.

'I'm not going to have a servant of mine making eyes at the stewards or playing with herself in the loo,' Ursula had said when Emma had protested.

As soon as they had passed through security in London, Ursula had taken back Emma's passport. Nor was Emma allowed even a handbag or any spending money.

'I'm not going to have you guzzling yourself on sweets or buying trashy magazines,' Ursula had said. She gave Emma a copy of *Little Women*. 'You can read this on the plane. It's all about little girls. I'm not going to have you mooning and lusting over pictures of some awful male pop star. You belong to me, don't you, little girl?'

'Oh yes, Madam,' Emma had whispered in reply, secretly excited at being treated like this by her imperious Mistress.

She had been given a seat at the back of the plane, amongst other servants: Arab girls, travelling back to Morocco with their employers. Some were pretty, but before the plane descended to Tangier they covered their faces completely with heavy veils that left just a little lace strip over their eyes for them to peer through. They even put on black gloves to hide their hands. With their long black shapeless robes hiding them completely, and wearing ugly black boots to hide their ankles, it was now impossible for anyone to see whether they were hideous old crones or beautiful young creatures.

Emma wondered whether perhaps they were not servants at all, but rather their Master's concubines, travelling and treated like servants, as was the Arab way, whilst their Masters travelled first class. Just like me, she thought, except that I am the secret concubine of a woman – or rather a lover, for of course Ursula did not have a harem of girls!

At the airport in North Africa, a fierce-looking official had warned Emma, after seeing her passport, that she would be arrested and imprisoned if she left Ursula's employment, or if she overstayed her four-month work permit.

'We do not allow European women to work here except as servants, or as registered prostitutes. If you try to run away from your employer, or if you try to leave the country without her written permission, then the police will pick you up and you will be returned to your employer after the normal punishment.'

'The normal punishment?' stammered Emma, taken aback.

'Fifty lashes for breaking our immigration laws,' replied the official coldly. He looked at her passport again. 'I see you are a married woman. Just also remember that this is a Moslem country. The punishment for adultery is two hundred lashes and five years hard labour.'

Emma gave a gasp of disbelief.

'And,' the man went on, 'if the proper Moslem law as laid down in the Koran was observed here, then a woman who commits adultery would be put to death by stoning.'

Emma was speechless when she rejoined Ursula.

'Did you get the usual little speech about not overstaying your work permit or leaving your employer, and not committing adultery?' asked Ursula with a laugh. 'Well, I don't expect you to want to run away from me anyway. And as for adultery, I'll certainly see to it that you don't have any opportunities for that!'

She laughed and gave Emma's little hand a squeeze.

'Now you must meet Ali, the only male in my life – my elderly Arab chauffeur! He's supposed to be meeting us. Now, carry my cases! Remember you are supposed to be my maidservant and walk three paces behind me. Now!'

Ali turned out to be a grizzled old man dressed in an ankle-length white jellabah with a hood, over which he wore a selham, a black cloak, also with a hood. He greeted Ursula respectfully, but ignored Emma and made no attempt to relieve her of the cases. In this society, Emma thought, it is clearly the women who fetch and carry.

Ursula's car was a big maroon coloured Mercedes with the tinted windows which are common in Arab countries, as Emma was to learn, so as to prevent curious eyes from seeing inside. Emma put Ursula's heavy suitcases in the boot of the car. She herself, of course, had no luggage, for Ursula had forbidden her to bring anything, saying that all she would need would be her chastity belt! Emma was uncertain as to whether she should get in alongside the chauffeur, or in the back with Ursula. In England, she knew, Ursula would have been outraged if she had tried to sit alongside her. Ursula came to the rescue.

'Get into the back, girl. You'll see there is a special folding servant's seat,' she said angrily, annoyed at having to interrupt a long conversation in French which she had been having with Ali whilst Emma struggled with the suitcases.

There was indeed a little servant's seat, almost on the floor, so low that she could not see out of the window properly.

Sitting at Ursula's feet, Emma simply had the impression of dry, dusty heat as they drove away from the airport. She tried, out of curiosity, to rise up in her seat to look at this new countryside, and strange new people, but Ursula angrily smacked her.

'Keep your eyes down on the floor, you stupid girl. If I want you to look, I'll tell you. Here in Morocco curiosity is not encouraged in a slave girl – nor is looking at men in the streets.'

'Slave girl?' queried Emma. It sounded rather exciting.

'Yes, you know very well that when you came back from the school in Paris I told you that in future you were to be merely my slave girl. Well, here in Morocco, that's exactly what you are going to be. The terms of your work permit effectively make you my slave, just as much as the indentured labour system here makes slaves of the servants and labourers of rich Arabs. Now, keep your eyes down and remember from now on speak only when you are spoken to, or you'll be sorry.'

Shocked by Ursula's angry tone, Emma lowered her eyes to the floor. She could feel herself becoming moist under her chastity belt, aroused despite herself, by Ursula's references to her being merely a slave. Ashamed, she felt herself blushing. Would she really be treated as Ursula's slave here? How exciting! How frightening!

Out of the corner of her eye she saw Ursula looking eagerly out of the window as the car drove on. She heard her exchanging remarks with Ali as they passed some building of interest. She did not dare open her mouth. She had no idea where they were going.

After perhaps an hour, she felt the car slowing down and turning into what seemed to be some sort of drive. She heard a gateway being opened, apparently electronically, and then the car stopped. Ali opened the door for Ursula. Emma made the mistake of looking up.

'How many times do I have to repeat myself?' said Ursula angrily, again smacking Emma's cheeks as she got out of the car. 'Keep your eyes to the floor and stay here.'

The door slammed behind her. Emma did not dare raise her head, as she squatted in the tiny little chair, wondering where they were, for Ursula had not told her anything about her villa in Morocco.

After several minutes the car door was opened again. This time Emma kept her eyes fixed on the floor. She heard a deep-throated female laugh and a woman's voice speaking in a harsh tone with a heavy German accent.

'All right, little girl, now you can look up!'

Emma raised her head and saw, framed in the door of the car, a very tall, strongly built, middle-aged woman, with straight hair, grey piercing eyes and a grim expression. She was dressed like a nurse in a long grey uniform, but to Emma she seemed more like a prison wardress with her thick black leather belt from which hung a bunch of keys. Horrified, Emma saw that hanging from the belt was also a short leather whip.

The woman reached into the car and without a word gripped Emma by the hair and dragged her out. Then she held Emma up by the hair, so that she was standing on the tips of her toes, right in front of her.

'Look up at me, you slut, or you'll get the whip!' she shouted menacingly. Terrified, Emma did so, feeling like a rabbit being hypnotised by a stoat. Then the woman went on slowly in her accented English. 'Now you listen, little girl! I'm in charge here. In charge of you! And I maintain discipline here; not your sloppy English-type discipline, but strict German discipline! And if you ever give me any lip, or answer me back, or ever try to argue with me or my assistant, then it will be the whip for you, my girl. You call me "Madam Warden", you understand? And you call my assistant, Miss Marbar. You curtsey when you report to us and you stand at attention, looking straight ahead with your head up and hands clasped behind your neck, when we speak to you. Understand?'

Dumbly, scared stiff of this frightening woman, Emma nodded – only to be rewarded by a stinging slap across her face as the woman shouted!

'Then into the proper position! Now! Head up! Hands clasped behind neck! Elbows back!'

Terrified, Emma saw that she was unfastening the short whip from her belt.

'Keep your eyes fixed ahead, you stupid girl!'

She brought the whip down across Emma's shoulders, through the thin material of her maid's dress. Emma gave a little scream of pain. She felt so foolish, standing in this position by the car but she'd do anything, she decided, not to make this terrifying woman angry.

Then, like a sergeant major inspecting a new recruit, the woman slowly walked round the trembling Emma, impatiently tapping her whip against the palm of her hand. Emma was petrified. She did not dare to move a muscle. The woman put her whip under Emma's chin to raise it slightly. She tapped Emma's buttocks with the whip, and instantly Emma clenched them together and straightened up even more.

'That's better, little beauty. That's a good little girl!'

Out of the corner of her eye, as she looked straight ahead, Emma saw the German woman smile slightly as she pulled Emma's hair back, but it was a smile that made Emma shiver as she wondered who on earth this woman was.

Behind the woman, she caught a glimpse of a sumptuous, white painted, Arab style house with arabesque stone tracery and elaborate black metal bars over the windows.

'Come!' the woman ordered. 'Follow me – and keep your hands clasped behind your neck and your head up. And make sure, you little slut, that your eyes keep fixed ahead and your elbows back!'

Feeling intensely embarrassed, Emma followed the woman into the house. It was spacious and cool, with typical Arab ornamental ceilings.

Emma remembered Ursula saying that her house had been built by a Moorish Caid, a cousin of the Sultan, who had been exiled to Tangier from Fez. He certainly seemed to have lived well to judge by the large house with its marble floors. Intrigued, Emma followed the woman down the passage. Through the elaborate arabesque tracery behind the windows, she could see that there was a splendid view of the haze-covered mountains on one side and of the vividly blue sea on the other. At the end of the passage was a heavy wooden door strengthened with iron bars and bolts.

'This is door to old harem quarters for when house belong to rich Caid,' explained the woman in her harsh broken English as she took a large key that was attached to her black leather belt by a chain, and inserted it into the lock. Then she pressed the buttons of a modern electronic lock on the adjoining wall. 'Now door also has clever modern lock as well. Only Miss Ursula, my assistant and I know the number for this lock.'

But what on earth do you keep behind the door these days that has to be kept so carefully locked up? Emma longed to pluck up the courage to ask. But she did not dare to say a word. Surely, she said to herself, Ursula wouldn't keep a harem of girls!

'Now you'll soon see what's going to happen to you,' grunted the woman as if in reply to Emma's thoughts, as she swung the big door open on its well-oiled hinges. She motioned Emma to pass through and then carefully locked the door behind her.

7

A harem with a difference

Standing behind the door as it opened was a large black woman, dressed in a long robe – rather like the terrifying German woman. Like her she wore a broad black leather belt around her waist, from which hung a short leather dog whip. Her glittering black eyes looked Emma over silently. My God, thought Emma. This must be Miss Marbar!

Scared stiff, Emma kept her hands firmly clasped behind her neck and her head up, in what was apparently the required subservient position.

'Keep an eye on this new one,' muttered the German woman to her assistant, as she strode off purposefully, as if going to check something.

Innocently, Emma wondered what was going on.

'You may look around,' said Miss Marbar. She spoke with a strong foreign accent.

Emma saw that she was looking down onto a very pretty and slightly sunken patio, with a tinkling fountain and brilliantly-coloured flowerbeds. Round the patio was a small, collonaded shaded walkway, with several rooms leading off it. Prettily barred windows looked out onto the patio. At the far end was a swimming pool, shaded by a curved roof. It was a picture of cool tranquility.

But what caught Emma's attention were the black, curved iron bars that went right across the top of the patio, giving it the look of a luxurious aviary. They would have clearly kept strangers out of the Caid's harem, thought Emma with a laugh – and have kept the inmates in!

'Caid not want concubines escape from harem – nor be stolen,' said the black woman in rather broken English.

'Once girl in harem, she stay here – no escape. That big door and those big bars make sure. Not even see another man – so soon even young girls fall in love with elderly Caid.'

'How awful for the girls,' said Emma, rather shocked at this example of masculine control over women. 'Would there have been European women here too?'

'Oh yes, black girls, Arab girls, Turkish girls, Berber girls, and, of course, white girls. Some Moroccan men like white girls best of all. They pay plenty money for white girls. Still do. And for white boys too.' She winked. 'Caid also keep castrated white boys in harem with white girls. And he like show off white boys. But keep white girls secret.'

Rather shocked and yet a little excited by the Arab woman's remarks, she asked, 'But how do you know all this?'

'I assistant harem mistress to Caid,' she said proudly. I keep girls in order. She tapped her whip and laughed. 'Madam keep me on!'

Emma followed her down the steps onto the patio, still curious to see what it was that Ursula kept locked up so carefully in this part of the former palace. Suddenly she heard girls' voices.

The big German woman came out onto the patio and clapped her hands. 'Girls!' she called out. 'Come meet new girl.'

There was a sudden silence. Emma heard Miss Marbar call out from behind her, 'Yes, girls, you put down little dolls and come see what Mistress has brought.'

There was a sudden patter of little feet from behind a door, and then four strikingly pretty European girls suddenly burst onto the patio. Clearly, Emma realised, the German woman and Miss Marbar were in some sort of position of authority over the four pretty young women. But she had no time to ponder over that, for it was the four girls who now caught her attention.

Silently they gave a little curtsey to the German woman and then quickly lined up, like well-drilled soldiers, with the tallest girl on the right and the shortest on the left.

All four of them were dressed in similar white caftans. They were of a thin cotton material and prettily embroidered. Emma was shocked, however, to see that, from the way that the girls' apparently painted nipples pressed against the fabric, they seemed to have nothing on underneath their caftans, just as she, too, had nothing on beneath her long maid's dress, except of course, her chastity belt.

All four girls were the same build as herself, with tiny waists and full bosoms – just like hers! Ursula, she knew, with her own tall, but straight and boyish figure, liked to see an old-fashioned hour-glass figure on a girl.

She saw that embroidered on the right breast of each girl's caftan was Ursula's monogram – an elaborate 'U de F'. She saw that the girls all had their hair hanging long and straight, like that of a little girl, which was how Ursula had told her to keep her own hair, in contrast to Ursula's close-cropped fashionable style.

The girls were all looking at her in amazement, their mouths wide open, as indeed was hers as she looked at them. What on earth, she thought, were they doing here in Ursula's villa, and in the former harem quarters? Who on earth were they? Who for that matter were the German woman and her Arab assistant? Why were the girls not decently dressed? What was that she had heard about dolls? These were grown women not little girls! And why did they all have Ursula's monogram on their caftans, just like she had on her nightdresses back in England?

'This is Emma,' said the German woman. 'Your Mistress brought her today from England to join you. Now you must all be very nice to the new girl, and tell her about our little rules. Now . . . Dismissed!'

The girls turned smartly to the right as one, paused, and then ran off squealing with delight at the news that Ursula was back.

'Madam's back! The Mistress is back!' they cried. 'Ursula's here again! . . . We must get ready for her . . . Hurry! . . . Come on! . . . I want to look my best! . . . So do I! . . . I want . . .'

The girls all made as if to rush off back to the room they had come from. But the big German woman barred their way, her arms spread out.

'Wait!' she ordered. The girls stood stock still. She continued in her German accent. 'I hear one girl call Mistress by name, Ursula.' She turned to the oldest looking girl, a strikingly beautiful blonde woman of about thirty. 'You did, Karen! You know that not allowed. She your Mistress, not Ursula. You get two black marks! And you also get this, Karen . . .'

The German woman brought her open hand down across the girl's white face. She gave a little sob.

'Oh no!' she cried. 'That's not fair! I was just excited. I don't deserve any black marks.'

'You now get four black marks for arguing with me,' shouted the German woman. She went over to a table on the patio, on which stood a big leather-bound book. She opened it and picked up a pen.

'Karen. Four black marks,' she called out as she wrote it down slowly.

'You asked for that Karen, you are silly,' Emma heard one of the other girls whisper in a very upper-class, educated English accent.

'I know, I know,' muttered Karen, 'but don't you start. It's bad enough being kept locked up here by that bitch, without getting a beating as well on the day she comes back. Just my luck!'

'What you say?' demanded Miss Marbar angrily. 'What you say?'

'Just that I love my Mistress and that I'm very sorry,' Emma heard the girl called Karen say in a frightened voice. Only a moment before she had heard her refer to Ursula as 'that bitch'. It was all very strange. And what had she meant by 'being kept locked up here'? Surely the girls were not prisoners? She looked up at the bars across the top of the patio and gave a little shiver of fear.

'Who is she?' Emma heard one of the girls ask in a French accent, as she pointed at her. 'And why is she dressed in a maid's uniform?'

'Don't you bother your little head about that, she soon dressed just like you!' came the reply from the German woman at the end of the patio. 'You know Mistress like all little girls in her harem dressed alike.'

Harem! What harem? thought Emma. Then suddenly an awful thought crossed her mind. Surely Ursula did not keep a harem of young women in her villa? Locked up in the old harem quarters? And was she now part of it?

'I don't understand,' she whispered to the older girl called Karen. 'What is this? Who are those awful women? And what's that book?'

'It's really very simple,' said Karen. 'Welcome to our beloved Mistress's harem of girls. You're her latest addition to it! And those awful women, as you rightly call them are the harem mistresses. We call the German woman the "Dragon" – she's very strict! And that book is our punishment book – deliberately placed there at the orders of our . . . beloved . . . Mistress to keep us all frightened and obedient.'

'No! No!' cried Emma. 'I'm her friend. She invited me here. She never mentioned a harem. And I'm a married woman.'

'All the more of a challenge for her,' laughed the older girl bitterly. 'Has she let you sleep with your husband since you met her?'

'No, but . . .'

'And if you are simply her friend, why are you dressed as a servant girl?'

'Because she made me,' admitted Emma in a whisper.

'Exactly! You're just one of her slaves, like the rest of us.'

'Slaves!' cried Emma. 'There are no slaves these days.'

'Perhaps not technically,' replied Karen in a whisper, 'but in effect that's what we are. Didn't you come here on a work permit? Didn't they warn at the airport what would happen to you if you tried to run away from Ursula? – You'd be flogged and returned to her!'

'Yes, but . . .' Emma tried to say.

'And didn't they warn you that the same thing would

happen if you were ever caught after overstaying your permit?'

'Yes, but . . .'

'So, don't you see? To all intents and purposes you're just a slave here, for the rest of your life if Ursula wants that – just like us,' she added bitterly.

'No! No!' cried Emma with tears starting in her eyes. 'I love her. She wouldn't do this to me.'

'But she has! And she did the same to the rest of us. But you're Irish and it will be lovely to have another Irish girl here to cheer me up!' The voice, in a strong Irish brogue, came from the youngest of the girls, a vivacious and fiery-looking redhead. She began to laugh.

'Cheer up! We'll stick together and see off these bloody Brits!'

Miss Marbar then came up and gripped Emma's arm.

'Enough talk! You come with me.'

She began to lead Emma across the patio.

'Please,' murmured Emma embarrassed. 'I want to go to the . . .'

It had been a long flight and so much had happened since. She sounded, she realised, like a little girl, but neither Miss Marbar, nor the woman she was now thinking of as the Dragon, seemed surprised.

'We'll take you to bathroom,' said the Dragon. She turned to the other girls. 'You wait outside – and no talking!'

Bemused and shocked by what she had just learnt, Emma let herself be led into a spacious modern bathroom. It had one extra large bath.

'This is where we wash the girls,' said the Dragon in a menacing voice 'Now we take off your dress.'

Emma was terribly embarrassed about the chastity belt locked over her body as the two women undressed her. But the women simply ignored it. Instead they produced a little Moorish brass bowl, and placed it on the floor. She saw that there were four others. The women pointed to it and explained to Emma just what she was to do. Emma was appalled. Ursula had controlled her back in England, and so too had the dreadful Achmet at the school, but these two big women with their hard, pig-like eyes, made it even more humiliating.

'All girls use bowl in harem, and always in front of Miss Marbar or me,' the Dragon told her. 'You never do it alone. We like to check girls fit and well for Mistress.'

The Arab woman had turned on the taps of the bath and, perhaps because of this, Emma was soon able to overcome her shyness and perform to the satisfaction of the German nurse who then called in the other girls.

Each girl took off her long caftan and fetched a bowl. Each was made to perform just as Emma had. Emma had noticed before that they were naked under their caftans. Now she was astonished to see that each wore a chastity belt identical to her own.

'You too!' said the dark-haired French girl with a laugh as she climbed into the bath with Emma. 'They're so terribly frustrating. Ursula only introduced them into her harem here a few months ago. But it feels like years.'

The other girls now climbed into the bath, all naked except for their chastity belts, each with its own elaborate artificial body lips, just like Emma's. Under the watchful eyes of the two women, the girls began to soap and wash each other.

'It's so frustrating for us girls, having to do this,' whispered the red-headed young Irish girl as she soaped Emma. She washed the plastic body lips on Emma chastity belt, but of course Emma could feel nothing. Nor did the Irish girl, whose name Emma learnt was Mary, feel anything when Emma washed her. She saw the nurse smile contentedly at the Arab woman. It was a smile that reminded her of Rafaela's back in London, when she checked that the special thigh chain was still in place, ensuring that not even the tip of a little finger could reach her real body lips and her little source of pleasure. Somehow it seemed even crueller here in this modern harem of girls to be kept completely frustrated.

Emma was longing to ask the other girls a whole string of questions. How long had they been kept here? Who were they? How were they treated? Could they escape? And above all, when would she see Ursula again?

But the two women, the Dragon and Miss Marbar, whom the girls addressed in very respectful tones, did not give her a chance to ask any questions, not even when she saw a cane hanging on the wall and wanted to ask about it. She remembered Karen being given four black marks and then fearfully saying that she was going to be beaten. Beaten by whom, Emma wondered, and with what? She was well aware of Ursula's enjoyment in beating a girl.

The women now brusquely ordered the girls out of the bath. Each girl started to make up and paint her face, and her body. Emma learnt that when Ursula was finally back in the palace they all had to paint their artificial body lips and nipples. Clearly each girl was painting herself so as to try and attract Ursula's attention.

'Oh God, I hope she chooses me and lets me take off this damn chastity belt.' It was the same educated voice that she had heard earlier. The educated voice of a pretty young blonde. Her name, Emma learnt, was Daphne and the French girl was Monique. She already knew that the older girl was Karen and the young Irish girl, Mary. She wondered how each of them had landed up here, in Ursula's secret harem. But there was no opportunity then to chat. Each girl was frantically busy getting herself ready for Ursula's forthcoming inspection of her harem.

Emma, shocked as she was by the way that Ursula had tricked her, found herself also caught up in the general excitement. These girls, she realised, may resent being kept by Ursula in her harem, but since being chosen by Ursula for her pleasure was the only way they might be allowed to have their chastity belts taken off – and so earn a little relief for themselves – they were genuinely desperate to catch her eye.

8

A touch of harem discipline

There was something vaguely familiar about the girls, thought Emma. But it was only when the Dragon opened a cupboard containing a row of beautiful bright Moorish dresses, that she suddenly realised that the girls had appeared in many of Ursula's paintings – those paintings of half-naked white women wearing eastern clothes that sold so well in London.

Ursula used her girls not only for her pleasure, but also as models for her paintings. No wonder they had seemed so lifelike. They were of white girls genuinely kept in a real harem – her own harem.

But to Emma's disappointment they were told that their Mistress wished to inspect them, on this occasion, dressed in their long transparent caftans. Emma soon found herself wearing one too. She looked in the mirror. With her long blonde hair hanging down over her back, her gorgeously painted eyes and the scarlet paint of her nipples and artificial body lips showing through the muslin-like material, she looked just like the other girls. She remembered the remark of the Dragon, about the Mistress liking to see all the girls identically dressed.

Looking again in the mirror, she had to admit that she looked exceptionally attractive – just like the other girls. Perhaps it was because of the feeling of competitiveness amongst the girls, she thought. Each girl driven by the frustration caused by her chastity belt, and by her natural female jealousy, trying to make herself look more beautiful than the others. What a clever idea it was from the Mistress's point of view!

For the next two hours the girls impatiently awaited Ursula's next move. Meanwhile she was, Emma learnt, bathing and resting in what were formerly the Caid's own quarters in the palace. These were alongside the harem and Emma saw the little trap door which the summoned girls had to crawl through, naked, into the Caid's sumptuous bedroom – now that of Ursula.

To prevent the harem women from trying to escape through the trap door when the Caid was not in his bedroom, it was, Emma learnt, a double door which could only be operated from the outside. The Caid, in his bedroom, would look through the grill onto the harem without being seen, and choose which girl or girls he wanted. He would then order his eunuchs to prepare and strip the chosen girls. His pageboy would then raise the trap door so that these chosen girls could crawl through it. They would then find themselves kneeling in a little cage hanging in their Master's bedroom – a cage from which they would be taken out, one at a time or all together, according to the whim of the Caid – when he was ready for them.

In the course of the night or afternoon, a girl might have found herself being taken out of the cage and replaced back in it several times, whilst she jealously watched her companions performing. It was apparently a custom that Ursula followed avidly, and one that her girls found both humiliating and yet also strangely exciting.

No one knew whether on this occasion Ursula would follow that course and simply inspect the girls through the grill as they paraded in front of it or whether, as she often did, she would come into the harem and have them paraded by the Dragon for her close inspection. The suspense amongst the frustrated girls was tremendous and even Emma, who had only been separated from Ursula for a couple of hours, instead of a couple of weeks like the other girls, found herself being caught up in the excitement and feeling of sensual arousal.

The atmosphere was made all the more tense by no talking being permitted as they waited. Meekly they sat on large leather cushions in the cool and airy main harem room, under the constantly watching eye of either the Dragon or her equally powerful-looking black assistant. Their role was similar to that of the eunuchs whom the Caid had employed both to enforce strict discipline in the harem, and to train the girls to give him pleasure; keeping them fit and eager to do so, and in particular to prevent them from playing with themselves, or with each other – something made very much easier in the case of Ursula's harem by their modern chastity belts.

Ursula, with her hatred of anything male, preferred to use women for this task. She reckoned that her strict and burly German and black women were probably just as effective as the strict and burly uneducated eunuchs that the Caid had employed. They were also, of course, easier for her to recruit since officially, to the outside world, it was not a harem of women that she kept but simply a school for girls.

This distinction was important to prevent any problems with the authorities or local Moslem fundamentalists. Lesbianism is, of course, not allowed by the Koran and is considered in the Moslem world to be an affront to men. But a blind eye is traditionally turned to what goes on in the privacy of a private house.

Emma learnt from the Dragon that Ursula would be attended in her quarters by her Arab maidservants who looked down on the European girls in the harem as merely the Mistress's chattels.

It was by now evening, and the Dragon motioned the girls to go up the staircase onto the roof of the harem to enjoy a little fresh air and the view across the countryside, after being cooped up in the harem all day. Emma eagerly wondered, as she followed Mary up the little steps, whether this might be a way of escaping from the harem. She was therefore very disappointed to find that the steps came out into a large cage built on the roof in the form of a pretty aviary with plants and even a swing. There were canaries and parrakeets fluttering about and sharing the aviary with the girls.

Clearly, however, the Caid had built the aviary like a cage, not only to prevent the little birds from flying away, but also to prevent his women from getting similar ideas. Emma looked despondently at the very solid bars of the aviary.

'There's no escape,' murmured Daphne giving Emma's hand a little sympathetic squeeze. 'And anyway where could we go if we did get out? The police would be ready to arrest us, and return us to Ursula after first giving us a thrashing, if they find us, or if we try to leave the country. And you can imagine what Ursula would tell the Dragon to do to us as well.' Daphne sighed. Emma realised that she was a highly intelligent girl and wondered how she came to be in this harem. Then she went on in a more cheerful tone.

'The view is lovely here in the cool evening. But don't think you'll ever even see a man. I haven't seen or spoken to one for months! That's just not allowed! I don't think any of the girls here are natural lesbians, and that's what makes not letting us see men all the more exciting for Ursula – and in a funny way for us too. That, and the very sensual and feminine atmosphere here, seems to make us all become obsessed with Ursula, and to accept the cruel way that she and her harem mistresses treat us. It's very strange, but I must admit that, except perhaps for Karen, most of the time we're all quite happy being kept locked up here, having no contact with the outside world, and just thinking about Ursula. It all seems to be part of the age-old harem system, a system that Ursula has adopted for her own use.'

Indeed, Emma saw through the bars of the cage only the distant mountains and the view of the sea that she had noticed earlier whilst being taken to the harem. It all made her feel very much like a caged bird, a feeling that was probably just what the cruel Caid, and now the equally cruel Ursula, liked their young concubines to feel.

The realisation that Ursula now had her locked up in her harem with these other girls both scared and excited Emma. What an extraordinary woman her Mistress was! To have a harem of young European girls kept locked up in a real former harem! And subject to the strict discipline of the Dragon and Miss Marbar.

It was all unbelievable. It just could not be true. But the bars of the roof cage and across the top of the patio, the special lock on the door and the horrible little trap door that led to what had been the Caid's bedroom, and was now Ursula's, all drove home the truth.

Suddenly it was sunset. Emma heard from a loudspeaker on the top of a nearby minaret something which she was soon going to recognise as the sunset call to prayer. Here in Ursula's harem it was also the call for punishment, the punishment of any of the girls who had been awarded black marks by the harem mistresses during the day.

Without any further orders having to be given, the girls all followed the Dragon down the stairs and back into the big harem room. Miss Marbar followed behind to make sure that none of them remained skiving in the cage on the roof, for all the girls had to witness any punishments. It made for better discipline!

Emma saw that Karen, despite being the oldest of the girls, was near to tears. She was biting her lips and trembling. Emma remembered her bitterness at earning a beating on the very day that their Mistress returned.

'Fetch the cane, Karen,' ordered the Dragon.

Looking very frightened, Karen ran off to where the long whippy cane was hanging on the wall. Doubtless, thought Emma, it was kept there on view to help coerce the girls and make them more obedient.

She saw a look of cunning cross Karen's face as she ran back to the woman with the cane in her hands.

'Oh please, Madam Warden,' she begged, 'can't I be beaten in front of our Mistress? Please, I'm sure she'd like that.'

And be more likely to choose Karen for her pleasure, thought Emma with a silent little laugh. How many times had she herself been naughty, and thereby earned a beating, merely to excite Ursula so that she would take her to bed! Clearly Karen was up to the same trick. But Miss Marbar was far too experienced in dealing with slave women to fall for Karen's attempt to turn her punishment to her advantage.

'No, you'll get all four strokes for your four black marks now,' growled the Dragon. 'Maybe, if you're lucky, the Mistress may be watching through the screen, or may later be excited to see the marks on your little bottom, and choose you. We'll see. But now you're going to bend over and put your neck and wrists in the punishment stock for your beating! And you other girls, line up properly behind her, facing away!'

She nodded to Miss Marbar, who raised the top half of the little stocks that would hold Karen's neck and wrists whilst keeping her neatly bent over. Then she gripped the trembling Karen by the hair to keep her still, and closed the stocks. Karen was now held helpless, bending over tight.

Emma saw that the girls lined up in order of height, with the English upper-class girl, Daphne, at the end, then the French girl, Monique, then Mary, the red-headed Irish girl and then herself as the most petite of them all. They all had their backs to poor Karen. Hearing but not seeing Karen's thrashing would make it all the more of a frightening lesson for them all in not being what the Dragon called 'impertinent'.

The girls clasped their hands behind their necks and stood quite still, their eyes fixed ahead.

'Say it aloud,' Emma heard the Dragon say to Karen.

'Please beat me hard,' sobbed Karen as if repeating a well-learned lesson, 'for I have been a naughty girl and deserve to be punished.'

'Good,' grunted the Dragon. She turned to the line of girls.

'Now you lot, say it!'

'Please thrash our sister hard,' Emma heard them chorus in perfect time. 'She has been a naughty girl!'

Emma did not dare look round. But out of the corner of her eye she saw the Dragon raise the cane. Miss Marbar slipped Karen's caftan up round her waist leaving her soft little white bottom quite naked, except for the curved bar of her chastity belt which pressed up tightly between her buttocks. There was an expectant hush.

Then the Dragon slowly lowered the cane and touched Karen's bottom with the tip, as if to warn her to expect the first stroke. Then suddenly she brought it down hard across the girl's backside. There was a little cry from Karen and the noise of all the other girls sucking in their breath in horror.

'Say it!' ordered the woman again, and again the wretched Karen had to beg to be beaten hard, and again the other girls had also to chorus their desire to hear their companion being well and truly thrashed – even though each was feeling that there, but for the grace of God, she herself might be bent over to receive a caning from the burly Dragon.

At last the long drawn out caning was over. The tearful Karen was released. The line of horrified watching girls was dismissed. Emma saw the Dragon smile up at the brass lattice grill that looked down into the harem room from the former private apartments of the Caid. Emma thought she saw a shadow move across it. Had Ursula been comfortably seated behind it, secretly getting herself aroused by watching a girl being flogged, before choosing which girls were to please her that night?

The girls were then left to sit around in the big harem room still in silence. Emma saw that it was beautifully decorated in a traditional Moorish style with big brass trays on little curved tables, huge Turkish carpets, elaborately patterned tiles on the walls and high but curved ceilings. All the heavily barred windows looked out onto the patio. From the harem there was no view of the outside world.

In an adjoining room was a huge bed, in which all the girls slept together – their chastity belts being considered sufficient to prevent any misbehaviour. They might rub their nipples against each other as they sought to ease their frustration, but frustrated they would remain.

Time dragged past.

Suddenly an internal telephone rang. The Dragon and Miss Marbar picked up separate receivers. Emma thought she heard Ursula's harsh tones giving orders. She saw the Dragon exchange smiles with her assistant, and then they looked at the girls as if they knew something which the girls did not.

Emma wondered what form Ursula's inspections of her harem took. Would they have to undress or line up in front of her? Would they have to crawl to her feet? Her mind was full of such questions when the Dragon put down the phone and ordered that all the girls, this time, were to crawl into their Mistress's bedroom through the little trap door. Emma could not help feeling that this sounded equally exciting.

Emma did not understand properly what was happening, but she saw that the other girls were taking off their caftans, brushing their hair, spraying on scent, touching up the make-up around their eyes and generally titivating themselves to look as attractive as possible.

The Dragon motioned to her, with a snap of her fingers, to do the same.

9

Emma's first night in the harem

The girls were all now stark naked, except for their little chastity belts. They were all feeling very shy and nervous. Clearly they were as mystified as Emma as to what little game their cruel Mistress was going to play with them.

Miss Marbar left the harem and the giris were made, by the Dragon, to line up behind each other on all fours with Karen leading the line and Emma in the rear. The German woman looked down the line, satisfying herself that her little charges were all looking their best. Then she picked up the internal telephone. Emma heard her speaking, but could not understand what she was saying.

A moment later the small trap door mysteriously opened. One by one the Dragon ordered the girls to crawl through it. As Emma crawled along the short passageway, she heard the little doorway shut behind her with a metallic clang. There was the sound of bolts being automatically rammed home. The Caid had certainly made sure that none of the concubines could escape to freedom. Emma wondered with a slight shiver whether any British girl had ever had to crawl to her Master's bedroom as she was now having to crawl to her Mistress's.

At the end of the passageway Emma found herself crawling into a small cage. It was suspended several feet above the floor. As she squeezed into it, for with four other girls in it already there was little spare room, a metal, barred door automatically shut behind her.

The cage was illuminated by a bright spotlight, making it difficult to see out whilst showing off the girls clearly to anyone in the room. She saw beneath the barred floor of the cage, a sloping metal tray down which water was running. It would, she realised with a shock, collect any liquids or solids dropping down from the cage. The water led away into a drain. The Caid must have enjoyed keeping girls in this cage for hours, if not days, on end.

Like the other girls, she blinked from the dazzlingly bright light as she tried to peer out between the bars. She had to kneel on the barred floor of the cage, for it was too low to allow the girls to stand up. As her eyes became gradually more accustomed to the light she made out a large and surprisingly high bed.

There, lying on the bed, she saw the figure of a woman dressed in a long satin negligée. It was Ursula. She was looking radiant.

Kneeling by her side on the bed, Emma could just see, was another slim, but younger woman. Emma saw that with one hand she was caressing Ursula. Emma saw her bend down and, keeping one hand on her, kiss Ursula on the lips.

'Darling, darling,' she murmered.

Emma's mind was racing. There was something very familiar about the relative positions of Ursula and this strange woman, something familiar about the way the woman was using her hand, and something familiar about the twang of her voice.

It was the American woman! The tall, beautiful grey-eyed Mrs Guggenheim!

It was indeed the American woman of whom she had been so jealous on that golfing weekend, and later in London and during that weekend in Ireland.

She must, Emma realised, have taken Ursula's invitation to come and see her in Morocco at her word. She must have arrived quite suddenly. This was what had disrupted the programme that the Dragon had arranged to celebrate the Mistress's return. This was why, instead of the usual parades and inspections, and the elaborate routine of choosing a girl for her pleasure, Ursula had unexpectedly ordered all the girls to be put naked into the little cage that hung in her bedroom.

Emma sensed the jealousy and arousal of the other women as they watched the rich young American woman bring Ursula to an ever increasing peak of excitement.

Minutes passed in a shocked silence, broken only by little cries and moans of delight from Ursula and her friend. Then her American woman spoke coaxingly.

'Darling, can't we now have your slave girls?'

Emma heard Ursula give a deep-throated laugh as she sat up in bed. She pressed a ball by her bedside. Miss Marbar came padding silently into the big bedroom. Emma saw that she was carrying a thick bundle of fresh twigs joined together at one end. It was a birch rod – something that Ursula had often spoken about as being the most effective weapon with which to control a girl. Emma put her hand to her mouth in sheer fear.

'Lie like me with your legs apart and hanging down over the side of the bed,' Ursula told the American woman. 'We'll each have a girl standing between our legs and rubbing herself against us to give us pleasure, whilst Miss Marbar uses her birch rod to keep them quivering and wriggling.'

'But that'll get the girls excited too,' objected the American woman. 'I don't want that! They're just sluts.'

'Don't worry, darling,' laughed Ursula. 'They've all got little chastity belts on. They won't feel a thing. And when I flick my fingers, they'll kneel down and use their tongues.'

'Oh yes, yes!' cried the American woman.

'There are five of them in the cage,' continued Ursula in her slow cool voice. 'We'll both try each of them out and we'll mark each girl out of five marks and tell Miss Marbar to keep the score. Up to five marks for the pleasure each girl's artificial body lips give us and five marks for her tongue. Then the bottom girl will get twelve strokes of the cane, and the other less, depending on how many good marks each has earned. That'll make them keen to please us!'

'And then,' continued the American woman eagerly, 'Miss Marbar can remove their chastity belts and we'll mark them again out of five for the pleasure they give us with their real body lips as they stand between our legs!'

'Exactly,' cried Ursula. 'And if a girl climaxes or touches herself without permission, then she'll also get five strokes of the cane! Come on Miss Marbar, let's have the first two girls out of the cage.'

The black woman went to the cage. She unlocked the little barred sliding door in front of the opening. She pulled out two girls by their hair. Mary and Monique. They climbed down the little ladder that led down to the floor. Then she led them, crawling, to the bed.

Monique stood between Ursula's legs and Mary between the American woman's. Their quite remarkable plastic artificial body lips were touching the women's real ones. Miss Marbar gave each girl a sharp stroke with the birch. Immediately they began thrusting and wriggling as if their lives depended on it.

'You'll like Mary,' said Ursula to the American woman as they lay back on the bed side by side, enjoying the intense pleasure that the two standing girls were giving them. 'She was a virgin when I got her from a convent in Ireland a year ago, when she was sixteen. Even now she's never seen a man's manhood. She doesn't even know what it is! Do you, little Mary? I brought her here into my part of the villa for a little honeymoon on her own. She had no idea about the harem on the other side of the door. On the second night I took her virginity with my dildo and the next day I took her through the door. She's been here ever since, haven't you my girl?'

'Yes, Madam,' replied Mary, blushing with shame.

'Well mind you give plenty of pleasure to my American friend, you pretty little colleen!'

'Oh yes, Madam, I will, I will,' she replied in her strong brogue.

'Half the pleasure from these girls comes from the knowledge that none of them are natural lesbians,' Ursula explained to her American friend as Mary and Monique, under the stimulus of Miss Marbar's birch rod, wriggled and writhed to give the women pleasure. 'They have to be beaten into giving us pleasure! The other half comes from knowing that they themselves can feel nothing, thanks to their chastity belts.'

A few minutes later it was Emma's turn to first stand and then kneel between the thighs of each of the women in turn. How she hated having to please the American woman! But the pain of the strokes of the cane, kept her straining hard. It was of course a deeply humiliating experience for all the girls, all of whom would have been far happier between the thighs of a strong man, even Mary, had she known what she was missing!

Finally Daphne was announced as the loser of the competition.

'Choose another girl to kneel between your knees as you watch that stuck-up slut getting her twelve strokes. I'm going to have one between mine! And I'm going to have the strokes given very slowly as the girl gets me more and more excited with her tongue, to match the visual excitement. It's a wonderful feeling!'

To Emma's dismay the American woman chose her. Her obvious repulsion for the American woman would make it all thc more pleasurable, she heard the woman telling Ursula.

'If you move your head away just as I am climaxing, Emma,' she warned, 'I'll ask your Mistress for you to have a dozen strokes of the cane as well.

This terrifying threat was enough to ensure that Emma bent her head down and kept it there, her tongue dutifully applied, throughout the long drawn out beating of Daphne. Emma heard Ursula's cries of pleasure as she reached her climax with Karen kneeling between her thighs, and moments later the American woman reached hers, reaching down with her hands to hold Emma's face pressed against her.

Then the girls were all put back into the cage whilst the two, now satiated women, slept for a while. Later, one by one, they had their chastity belts removed and had to give more pleasure to the two women, standing between the women's thighs but now with their real body lips rubbing against those of the women, whilst Miss Marbar, with her birch, drove each girl to wriggle more and more tantalisingly. Emma noticed that the other girls had had their body hair removed like herself, unlike Ursula and her friend.

'I like them to look like little girls down there,' she had heard Ursula telling the American. 'But you'll also find that it feels much more exciting for their Mistresses.'

By the time it was Emma's turn to stand between Ursula's thighs to give her pleasure, both the women were again in a high state of arousal, as indeed was Emma, who remembered what Ursula had said earlier and was terrified lest she might climax without permission as had already happened to young Mary. However just as she felt she could no longer stop herself, Ursula suddenly kicked her away and seized her American friend.

In no time, as the girls were put back into their cage, except for Mary who was to be beaten for disobedience, ecstatic cries of 'Darling, darling!' from Ursula were mixed with similarly rapturous cries from the American woman, until they both fell back exhausted and slept in each other's arms.

Meanwhile the aroused but frustrated girls were made to put their hands through the bars where they were handcuffed so that they could not touch themselves.

Several times that night one or more of the girls were taken out of the cage to give pleasure to Ursula or the American woman. As a special reward, Monique was even allowed by Ursula to reach a climax herself as the other girls watched, mad with jealousy, from behind the bars. Each was then desperately hoping that she too might be allowed this privilege before the night was over. Their hopes were gradually increased when Ursula told her American friend to choose a girl and make her climax in her hand. The girls all held their breath, each hoping desperately that she would be chosen. But it was Mary who, standing by the bedside, was brought to a sudden climax by the American woman's touch.

At last whilst the two women slept late, the girls were quietly taken back into the harem, and their chastity belts replaced, before they too were allowed to sleep late into the morning.

Several times Emma awoke in the big communal bed in which the girls all slept – watched over by the horrible Miss

Marbar. Did she never sleep, Emma wondered, as the black woman firmly put Emma's hands back on top of the bedclothes again – for the girls all had to sleep on their backs with their hands innocently on display above the bedclothes so that the harem mistresses could see that they were not getting up to any naughtiness with each other or themselves.

'You keep hands where I can see them,' Miss Marbar whispered. 'You put below sheets again and you get caned!'

Aroused and frustrated by the recent scenes in Ursula's bedroom, Emma found it difficult to sleep. She was, in any case, too overcome with the shock of finding herself locked up in Ursula's secret harem. Was this Ursula's ultimate revenge for her escapades with Henry, 'The Brute', she wondered?

Even the chastity belt did not give Ursula a complete feeling of security that Emma would not secretly meet him again. It would certainly prevent her from getting any pleasure herself, and of course, would prevent her from being penetrated in the normal way. However, Henry had always had a predilection for asserting his control over Emma and his masculine superiority, by penetrating her from behind. It was something that Emma had hated, but had to submit to from Henry. It had made her feel he really was a brute.

Moreover, as Ursula knew, her chastity belt did not prevent her being made to use her mouth and tongue to give 'The Brute' pleasure – and this was something to which he was also very partial.

But here, locked up in her harem, Emma realised, Ursula would have no fears. Her control over Emma would be complete and unchallenged.

She remembered what the French girl had said about Ursula only introducing the chastity belt into her harem a few months ago. That was when she came back from Morocco, picked Emma up from the school in Paris, took her back to London and locked her up in a chastity belt too. So that must have been when she had the belts made especially for her here in Morocco after Emma's second escapade with Henry in Bruges.

Goodness, thought Emma, how angry the girls would be if they knew that she was the cause of them all having to wear the dreaded chastity belts!

10

Karen's story

Three days had passed. The American woman had left. They had been three days in which Emma had begun to settle down to life as one of Ursula's pet concubines. Three days of submitting to the close supervision of the Dragon and Miss Marbar. Three days of being completely cut off from the outside world – no radio, no television and not even a newspaper. Just as the Caid had kept his girls in this harem ignorant of the outside world so that they would concentrate their thoughts all the more on him, so too Ursula liked her girls, like real little girls, to be kept similarly ignorant.

They had also been three days of not seeing even a photograph of a man, or hearing a man's voice, even on a recording, for Ursula had given strict instructions that, like girls in the Caid's old harem, her girls were not to see or hear any male. But whereas the Caid, like other elderly male owners of harems, enforced this rule so as to make sure that his girls were not excited by the sight of younger men, Ursula enforced it so as to eliminate any males whatsoever from the lives and thoughts of her girls.

Accordingly, the girls were only allowed children's books, magazines, games and videos and recordings of children's radio and television programmes. But even so, the Dragon very carefully vetted them all beforehand to make sure that they contained nothing masculine.

Emma already knew that Ursula got her kicks by completely controlling the sexuality of young women. By keeping them in a real harem, under the supervision of a strict German woman, Ursula must have reached the very apogee of sexual control of her girls. And, of course, keeping them locked up in their highly effective chastity belts and preventing them from seeing even a photograph of a man or hearing a man's voice on a recording, must make it all even more exciting for Ursula, she thought ruefully.

'Missing the company of admiring males?' said Karen and Emma one day as they lazed, naked except for their chastity belts, by the side of the swimming pool on the patio, exchanging commiserations on being kept so frustrated by Ursula.

'Well, don't get caught trying to send a letter to a boyfriend or caught mooning over a photograph of some pop star,' laughed Karen bitterly. Emma did not understand what she meant.

'Don't you see?' whispered Karen, looking round anxiously to see that they were alone. 'I wrote letters once to my boyfriend saying where I was and that I still loved him, despite the awful letter that Ursula had made me write to him saying I never wanted to see him again. I had thought that one of Ursula's maids had taken pity on me and was posting them. How wrong I was! One day I was led by the Dragon up in front of Ursula. She was looking furious. Horrified I saw that she had a pile of letters in front of her: my letters to my boyfriend.

' "As you seem so keen to be unfaithful to me, your Mistress, I shall send you to a little private prison for adulterous wives and concubines," she said. "Here in the Moslem world, the official punishment laid down in the Koran for unfaithful wives or concubines is death by stoning. Several Moslem countries have brought back the law. Here, however, some people have set up a corrective establishment for women. Any man can send his erring wife or concubine to be judged and, if they are found guilty, then they will be sent to a special establishment for punishment . . . and that, Karen, is just what's going to happen to you!"

'Dressed like an Arab woman, and heavily veiled, with my wrist chained to the Dragon's, I was driven off to the private women's prison. There was a sort of court. The judges were stern looking men. I saw them wave my letters angrily, as they spoke to each other in Arabic. I did not understand what was being said. I just stood there in the dock, like a prisoner. I was not given any chance to say anything. Apparently errant women are not allowed to speak. The presiding judge banged his hammer and said something. I was told that I had been found guilty of adulterous behaviour and that I was to be punished by being sent to their special, private women's corrective prison. I tried to cry out in protest under my veil, but I was ignored and led away.

'There I was stripped by guards. I felt so ashamed. Then I was given a simple cotton shift to wear, and put into a cell with a dozen other young women. They were all Arab women, mainly rather young and pretty. They had been caught seeing or writing to young men – what was regarded as being unfaithful to their older husbands or masters. They all bore the marks of recent beatings. One of them spoke a few words of English. I learnt that most of them had merely been caught talking to another man or had written a letter to one, like me. But that was enough for them to be sent here for a few months' severe punishment.

'Conditions in this private women's prison were terrible. We had to sleep naked on the floor. To prevent the women from misbehaving we had to sleep head to tail like sardines with the feet of the two naked girls on either side of you level with your head, and a light burning all night so that the guards could see that we were lying still. At dawn they would hose down the women and the floor of the cell. Then still naked we were taken out into the passage to be fed. We had to kneel in front of a trough of nasty looking gruel. When the guard in charge rang a bell, we had to start licking up the food, keeping our hands flat on the floor. Any hesitation and your face was thrust down into the gruel and kept there until you felt as if you were drowning. When the bell rang again, we had to kneel up, even if we were still hungry.

'Then wearing our cotton tunics we were taken out into

the prison yard. All day we had to work in the hot sun chipping little paving stones until they were exactly square. When we had a load of these stones we had to run across the yard, carrying them in a basket on our heads, to a fat guard sitting comfortably in the shade, for the stones to be weighed and examined. Then we had to run back across the yard and lay them down in a pretty curved pattern like paving stones in a real road. The road was curved and so was never finished. As some girls would be laying stones at one end, other girls would be picking them up and loading them into lorries to be taken to real roads outside the prison.

'Although the road in the yard was only a temporary one, the guard supervising the women's work was very strict. The stones had to be laid in an exact pattern. The slightest mistake and he would kick them aside, making you start all over again. This would be fatal, for each girl had to chip and lay a certain weight of stones by the end of the day. At the end of the day we had to line up whilst they checked whether we had met our quota or not. Any girl who was under her quota was called forward, stripped and caned there and then across the back and buttocks.

'It was almost impossible to meet these quotas, though you would be trying desperately all day to do so. The guards clearly enjoyed humiliating the Arab women and, so as to make sure that the prettiest ones were beaten, would trip them up whilst they were running with a load of stones. Or to humiliate the slightly older women, they would talk idly to each other as they were anxiously waiting for a load to be inspected or weighed. Another trick would be to show off what they felt about white women by angrily rejecting as not properly shaped, or as badly laid, all the stones a girl had spent hours beautifully shaping with her chipping hammer, or carefully laying.

'There was a little viewing gallery for visitors. The husbands or owners of the women used to come and see us being made to work under the whips of the guards. Punishment time in the evening was a particularly popular time. Several times I saw Ursula come to watch me being flogged.

'It was the most awful period of my life. But at last my three months were up. I was collected by the Dragon and brought back into the harem. I can tell you straight, I'll never dare to try and contact my boyfriend again. I may hate Ursula for what she has done to me, but I'm now far too scared of what she can have done to me not to be her obedient slave.'

'But if you've got a boyfriend how did you ever end up in Ursula's harem?' asked Emma.

'Well, it all began when I was working as a very successful model in London, earning a jolly good screw. I have always been attracted by men and I had a series of affairs with some quite well-known ones, and even a few women! I had met Ursula several times at parties and I could see that she was very attracted to me. I got rather fed up with the passes she kept making at me, and one day at a smart party where she had once again propositioned me, I flung a glass of wine in her face, ruining her dress and making her look an awful fool in public. She swore she would get her revenge but I did not take her seriously.

'I was then involved with a young man, Phillip. Ursula learned that we were planning to go to Morocco for a holiday together. She arranged for my boyfriend to be sent a telegram just as we arrived, calling him back to his office for a few days. Naturally I said I would stay on until he could rejoin me. It seemed the obvious thing to do.

'Ursula then had me kidnapped and brought here to her harem. She told me to write a letter to Phillip saying that I had met a man who had offered me a new job in Paris and that I never wanted to see him again. Of course I refused. So Ursula handed me over to the tender mercies of that swine the Dragon and Miss Marbar.

'I shall never forget it. Ever! Every four hours for a whole day, even during the night, they tied me down and beat me. Four strokes of the cane and eight from a stiff leather paddle. The four-hour treatment they called it. I'd been spanked before by my boyfriends, and had even quite enjoyed it. But there's a world of difference from being spanked by a randy, but handsome man, who can't wait to take you, and being beaten repeatedly by a couple of huge ugly women. The worst part about it was knowing that no matter what I said or promised, I'd still get the next beating in four hours' time – for Ursula had said she would not see me for twenty-four hours – until I had been thrashed six times.

'The next day, sore and stiff from all the beatings, they took me in front of Ursula again. I had to stand to attention in front of her desk. She asked me whether I was now ready to write that letter. She had even typed it all out ready for my signature. I hesitated.

'That hesitation was enough for Ursula.

' "Take her away," she said coldly. "Double the number of strokes and bring her back to me in two days' time. Meanwhile I'll forge her signature and send off the letter anyway, and leave a copy in her hotel, in case her precious boyfriend returns before he gets the original letter in London. If he does, then the hotel will simply say that she left, taking a taxi for the airport – which is all they know."

'The next two days were awful. They made me stretch across a table and beat me every four hours. I was calling out that I would do what Ursula wanted and begged them to take me to her. But they paid no attention and just went on beating me every four hours. The Arabs say that the cane will make a woman do anything. How right they are!

'When at last they took me before Ursula again, I begged for mercy and said that I would do anything not to be beaten again. But this time, the bitch said that I was not fervent enough, and that I did not seem to mean it. Anyway, she added, Phillip had returned, had been given the letter and had left for England. You can imagine how dispirited this news made me. She told the women to carry on the good work and bring me back again in another two days' time.

'I returned to Ursula's study, two days later. I was desperate this time to show her that I loved her and her alone, that I would happily be her slave and that I would write any letter she wanted to Phillip. Thank God, she did not send me back for another dose of the four-hour treatment. I just couldn't have stood any more.

'Then Ursula set about making me one of her most loving and attentive concubines. The slightest hesitation on my part would result in the threat of another bout of the four-hour treatment. I can assure you that I became a most accomplished lesbian lover.

'The rest of the story you know,' Karen sighed. 'Ursula made me write another letter to Phillip confirming that I never wanted to see, or hear from him again.'

'Goodness, how sad,' said Emma with feeling. She was, of course, thinking back to her own rather similar escapade with Henry and how Ursula had very effectively put paid to that with the cane – just as she had stopped Karen from marrying her boyfriend. What a determined woman Ursula is, she thought, half admiringly and half feeling rather jealous that she should have taken so much trouble to get Karen into her clutches.

'It was even sadder,' said Karen, 'when, a few months later, Ursula gleefully showed me a cutting from *The Times* announcing Phillip's forthcoming marriage to another girl. I could do nothing about it, and anyway did not dare – for Ursula said that if I tried to contact him again, even to wish him well, she would send me back to that terrible women's prison. I just couldn't face running the risk of being caught again.'

'What will you do now?' asked Emma rather naïvely.

'There's nothing I can do,' replied Karen bitterly. 'Ursula has said that she will never let me go now – and if she does tire of me, then she'll sell me to a brothel here. She says there are several brothels catering to rich Arabs which are staffed only by European women. She says the women are treated as complete savages. So, she repeatedly tells me that I'd better just go on doing my best to please her!'

'How awful!' said Emma sympathetically. 'And do you still want Phillip?'

'Yes, of course,' whispered Karen conspiratorially. 'But you must not mention his name here in the harem or I'll get into serious trouble again. I'm supposed to hate him now. Ursula made me record a tape saying that I hate him and made me play it over and over again.'

Just like she did with me over Henry, thought Emma.

'Of course it's all the more exciting for her, knowing that I still like men and that I secretly hate having to please her. She knows that I'm terrified of being given more of the dreadful four-hour treatment, or being put back into Pedro's cage, or being sent back to the awful women's prison, if I don't do my utmost to give her complete satisfaction whenever she summons me to please her. This makes it all the more thrilling for her. She really enjoys having a girl who isn't a natural lesbian.'

Yes, thought Emma, that was why Ursula had been attracted to her in the first place and why she had enjoyed binding to her subsequently.

'She really enjoys having complete power over a girl,' Karen went on, 'and is utterly ruthless in how she establishes it.'

Yes indeed, thought Emma. It was that power and ruthlessness that had attracted her to Ursula, and which made her the most exciting person she had ever met.

But nevertheless Emma had been horrified by Karen's story. It made her feel that she had got off very lightly after Ursula had found out about her two meetings with Henry. She had thought that the beatings, the brainwashing and being locked up for the night in the fisherman's hut had been terrible. But they were nothing compared to what Ursula had put Karen through. And all she had done was to write letters secretly to a man. Emma had actually made love to a man behind Ursula's back! She shivered at the thought of what might have happened to her if she had met Henry here in Morocco, where Ursula seemed to have almost the power of life and death over the girls in her harem.

Indeed, Karen's terrible story dominated Emma's thoughts for several days – just as, doubtless, Ursula knew and had intended it would. She would, Emma resolved, do anything rather than risk being punished by being sent to the women's prison, or by being given the four-hour treatment, or by being disposed of to an Arab brothel.

11

Life in Ursula's harem

How long had Emma been in Ursula's harem? Was it a couple of weeks or was it a month? Emma wasn't sure.

There were no calendars in the harem. The Dragon kept a record of each girl's monthly cycle but did not allow the girls to see it. They had no idea if they were late or early and questions on the subject were brushed aside by the Dragon patting the girl's head and saying: 'Don't you worry your head about it, little girl, just leave it all to me.'

However oppressive the atmosphere might have been in the Caid's old harem, Ursula clearly wanted the atmosphere in her harem to be that of a nursery of pretty little girls without a care in the world.

Once a week the Dragon had told Emma that she must write a letter to John, saying how happy she was and how wonderful Ursula was. It was the innocuous letter of a schoolgirl writing home, and before being posted it was shown to Ursula for her comments. This was of course all intended to make Emma feel even more under the complete control of Ursula. She could not even write a letter to her husband without it being vetted first.

Life in the harem, thought Emma, seemed surprisingly busy. Early every morning the girls were got up by Miss Marbar.

'Come on, little girls, up you get!' she would cry.

Several times during the night, she or the Dragon would have come quietly into the night nursery, as the former harem dormitory was now called, to make sure that the girls all had their hands above the bedclothes and were lying on their backs. Despite the security that the chastity belts gave Ursula against any attempted misbehaviour by her girls, she still insisted on them sleeping on their backs with the right ankle of each girl being fastened to the left ankle of the girl on her right and her left ankle being fastened to the right ankle of the girl on her left. This kept their legs wide apart and so made sure that each girl lay chastely on her back – and woe betide any girl who was caught with her hands under the bedclothes.

Sometimes Ursula might keep one of the girls in her bed or in the cage in her bedroom at night, but more often she would kick them out through the trap door back into the harem. The girls would then be taken by the Dragon, or Miss Marbar, to the bathroom to wash and perform under their supervision with the results of each girl's performance being carefully noted down.

Ursula liked to keep her girls on a light diet. Breakfast, and indeed the other meals, usually just consisted of fruit and fruit juices with yogurt.

The mornings were very busy. First came the girls' dancing and singing classes with a well known Arab woman entertainer. She was delighted to find an apt pupil in Emma. Ursula liked to have her girls taught to belly dance and to do the dance of the seven veils – an erotic form of striptease. She also liked them to be taught to sing in the rather high-pitched and girlish Arab fashion. Not only did she enjoy being entertained in these ways by her girls, but she also liked to produce them as an after-dinner entertainment for her dinner parties. She was delighted when the Arab dancing mistress reported that Emma had the makings of an excellent dancing girl.

The dancing mistress had the right to award any of the girls black marks for laziness or inattention, but usually preferred to use the dog whip which she carried and used as part of her instruction.

When she had left, the girls were taken back to the bathroom again for a shower and then it was the turn of Madamoiselle, the French governess. She gave the girls lessons in deportment – carrying heavy books on their heads as they walked elegantly round the room – and in maths and copybook writing. She also made them read out aloud from a variety of children's books and they had to write little fairy stories. The fact that Daphne was a very clever girl who had passed all her examinations to go to university with flying colours, or that Monique was also well educated, did not affect the regime. She treated them all as little girls who had to be taught the basics of education: reading, writing and long division.

Ursula had considered at one time, putting Madamoiselle in charge of the harem. She was a tall, thin-lipped woman who stood no nonsense from any of the girls. Indeed, they were all scared of her. She kept a tawse in her desk in the little school room and was not slow in using it on the hands of any girl who she felt was slacking. Ursula liked her and applauded her strictness. Finally however, she decided that the German woman would maintain even better discipline.

By the time the lessons with Madamoiselle were over, Ursula had dressed and was demanding one or more of the girls to pose for her in her studio, dressed in voluptuous harem clothes: transparent silks, heavy brocades, open fringed boleros, and little Turkish caps and slippers. They would have to keep quite still whilst Ursula painted and, to make sure they did so, either the Dragon or Miss Marbar was usually also present, a cane or dog whip in her hand.

Ursula's women friends would often look in whilst she was painting, partly to gossip, and partly to have a look at Ursula's latest girls, and compare them with their own. Whilst Emma was posing for her half-naked, Ursula would toss the latest letter from her husband John to her guests.

'Do you think we should let her read it all?' she would ask them. The women would laugh and giggle over what had been written as a private letter between husband and wife – a letter which Emma was longing to read herself. John might be a rather disappointing lover when he came back to England, but absence made him both fonder and randier. His letters were full of both endearments and erotic suggestions, much to Ursula's amusement, now that she had his wife firmly under her own control.

'Oh, I don't think you should allow her to read this part,' one woman would say with a giggle.

'Oh, I think she's too young to be allowed to read this bit,' another woman would say, crossing it out.

It was therefore a heavily censored version of John's letter that Emma would eventually be allowed to see momentarily before it was torn up in front of her.

Emma was being painted kneeling up on a couch with Daphne. The girls were both dressed as harem concubines wearing gauzy lace transparent harem trousers, through which the outlines of their legs and buttocks were clearly visible, and short, heavy brocade boleros which scarcely covered their breasts and which left their bellies quite bare.

The girls were facing each other. Daphne had to look tenderly at Emma with one hand on her shoulder and the other stretching down towards Emma's belly. Emma had to be looking over her shoulder as if making sure no one in authority could see them. Ursula said the painting would be called 'A Stolen Moment of Pleasure'. It was typical of the painting of harem scenes that she found sold so well.

It was a position that both girls found hard to maintain for long. Indeed only the presence of the ever-watching Miss Marbar, her dog whip ready, made them remain still.

Having to pose with Daphne for hours on end gave Emma the chance, whenever they were left alone for a few minutes, to learn how she came to be in Ursula's harem. She was twenty, an English girl of good family, whose parents had been killed in a car crash when she was a teenager. She had decided to take a year off before going on to university and had accepted the job of looking after the teenage daughter of a Saudi Princess. She had imagined that she would be a sort of governess, but found in fact that she was merely the girl's servant. On holiday in the South of France, for instance, she had been forbidden to wear a bathing suit on the beach, unlike her so-called charge, for fear of exciting the male Arab servants. Nor had she been allowed to water ski, or even to talk to any man.

Once when her young charge had caught her mildly flirting with a young Frenchman, she had told her that she would either report her to her mother who would sack her, or she could accept six strokes of the cane from her. She had accepted the latter but from then on had been completely under the girl's thumb – fetching and carrying for her like a slave.

Back in Morocco where the Princess lived, separated from her husband, the girl had demanded that Daphne should please her sexually, on pain of being reported to the morals police for stealing a diamond ring which she had 'discovered' in Daphne's belongings. The morals police, the girl told her, had a standard punishment of two hundred strokes of the cane, spread out over three months, for foreign women who stole from their mistresses. Terrified, Daphne had agreed to the girl's demands, despite her deep-felt repugnance.

Her degradation at the hands of this young girl was, however, not over. Arab girls get married off very young and this young girl, having become engaged to be married to a rich Moroccan, announced, without bothering to consult Daphne first, that she would be accompanying her to her new home as a wet nurse for her first child. Horrified, Daphne learned that this meant that the girl had arranged to have her mated shortly to one of her mother's servants. In this way she would be well and truly in milk by the time the girl herself could give birth to her own first child.

Even worse was when the girl offered Daphne's virginity to her younger brother as a birthday present, saying that it would be wasted on the servant with whom she was soon to be mated.

Strapped down on the watching girl's bed, Daphne had been quite powerless to prevent the boy from having his way with her. But she had then gone to the Princess and told her all that had happened.

Horrified lest the story would bring dishonour onto her family when Daphne returned to England, the Princess had consulted her friend Ursula. When Ursula saw how pretty Daphne was, and how obedient and docile she was after her experiences in the Princess's household, she offered to keep Daphne locked up in her harem for several years by which time her story would be too old to be of interest to the press. Meanwhile Daphne, an orphan, had no family anxious to know what had happened to her.

Daphne was a willowy blonde girl. She was grateful to Ursula for, as she understood it, getting her out of the clutches of the Princess and her family. However, although the girl had forced her to please her, she was not a natural lesbian – something which, of course, made her of greater interest to Ursula. Indeed Daphne badly missed all the male company she had enjoyed in England.

Now, however, deprived in Ursula's harem of any contact with men, driven half-mad with frustration by the chastity belt that, of course, Ursula had made her wear, and living therefore only for the occasional relief that Ursula deigned to allow her as a special treat when she had performed exceptionally well in her bed, she now, like all the other girls in the harem, felt that she both loved Ursula deeply and yet also hated her.

'Just like me!' Emma had whispered thinking back on how she had hated Ursula for stopping her seeing Henry and for sending her to that awful training course in France. At least, however, she also thought, Daphne's virginity had been taken by a male, even if he was only a boy. Ursula, of course, really enjoyed taking a girl's virginity herself and then making sure that the girl had no contact with a man.

Emma wondered what it would be like to have to submit to a young boy. Not that it seemed likely that she would have to do so in the foreseeable future! Poor Mary's virginity, she reflected, had been taken by Ursula with her dildo and she boasted that Mary had never seen a man's penis, and never would as long as she remained the girl's Mistress!

'But what about you,' Daphne had asked. 'Surely you are not in Ursula's harem of your own free will?'

'Well, I suppose I am really, though I certainly didn't know when I came to Morocco with Ursula that she would shut me up in a harem of other girls!' Then Emma had told Daphne the whole story of her original meeting with

Ursula in London, of all that had happened, of the training course in Paris, of what had happened in Bournemouth and in Ireland, and finally about Henry, all about Henry.

'Of course, it was Henry and the fact that you were still attracted to men that settled your fate and made it inevitable that you would end up here,' said Daphne wistfully.

Emma knew that she was an intelligent girl and valued her opinion.

'She knows that she can't trust you completely. She knows that given the opportunity you would be off with another man. It's the same with me and with Karen and Francoise, of course. That's what particularly excites Ursula. Or having a girl totally innocent of any contact with the male sex, like poor little Mary.' Daphne paused wistfully before continuing.

'You see, Ursula enjoys keeping us here completely under her control and deprived of the sight of men so that we are driven, whether we like it or not, into longing for her hands, longing to be chosen for her bed, and madly jealous of each other. It's just like being an educated European woman in the harem of a fat old repulsive sheik. If he's the only man a woman is allowed to see, then she will end up adoring him no matter how much she may also hate him and resent being his prisoner. With us it's even worse, we don't even have a master we can see, just a very cruel and ruthless mistress. Like the other girls, I can't get her out of my mind, and, equally like the other girls, can't help loving her passionately.'

'Just like me,' murmured Emma unhappily.

12

Ursula's women friends

When Ursula's women friends came in to see her in the mornings whilst she was painting, she would often invite them to stay on for what she would call a women's gossipy lunch. This was not entirely what it sounded. Ursula appreciated intelligent discussions with other clever and well-informed women. She also felt that good conversation was enhanced by good food and wine. But she also felt that it was greatly enhanced by the silent and pleasurable attentions of a girl – and if one of her guests had not brought her own girl with her then she was only too pleased to oblige with one of hers.

Thus Emma frequently found herself kneeling, with other girls, on all fours, naked but hidden under the tablecloth of Ursula's round dining table, as they waited silently for Ursula and her women guests to finish their pre-lunch drinks. Each girl would have been fitted with a dog collar and lead by the Dragon, with the end of the lead coiled neatly by the side of each woman's plate.

When the women came over to the table for lunch, Ursula would seat each of them in accordance with a little seating plan. All that the still naked and hidden little creatures would see of the guests would be the sight of their legs as they thrust aside the tablecloth with their knees as they sat down . . .

Then, in the half dark they would silently wait, often for quite long periods, before their particular guest, or Ursula herself, felt she needed the extra stimulus of a girl's tongue to make her conversation even more amusing, or the food more invigorating. She would indicate this by a pull on the girl's collar as the woman gave the lead a surreptitious little jerk, without in any way interrupting either her meal or her conversaion.

Emma, like the other girls, found this all highly degrading, but also rather exciting. They were being brought down to the level of playthings, which was, of course, why Ursula enjoyed offering this service to her guests. The girls could hear what interesting things their betters were saying and could smell the delicious food that was being served to them. But they knew that they would not be allowed to participate in either.

Their role as they huddled naked and silently under the table, was merely to wait until the unknown woman at whose feet each knelt gave the signal, whereupon the girl would have to very carefully slide under the woman's dress and tantalisingly apply her tongue between the woman's outstretched legs, until she was roughly thrust away and later brought back again with the next course.

The Dragon would warn the girls required for this duty that she would be asking each woman as she left whether she was entirely satisfied with the service provided and woe betide any girl on whom a guest gave even a moderately critical report.

After some very painful appearances at the daily punishment parade after the Moslem evening prayers, Emma soon learned to apply herself very diligently to please whatever woman she was allocated. Some she learned, would like to be merely slightly aroused, others would like to be kept at a high level of arousal throughout the meal, whilst others would quietly enjoy reaching a climax as they delicately raised a forkful of lobster or pâté de foie gras to their lips. Others would wait for the coffee. It was all very shame-making.

It was in this way that Emma got to know by sight several of the girls brought by other women as their personal attendants. Some it seemed were part of a harem of girls, like herself. Others were merely treated as European servant girls, registered with the Moroccan authorities as such, just as she was.

All these other girls had had their body hair removed, just like Ursula's girls, but the girls of a rich Italian woman friend of Ursula had the heads of her girls made smooth as well.

'A smooth, shiny, bald head is so much more fun between your thighs, my dear, and gives so much pleasure,' she would constantly tell Ursula, much to the dismay of any of Ursula's girls who might be listening. 'You really should try it. And I think it improves the appearance of these little sluts. Of course they hate it, but that's half the fun! And you can always have the girl's number written with a marker pen on her cranium to help you remember just which girl it is you have kneeling between your thighs. And I always have the girl's name also written on her belly, so that I can also be reminded which girl's juices I'm sucking. When the girl is kneeling over me to offer me her nectar, I can see her name just in front of my eyes without the bore of having to remember a lot of girls' silly names. I find it all very convenient.'

Indeed Emma had been terrified to see that the girls had a large number written on the tops of their hairless heads and the same one on their tummies. To their Mistress, she realised, they were just numbered slave girls. At least Ursula allowed each girl to keep her name and a little individuality.

One day one of Ursula's friends, a rich and very sophisticated Arab widow, a Saudi Princess, brought along one of her girls, a blonde Scandinavian woman. Emma saw to her astonishment that she was pregnant.

'Yes, I had her covered several months ago. The girl's so excited by it now. But she was getting rather above herself. You've no idea, Ursula, how interesting it is to breed from one's girls. It's given me a new interest in life since my husband died – and you can still get just as much pleasure out of them when they are pregnant as when they are not.'

Emma had been horrified, listening to this woman. Suppose Ursula were to get the same idea? But, she felt there was little chance of that. Ursula hated the entire male sex far too much to be interested in having a man mount one of her precious girls. She felt desperately sorry for the attractive Scandinavian and wondered whether, like herself, she had half-willingly fallen into the clutches of her rich Arab Mistress. Indeed the woman's next remarks answered her silly question.

'I suppose, my dear Ursula, you wonder how I got hold of such a lovely creature as this Greta. It's easy – they come for money! I simply advertise for a governess and offer a very high salary to a girl without ties. I must remember to bring round my latest acquisition: a quite delightful Austrian divorcee and her equally pretty young daughter. And no family at all to wonder what has happened to them. This was a chance that I could not miss.'

Later Emma saw what the rich Arab woman had meant by a pregnant girl still giving as much pleasure to her Mistress, when she and Greta both knelt down under the overhanging tablecloth of Ursula's dining room table. Whilst waiting for the tug on her own collar from Ursula, she saw that Greta was already being put to work.

But she really was shaken when two days later the Princess turned up with two figures hidden under black shrouds. When the shrouds were removed, two very very pretty blonde-haired white women were revealed. They had been handcuffed together to prevent them from trying to escape, and also muzzled under their thick veils to prevent them from speaking to each other. It was the young Austrian mother and her teenage daughter! The Arab woman was very proud of them. She patted their flat little bellies.

'Not long now before they pay an interesting little visit!' she whispered. 'Perhaps you'd like to come and watch?'

Clearly both the mother and the girl were scared stiff of their cruel Mistress, as they stood silently in front of her. The Dragon took off their muzzles but kept their handcuffs on when she stripped them to put them under the table with Emma and two more of Ursula's girls – for there were several women for lunch that day. Emma was also fascinated to see that they had been trained to work together and that when their Mistress gave a little tug on their lead, both of them hastened to apply their tongues for their Mistress's greater pleasure.

But even more unexpected was one of Ursula's French friends, an amusing woman in her fifties who clearly enjoyed the good things in life. There seemed something a little odd about the tall and strangely attractive young blonde girl who attended assiduously to her. Emma was surprised to hear that Ursula had given the Dragon orders to keep Mary locked up in the harem and not to allow her to come to her studio.

'Yes, I got him from a dealer,' Emma was astonished to hear the French woman say. The woman spoke slowly and Emma's French was getting better thanks to her daily lessons with Madamoiselle. 'There's a big demand for these pretty creatures from the rich Arabs. Of course you have to catch them when they're still young and their skin is still soft like a boy's and they have not yet had to start shaving seriously. But their little manhoods must be capable of having a nice big erection. Have the boy cut then, and you will keep him just like that for the rest of his life.'

'But why bother,' said Ursula, 'when you can still get a real girl?' Emma was listening to the conversation open mouthed.

'Because, cherie, he becomes a girl with a manhood! Of course I know that doesn't interest you, with your hatred of everything male, but it certainly does interest me! I call him my living dildo. And what's more, since he has been cut he can keep an erection for hours on end without having a climax. Think of all the secret pleasure that a woman can have from a creature like this. To the outside world he's just a pretty girl with nice little breasts and a slim waist. But underneath he still has that manhood – and moreover one that can remain erect for almost as long as you like and which won't make you pregnant – since he's been cut. That's why age is so important and it's best to buy from a good dealer who knows what he is doing.'

'But can the dealers get their hands on suitable European boys?' asked Ursula.

'It seems so,' laughed the French woman. 'The boy must be small-boned like a girl, of course, which eliminates many northerners, but they still seem to bring a steady stream of boys to Africa to be cut. Money talks and the Arabs have it these days.'

This conversation had been a little over Emma's head, until she saw the naked boy–girl under the dining room table. The French woman was right. The figure, the breasts, the waist, the buttocks and the soft skin were those of a teenage girl. But there, dangling between the legs, was a boy's manhood which was already showing signs of reacting to the presence of the naked Emma. No wonder, she thought, that Ursula had ordered the still-innocent Mary to be kept away from this half-girl, half-boy.

When his Mistress later gave his lead a little pull, Emma saw that the boy had been trained to please a woman just as she herself had been trained.

13

Jealousy!

The all-female atmosphere of Ursula's harem, Emma realised, certainly brought out one feminine trait: jealousy. The harem system had, of course, been developed to make young women fall helplessly in love with their Masters – often much older men, but the only men they were ever allowed to see and speak to.

In Ursula's harem, however, the girls did not have even one man to see, dream and fantasise about, or to please. Ursula had achieved her dream: a society in which girls did not see a single man. They dreamt and fantasised only about her, and pleased only her; and occasionally one of her women friends. However the harem system ensured that the girls were as madly jealous of each other, and anxious to please their owner, as were the women in a man's harem – even if none of them were naturally inclined to lesbianism or to their own sex.

In a man's harem, the women were driven towards lesbianism by the absence of more than one man, though the eunuchs would make sure that their mutual feelings were never consummated and were instead sublimated into a longing for their, often elderly, Master.

In Ursula's harem, however, the absence of any men at all, with a little assistance from the Dragon's cane, drove even normal girls like Karen, Monique and Daphne, into longing for their Mistress's arms, and into being very jealous of each other.

Emma soon found that she was no exception. She too found herself becoming madly jealous of the other beautiful girls in the harem, as she competed with them daily for

Ursula's favours. She had, she remembered, been jealous of Ursula's other girls back in London and of the lovely American woman, Mrs Guggenheim. But that was nothing compared with the continual, mutual jealousy that now consumed her and her companions, as they competed to catch their Mistress's eye.

It was, moreover, a jealousy that it amused Ursula to encourage in several clever ways.

Whenever Ursula was enjoying herself with one of the girls in her bedroom, a red flashing light would show in the harem. This was the signal for all the other girls to go and lie down in the dormitory in complete silence. They then found themselves inevitably only able to think jealously about what was going on in the bedroom, and wondering equally jealously if their companion had had her chastity belt taken off. And if so whether she had been allowed a little pleasure.

The Dragon kept a record in her private book of every time Ursula allowed a girl relief. She would frequently show it to Ursula and discuss with her both the sexuality of each girl and the number of orgasms each should be allowed to reach. But the girls were not allowed to see it and each frustrated young woman was convinced that the other girls had been allowed to yield to their Mistress more often than she had.

It was clearly a system that worked very well from Ursula's point of view.

Emma indeed found that, like the others, she would be thinking, whenever the red light was flashing, of how she could have pleased her Mistress more than the girl who had been chosen. She would be furious with herself at not having done more to try and catch her Mistress's eye. Indeed each girl, desperately, was continually trying to make herself more beautiful, more alluring, and more amusing than the others. Each would be constantly looking in the mirror and trying out new make-up, new hairstyle, new more coquettish ways of laughing and smiling, new ways of looking, talking and behaving like a little girl, and even new ways of walking and moving more provocatively.

The flashing red light certainly made each girl reflect on her failure, and how unfair it was that she had not been chosen. It also, of course, yet further aroused each girl's jealousy.

Ursula knew that when a girl returned to the harem from her bedroom, the other girls would crowd round her. Under the approving eye of the Dragon, they would listen breathlessly as the lucky girl proudly gave an often highly exaggerated account of what had happened. She would proudly describe not only how she had brought her Mistress to what Ursula had said were new heights of exquisite delight, but also how her Mistress had allowed her to have pleasure as well – something which the smiling Dragon knew was blatantly untrue.

Enjoying her moment of glory, the lucky girl would look in a superior way down at the other, still-frustrated, girls. They would be listening both eagerly and jealously to what she was saying.

Indeed, since any talk about men was strictly forbidden by the Dragon, the normal topic of conversation in the harem was of memories of pleasing their Mistress. Each girl would be listening carefully, thinking of how she might improve her performance when she was next summoned to Ursula.

It would, each girl realised, have been more sensible to keep quiet and not tell the others of her own little tricks and ways of thrilling her Mistress. But, as the wise Dragon knew, the temptation amongst the girls to show off was too strong. Each girl found herself trying to make the others accept her superiority as an accomplished concubine. Each was trying to show that she was her Mistress's favourite.

Ursula also used the cage hanging in her bedroom to heighten her girls' jealousy of each other, and hence their eagerness to please her all the more. It amused her to have one girl in the cage whilst she was being pleasured by another. The girl in the cage would be driven almost out of her mind with jealousy. Of course, it also served to drive the girl in her bed to perform even better, since she knew that at any moment she might be replaced by the girl in the cage.

Sometimes it would amuse Ursula to have the curtains drawn around the cage. The girl could then hear and jealously imagine what was going on, but not see it.

Several times Emma had found herself in this situation, furiously jealous as she heard one of the girls giving Ursula pleasure. She would be longing and hoping that the other girl might annoy Ursula by slackening off at a critical moment, and that she might herself then be taken out of the cage and given the chance of showing off her skill in bed. But usually her mere presence was enough to drive the other girl on and on, and it would be a still-frustrated little Emma who would have to crawl back into the harem, with her happily smiling companion, and then listen to her showing off to the others.

Another little game that Ursula liked to play with her girls was to have one of them kept in the bathroom next to her bedroom. Not merely did the girl have to attend to her Mistress, or a visiting woman friend, whenever she carried out her natural functions, she also had to arouse and prepare her Mistress before she enjoyed another girl, and to wash and clean her afterwards. All this would arouse terrible feelings of jealousy, as did having to listen to their lovemaking through the open door. It was a task that Emma was constantly being chosen by Ursula to carry out.

Another cause of jealousy, this time amongst the four older girls, was young Mary. None of the girls were naturally interested in their own sex. If they had not been incarcerated in Ursula's harem, without ever seeing any man, they would probably have paid no attention at all to the pretty little Irish girl. But kept desperately frustrated, as they were, each found the presence of the innocent young girl to be a disturbing influence.

Each girl found her own reason for regarding Mary as her special concern. Karen felt that, as the oldest girl, she was entitled to look after the young girl, whilst Emma felt that as another Irishwoman, she had prior rights. Daphne and Monique both simply found themselves desiring Mary as much as the other older girls did. It was of course a common desire that the Dragon, and the chastity belts, made certain was never consummated by more than a chaste kiss or a little tweak to the young girl's nipples.

But even this was enough to ensure that each of the older girls was jealous of each other over Mary, as well as over Ursula. It also ensured that they were jealous of Ursula's exclusive use of the girl. The usual little sighs of disappointment turned to growls of jealousy whenever Mary was chosen by Ursula for her bed. To be put into the cage when Ursula was enjoying the younger girl in her bed was particularly poignant – as Ursula well knew.

Normally the girls secretly rather enjoyed it when one of their rivals was ordered to be beaten for some minor offence. But they felt quite differently when it was Mary who was going to be beaten. They all hated it, and hated having to watch it. Each girl's heart went out to the pretty little thing. When it was all over, they would fight to cradle the sobbing young girl in their arms and to rub away the pain of the cane on the girl's soft little bottom, and to kiss and caress her rosy nipples.

Ursula was well aware, of course, of the feeling of her older girls towards her little Irish virgin. Sometimes if they had annoyed her in some way, perhaps not being sufficiently submissive in front of her women friends, she would order Mary to be thrashed simply as a way of asserting her power and authority over all her girls. It was a very effective way of doing so.

On one occasion Ursula had become dissatisfied with the combined efforts of Emma and Daphne, both of whom she had taken into her bed to please her whilst she had her siesta. Instead of having them both beaten, she had lifted the phone and ordered the Dragon to bring little Mary into her bedroom to be beaten. The poor girl's cries as she was given six strokes of the cane as a punishment for the lack of zeal of Emma and Daphne, shamed these two into really applying themselves to their Mistress's pleasure. They even felt that they deserved the six strokes which they learnt, on their return to the harem, that each was to be given that evening in the presence of Mary.

Indeed, if anyone had asked Emma for her brief overriding impression after a month in Ursula's harem, then her reply would certainly have been: 'Jealousy, frustration and the cane'.

They would have been sentiments that both Ursula and the Dragon would have welcomed with delight, as proof that their system was working well.

Ursula was painting hard every morning, but on Fridays, the Moslem sabbath and holiday, she would go and join her friends at a swimming club at one of the big hotels, where she rented a chalet near the pool. She sometimes took one of the girls with her. This was regarded as a great treat since it was the only time that they were allowed out of the harem. None of the girls dared say so, of course, but it was also a chance to at least see a man!

Emma had been shut up in the harem for nearly a month when the Dragon told her that, for the first time, she was on the shortlist to accompany her Mistress the following Friday.

It had been a month of intense devotion to Ursula, driven on as she was by her desperate frustration and by the complete absence of seeing even a photograph of a man, any man, or of reading about one, never mind actually seeing one or hearing a man's voice.

She could not help thinking back about Henry. He had dominated her, it was true, but only really in the bedroom, and she had enjoyed that. But Ursula's control over her was something quite different, far more absolute and total. She resented it bitterly, and yet it made her regard Ursula with increasingly passionate love. Perhaps the main reason was simple: only Ursula could give permission for the removal of her hated chastity belt and thus Ursula was the only person who could permit her any sexual relief.

Now suddenly, there was a chance that she might, for a few hours, actually be allowed to see something of the outside world. And, according to the other girls, actually see bronzed young men in bathing trunks. She had never considered that such a prospect would really excite her – but goodness, she thought, it did now!

Traditionally, it had been the custom in North Africa for a female slave to be branded or tattooed with the mark of her owner. This was partly to ensure that if she escaped she would be returned to her rightful owner. But it was also to make the slave, usually a black woman but occasionally a European one, perhaps captured by the Barbary pirates in the days of yore, realise deep down inside her that she was now an owned slave, with little more than the status of an animal.

Ursula had naturally been attracted by the idea of carrying on this rule, which was still widespread in many real harems, even though slavery had officially been abolished.

For the time being, however, she had compromised by making it a strict rule that no girl was ever to leave the harem and her palace unless, as well as wearing her chastity belt, she had also been temporarily marked with the emblem of her Mistress's initials (U de F), in a distinctive diamond-shaped surround, together with the girl's police registration number.

This was done by putting a transfer onto the girl's right breast, above the nipple, and on the back of the left hand, using a special liquid. It lasted at least a week or ten days. Long enough, Ursula reasoned, for the girls, all of whom were registered with the police as only allowed to stay in Morocco if working for her, to be picked up and returned to her irrespective of what cock-and-bull story they might try to tell. Registered servants were liable to be arrested if ever found out alone without their employers' permission, and everyone knew that a reward would be paid for their return.

So it was that one Friday morning Emma found herself, in the palace garden that she had not seen since the day of her arrival, and being hustled into the same Mercedes car. This time, however, she was dressed as an Arab servant girl, covered from head to foot in a loose grey robe with only a grill in front of her face for her to peer through. No one would ever have guessed that underneath this voluminous shroud was a very pretty Irish woman, stark naked, except for her cunning chastity belt.

Even Emma's hands had been gloved to prevent the sight of her hands from exciting true believers of the Moslem faith and her ankles were hidden in ugly boots. A slim chain joined her left wrist to the Dragon's right wrist. Once again she had to sit on the little folding servant's seat, whilst Ursula and the Dragon reclined in comfort. Once again therefore, she could not see out properly. This time, she did not dare to try to look out, but kept her eyes to the floor whilst Ursula chatted to the Dragon about the friends she was expecting to meet her and see her smart new swimming costume. Emma knew that she was to remain shrouded and veiled even in the hotel, as befitted an Arab servant girl.

Not until they arrived at Ursula's little cabin with its pretty veranda, was Emma's almost-invisible little wrist chain removed. Her duties, she had been told, were to assist Ursula into her many different swimsuits; to make sure that she was properly dried after each swim and given a dry costume to change into; and to wait silently on Ursula and her guests. Under no circumstances must she open her mouth or show her face.

Poor Emma, hot and flustered under her heavy loose robe, was deeply affected by the sight of all the many gorgeous men and women she could see, through the little lace grill in front of her eyes, swimming in the clear cool water and parading around the large pool in fashionable swimsuits. How she longed to be allowed to join them! But there was no release.

'Hurry up, girl,' Ursula said as Emma carefully undressed her and slipped the new swimming costume up over her slender hips and small breasts. She was shaking from nervousness and caught some strands of Ursula's hair in the neck strap. 'You stupid clumsy girl,' raged Ursula as she turned to the Dragon. 'Make sure this girl gets two black marks when she gets back – for not paying attention when she's attending her Mistress.'

Then she glided out majestically to greet her guests, leaving Emma almost in tears behind her veil at the thought of the painful punishment which awaited her. But worse was to follow, for unaccustomed to the voluminous robe, she slipped and poured a glass of orange juice over the legs of one of the women guests who was reclining on a sun bed. That little episode earned her another two black marks and she now regretted ever having been chosen to accompany Ursula to this hotel pool.

When she had a few minutes to herself, she looked admiringly at the slender tanned bodies of numerous young women and with increasing interest at the many handsome young men. One of these came over to greet Ursula and was invited to sit down and have a drink. Ursula was watching the veiled Emma carefully as she silently brought the drink on a tray to the young man. Emma was aware of Ursula's gaze and terrified lest she earn any more black marks. But she could not help her gloved hand from accidentally touching his shoulder as she served the handsome and muscular young man. It was the first time that she had been so close to a half-naked man for months. The young man suddenly gripped her arm to prevent her slipping again. It was the first time a man had touched her since Henry in Bruges. She caught her breath under the veil. She suddenly felt terribly excited. Overwhelmed with shame, she smelt her own arousal under her wretched chastity belt. None of this was missed by Ursula who quietly hissed at her: 'Another six strokes!' and then turned smilingly to the young man, an Englishman Emma realised, and, indicating Emma, asked innocently: 'Well what do you think of our Moroccan girls?'

Before he could reply she turned to Emma and, speaking slowly in English, as if to a foreigner, said: 'Take off your gloves girl. You need not keep them on here.'

Blushing deeply under her veil, Emma reluctantly drew off the big shapeless gloves. Desperately, she put her right hand over the back of her left one to hide the shameful mark of Ursula's initials and her police registration number from the eyes of the young man. She was not particularly worried about Ursula's women friends. They all knew or guessed her identity. But not the young man! Maliciously Ursula told her to pick up a towel lying in front of him.

He could not have helped seeing Ursula's well-known mark on the back of her hand. He turned away. It was a moment of bitter degradation for Emma. She felt almost worse about that than about the caning she knew awaited her on her return to the harem.

How could she have allowed herself to be so stupid? she wondered. She had behaved like an alley-cat – and right in front of Ursula! She remembered the punishment and brainwashing that had followed her meetings with Henry in London. She remembered with a shiver what had happened after the incident with the young man in Bournemouth and her terrifying ordeal after Ursula had beaten the truth out of her about meeting Henry in Bruges – a meeting that had led to her even more terrifying ordeal at the school in France. And yet despite all this she had been helpless to prevent her body from reacting with lust at the mere touch of this young man.

Not surprisingly, Emma had a feeling of dread later that afternoon when the heavy big harem door closed again behind her. The Dragon unlocked her wrist chain, took off her shroud, and led her into the bathroom. She always made the girls wash their mouths out with soap if she ever caught them saying even the name of a man. Now she grimly took off Emma's chastity belt and told Miss Marbar to douche with nasty burning lysol that part of her body that had behaved so badly in the presence of the young man.

It was indeed a very contrite Emma who then, dressed as a little girl, joined the other girls for their afternoon dolls tea party. At least, she thought, as she dressed her pretty little doll in its prettiest frock, this would all take her mind off her forthcoming caning.

However the news that Emma had actually seen and touched a man, and was going to be punished for disgracing herself in front of Ursula, had spread like wildfire in the harem.

'What was he like?' they whispered as they poured cups of tea for their dolls and pretended to compare their dresses. 'Was he good-looking? Was he big and strong? Had he been wearing only bathing trunks? And if so had she seen how big his . . .'

They were the questions of healthy young women deprived of the company of young men. But they had then stopped abruptly when Mary, the young Irish girl, arrived. Having been kept in her convent since she had been a child, she had only the vaguest idea of the facts of life and Ursula wanted her kept that way. Woe-betide, she warned, any of the girls who ever told her about men's revolting manhoods.

'But I don't understand, why should he have such a big bulge in the front of his trunks,' she asked innocently. 'We don't have one, do we?'

Remembering Ursula's warning, the other girls changed the subject quickly.

'It must have been terrible for you being so near to this handsome young man in front of Ursula,' Francoise murmured sympathetically. 'And now you're going to be caned this evening in front of us! Poor you. I'm sure I would have reacted just like you did.'

She looked around to make sure they were out of earshot of the Dragon. 'I still like men! I have to love Ursula, but I still like men!' She paused. 'I was a beauty consultant in Paris, and I had lots of boyfriends. I wasn't the least bit interested in women. But Ursula had seen me at several parties and seemed very interested in me. I was trying to get over an unhappy love affair when Ursula suggested that I should come and stay with her here. She said it would be much easier if officially I was working for her, then I could stay on if I wanted to. Like a fool I believed her.

'Not until I got here did I learn, like you, that having a work permit means that you can't leave the country without the permission of your employer. So here I am, a prisoner in Ursula's harem, and even if I escape I can't leave the country and I am liable to be arrested by the police, and returned to Ursula. Yes, it's certainly the nearest thing to slavery.'

Just then Ursula came into the harem. It often amused

her to see her concubines, dressed like little girls and having to play with their dolls under the watchful eye of the Dragon. She would stand discussing the girls with her, and then go and sit on her special chair. There, she would call the girls over one by one to come and sit on her lap and show off the dresses that they had made for their little dolls, lisping like real little girls as they did so.

It was a worrying experience for the girls as they wriggled on Ursula's lap, for the failure to act the part of a little girl would result in black marks being awarded. But it was also a chance for each girl to look as appealing and winsome as possible, so as to try and attract Ursula's attention and hopefully be chosen for her bed that night.

When it was Emma's turn to sit on her lap, Ursula patted her hair and said: 'I hear you've been a naughty little girl, Emma! I'm going to enjoy coming to watch you being caned.'

'Oh please, Madam, please don't have me beaten. I didn't mean to be naughty. I do love you – and only you.'

'Yes, little Emma, I'm sure you do,' said Ursula with a cruel little smile. 'But you'll love your Mistress even more after you've had a good thrashing.'

How true that was, thought Emma bitterly a few hours later as she crawled to Ursula's feet, her little bottom on fire from the caning that the Dragon had given her, and pressed her lips to Ursula's foot. Thrilled she felt her Mistress stroke her hair.

'Let this little creature crawl through the trap door into the cage in my bedroom,' Emma heard Ursula say to the Dragon. 'I'm going out to a big dinner party tonight, and I want her ready and keyed up. I shall enjoy the party all the more knowing what is waiting for me on my return. And knowing that it is in my little cage with a well-striped little bottom.'

With a strange mixture of cruelty and affection, Ursula went on stroking Emma's hair and then abruptly kicked her away.

'Go on crawl into the cage, little bitch, and get ready to please your Mistress as you've never pleased her before.'

* * *

Driven on by fear of the cane and genuine adoration for her Mistress, Emma did intend to please Ursula that night.

But Ursula would have been most concerned during the subsequent days and nights if she had known what Emma was thinking about the whole time, as she lay frustrated under her chastity belt by the side of the pool, or as she lay equally frustrated on her back in bed at night.

She was not daydreaming about her beloved Mistress and her tall slim body. She was not daydreaming about her beautiful companions who lay alongside her by the pool or in the big harem dormitory bed. She was thinking over and over again about that handsome muscular young man at Ursula's cabin by the hotel swimming pool, and in particular about the big, prominent bulge in the front of his swimming trunks. When she fell asleep, she dreamt of what lay beneath the trunks, and would wake up feeling more frustrated than ever.

In London she had served Ursula largely as a maid servant. This did at least allow her to see and occasionally talk to men – quite apart from the escapades with Henry. But here she was simply one of Ursula's concubines, kept locked up to await Ursula's pleasure, and completely denied any sight or contact with a man, any photograph of a man, any description in a book or magazine of a man, any sight of a man on the television, and not even allowed to hear a man's voice on the radio or on a recording. All the girls had been deliberately brought down to the same level of ignorance of the male sex as Mary.

In a real harem, the girls were denied the sight of any man except their Master. In Ursula's harem they did not even enjoy that. Ursula was the Master!

No wonder, Emma thought, that the sight of the handsome young man in his bulging trunks had made such an impression.

But it was not a sight that Ursula had been happy about, even if she did enjoy occasionally teasing her frustrated girls with the distant view of handsome young men from her chalet near the hotel swimming pool. The visit of the young man to the chalet itself had been unexpected and unintentional. Ursula had determined not to allow it to happen again when she had one of her girls with her!

PART III

IN THE HANDS OF THE CAID

14

The Caid

Emma's prowess as an Arab dancing girl was growing fast. Her childhood ballet training helped enormously in giving her the grace and suppleness that forms such an inherent part of oriental dancing. The hours that she had been forced to spend rubbing her belly against the oily post in the French training school had also developed her stomach muscles considerably. This had been intended, of course, to enable her to give a woman greater pleasure whilst writhing under her, but it now also enabled her to put on a very fair impression of an Eastern belly dancer.

She had also developed a good girlish Arab singing voice – though she had no idea of the meaning of the, often lewd, words she had been taught to sing in both Arabic and French.

Her chastity belt removed, she was fast becoming the star of the little after-dinner entertainments with which Ursula liked to amuse her guests. In particular, her dance of the seven veils, in which she ended up stark naked and still dancing, was highly popular. Emma hated this dance and its long-drawn-out finale in which she had to mime reaching a climax with her glistening sex lips showing her genuine state of arousal. However, she knew that the slightest failure to please would result in the application of the Dragon's cane to her backside – often in front of the guests.

Another favourite dance she had to perform was one in which she was dressed only in a ring of long ribbons which were clipped onto a ring fastened round her neck, with the ends flowing down over her shoulders, breasts, buttocks and thighs down to the ground. As the taped Arabic music progressed, she would have to unfasten the ribbons, one by one, and drop them on the floor whilst thrusting her hips backwards and forwards – again in a mime of sexual love – until the last ribbon fell to the ground. Once again, she had then to continue her lewd dance, stark naked, for several minutes more whilst the sweat ran down her back and between her shoulders.

It was not only Arab dancing that she was made to perform, however, but also, since she had had ballet training, a simple ballet dance. For this she was dressed only in a white tutu and ballet shoes, and nothing else, so that once again her little bare, and now well-powdered, body lips were constantly on display as she pirouetted, posed and spun round and round.

It was to one such dinner party that one of Ursula's women friends, unexpectedly brought along as her guest, not another woman with the same tastes as them all, but a Moroccan Caid; the governor of a province and a man of great influence. Dressed in a spotless white gandoora that reached to the ground and with a hood that covered the top of his head, he looked the very image of what he was: a tribal chieftain, who by a mixture of cunning, cruelty and ruthlessness had reached the very top.

He was a man of about fifty with a small black beard, a hooked nose and expressionless eyes. He was indeed a frightening figure, and yet his cruel and expressionless face made him somehow attractive in a perverse sort of way.

'Why have you brought this man?' hissed Ursula when she saw him arrive with her friend.

'He simply insisted on coming when he heard you lived in this palace,' explained the friend hastily. 'Apparently he knew it well formerly and said that he was eager to see what changes you had made. He's a terribly important person and has had foreigners who offended him jailed and thrown out of the country. So I did not dare to refuse to bring him along. Keep him sweet – if you want to go on living here! He'll probably leave before dinner.'

But the Caid, whilst complimenting Ursula on the way she had modernised the palace, showed no sign of wanting to leave. Indeed he clearly enjoyed being the only man present.

'I wonder what you have done with the former harem quarters?' he asked in good French. 'They should be filled with pretty girls.'

'Perhaps they are,' laughed Ursula, wondering how much he knew. 'Would you like them to dance for you after dinner? I had arranged for them to do so before I knew you were coming.'

'That would be delightful,' the Caid answered gravely. 'Please do not change your plans on my account.'

Ursula remembered her friend's whispered warning of the man's importance. She did not dare offend him now by cancelling the dances.

So it was that Emma, performing her little ballet, naked except for her tutu, was horrified to see that an ugly-looking Moroccan man was watching her, as well as Ursula's usual coterie of like-minded women. However, deprived as she had been of the sight of men, she could not help also feeling rather excited at having to dance almost naked in front of one. Moreover, he was clearly fascinated by the sight of a European girl dancing on her toes, and by her bare breasts and the glimpses from under the tutu of her equally naked little bottom and body lips.

As she finally lowered herself gracefully to the floor in a gesture of humility and submissiveness, he applauded loudly. He beckoned her to come and sit at his feet. Emma, taken aback and terrified of infuriating her Mistress yet again with a man, looked at Ursula imploringly, as if asking what to do. To her great surprise Ursula gave a little gesture of acquiescence. It would indeed have been very difficult for Ursula to have done anything else without insulting this very influential man, though she bit her lips in inward rage as Emma dutifully sat at the Caid's feet, looking up at him with carefully concealed repugnance.

As the Caid watched the other girls perform, he absentmindedly stroked Emma's breasts whilst talking to his hostess about Moroccan politics and the importance of foreign residents not offending the regime in any way. As

Emma felt herself becoming excited by the Caid's hands, he continued to talk to the increasingly alarmed Ursula.

He spoke of the growing fundamentalist movement and the strict curbs it was placing on women. He even mentioned how lesbianism was against the tenets of the Moslem faith, whilst also saying that no one minded, of course, what went on inside a private house – provided the fundamentalists did not get to hear about it.

He told Ursula of how two foreign women, notorious lesbians who had paraded their affection for each other in public, had been seized by the fundamentalists and publicly thrashed. Ursula gave a little shudder of fear on hearing this story.

'But, madamoiselle,' he reassured the worried Ursula, 'you need not worry – whilst you are under the protection of people like myself. I shall speak to the police to ensure that you and your friends are properly protected.'

Ursula, greatly relieved, was expressing her gratitude to this important man, when the Dragon came to take Emma away so that she could get ready for her next dance. She was to perform her full repertoire that evening. Indeed as the evening went on the Caid became more and more taken by Emma. When finally, after her ribbon dance, she had crawled to his feet, he had turned to Ursula.

'I want this girl in my harem. I am returning to my estates tomorrow, my eunuchs will collect her in the morning,' he said in an offhand tone.

Ursula could not believe the man's insolence. The situation was incredible! She was completely taken aback and also shocked at her own stupidity at allowing her girls to dance for this awful, but important man. She felt helpless. What could she do to prevent him from taking Emma?

'But, your excellency,' she stammered, anxious not to offend him. 'She is a married woman, an English girl who is staying with me for a couple of months whilst her husband is abroad.'

'So, she has a husband too! In Moroccan eyes that makes her all the more interesting. Taking a woman for your harem, whilst keeping her husband in your dungeons and only feeding him after his wife has performed well in your bed, is an old Moroccan custom! A pity he is not here to taste the sordid delights and darkness of my dungeons!'

'No, no, you can't have her,' gasped Ursula.

'Or perhaps in this case,' the Caid went on imperturbably, 'it might be more suitable to have you in the dungeon. Have you ever seen a dungeon in a Moorish castle? The rats have to be seen to be believed, and as for the scorpions and visiting snakes . . .'

'No! No!' cried Ursula in genuine terror.

'Perhaps we could do a deal,' smiled the Caid cruelly. 'I will keep the girl for a couple of months and then return her to you to be restored to her husband. There! That seems a very generous compromise by me. For understand, one thing, madamoiselle,' said the Caid in a harsh voice, 'I want that girl and if I don't get her then I shall denounce you to the fundamentalists who will undoubtedly have you flogged.'

'Oh!' cried Ursula, not knowing what to say.

'So that's settled,' said the Caid, getting up to leave. 'Have the girl ready tomorrow morning. She will not need any luggage! I promise I will return her to you in a couple of months' time. And in exchange you will have my protection.'

Ursula did not know whether to be relieved or furious, but the next morning she had a tearful farewell with the incredulous Emma as she explained that she was going to the Caid's harem for a few weeks.

'But I love you,' Emma had cried piteously.

'Yes, I know, little Emma, and you'll soon be back with me. But, meanwhile, there is no alternative.'

Poor Emma was sobbing, stark naked, and not even wearing her chastity belt, under an all-enveloping black shroud with just a little lace grill for her to see through. Talking in Arabic, Miss Marbar handed her over to a burly, brutal-looking eunuch, wearing an Arab-style robe and a grey felt fez-like cap. Except for his high-pitched voice he reminded her, she thought with a shudder, of Achmet, her trainer at the French school.

She could not believe that she was really now being lent to the cruel-looking Caid, for whom she had danced the previous night. Handed over to him for his sexual use. It was all too awful.

She was even more shocked when she saw Miss Marbar also handing over to the eunuch a little book which she recognised as the one which had been started by Miss Perkins, and subsequently kept up to date by Rafaela in London and by the Dragon here in Morocco. It recorded her monthly cycle, her natural functions, her weight and measurements and every occasion on which she had been allowed to reach a climax. She had even had to give Rafaela details of every time she had climaxed with Henry. Now this awful eunuch was going to keep it up to date. It was really all too embarrassing.

The eunuch pushed her roughly into a large car with tinted windows. She looked around to wave goodbye to Ursula, but Ursula had decided that it would be too painful to witness Emma's departure. In the back of the car she was surprised to find another shrouded figure. The figure was being held by another eunuch. She wondered if she was another girl destined for the Caid's harem. She saw that the woman's hands, all that she could see of her, were pitch black. Perhaps, she thought, the Caid liked women of all colours. She saw that the woman's shroud had been covered with a hood that even covered the lace grill in front of her eyes.

The car drove off. The eunuchs exchanged comments in a strange tongue. Emma was sure that they were talking about her. She tried to say something but clearly neither spoke any English. She wondered if the Caid did either. He had been speaking to Ursula in French, a language of which she still had only a rudimentary knowledge. Perhaps, she thought, the master of a harem did not bother to actually speak to his girls.

Emma remembered being told that, traditionally, Moorish girls, although often very pretty, were often also virtually uneducated and even illiterate – and deliberately kept like that lest, by having other interests in life, they might revolt against merely existing to please and obey their masters. Women were not companions to men in this world. They existed merely for a man's pleasure and to bear his children. Presumably, thought Emma, a common language was not important.

Her thoughts were interrupted, as they drove out through the gates of Ursula's villa, by a hood being pulled down over her head. Now, like the black girl, she could see nothing. She tried to pull the hood off, but her wrists were seized and she felt them being handcuffed behind her back. She felt utterly helpless. It was very frightening.

Here she was, she thought, a respectable married English woman, being driven through the streets of a modern town to be put, against her will, into the harem of a terrifying-looking Arab Caid whom she had only seen once, and with whom she had no common language. She wondered if the European tourists who saw the car passing would have the slightest inkling of the drama that was taking place under their very eyes. The veneer of Western civilisation was very thin in this still very traditional country.

At last after what seemed to be a long journey, the car stopped. Still hooded and handcuffed, she was dragged out and pushed into some sort of building.

She heard a rustling sound. She guessed that the black girl's hood was being removed. A few minutes later she heard a grinding noise as if something was being engraved in metal. Then she heard a repeated hammering noise. She also heard the noise of a girl sobbing. What were they doing to the girl? she wondered with a shiver. What were they going to do to her? Even in these modern days, she knew, a Caid had almost limitless powers to do what he liked to his women.

She heard the high-pitched voices of the eunuchs. But she could also hear a deeper-pitched voice. She could not understand a word of what was being said. Then she heard a sharp cry, apparently from the black girl, followed by more talk and laughter. The eunuchs sounded pleased with whatever had been done to the girl.

Then, she heard the noise of the sobbing black girl led

away. She heard a distant clang as if a metal door had been closed. She could no longer hear the girl's sobs. She felt quite terrified again.

She felt herself being led forward. She felt her black shroud being slipped back over her head, under the hood. She felt the hood being raised slightly to bare her neck. She could still see nothing.

She felt an iron post by her side. She felt something cold and metallic being put round her neck and moved as if to check that it fitted properly. She heard the same grinding noise as if metal was being carefully engraved. Then the collar, or whatever it was, was fastened round her neck again. She felt a piece of metal plate being inserted between her skin and the metal collar round her neck. It held her neck tightly up against the post.

Then Emma felt a man's hands on the side of her neck. It was in fact a blacksmith inserting a rivet into the matching holes at either ends of the hinged metal collar. Suddenly she felt a series of hammer blows on the side of her neck as the rivet was hammered flat. The steel plate protected her from the full force of the hammering, of course, but even so it was a nerve-racking experience especially as she could not see what was happening, and since it was repeated three times as three separate rivets were inserted into the matching ends of the collar and hammered flat.

The burly blacksmith stood back to admire his work. He was used to wealthy Arabs having their women permanently collared even in this day and age – it had after all been customary for centuries. So he was not particularly surprised to be riveting a collar round a European woman's neck.

He had suggested a heavy brass collar, saying that its golden colour would match the girl's hair. However the eunuchs said that they had orders to make sure that she was fitted with a simple black iron collar, similar to those of the Caid's other concubines. He checked that it was sufficiently wide to make the girl keep her chin up well, and that the rounded edges would prevent her from rubbing her skin on it.

He reached forward and moved it slowly round her neck. Normally she would wear it with the hinge and the riveted end on opposite sides of her neck, so that the two strong rings attached to it hung down the front and the back. Swivelling it would enable, for instance, girls to be chained side by side in the Caid's bed. The Caid, the blacksmith knew, was a demanding man when it came to his pleasure.

The blacksmith examined the Caid's crest, prettily engraved on one side of the front ring, with his name in Arabic engraved on the other side. These would not only ensure that the girl would be returned quickly to the Caid should she ever try to escape, but also played an important psychological role in making the girl feel that she was the Caid's property. Satisfied with the engravings, he examined the rivets. It would take careful work with a special tool to remove them to enable the collar to be taken off.

It was time, he decided, to fit the matching iron manacles to the girl's wrists. He measured her slender wrists and from a cupboard produced a pair of manacles joined by a two-foot length of light steel chain. Each of the manacles was several inches long and like the collar was hinged and would need three rivets to close it permanently on the girl's wrists.

The Caid insisted on his concubines being kept lightly chained and manacled. It was something that had been traditional in his family for generations, and he saw no reason to change it now. The two-foot length of chain allowed a girl to use her hands almost normally, but it did have a strong psychological effect on her in making her feel the Caid's helpless possession, and in making her realise the hopelessness of trying to escape. But, of course, the blacksmith laughed to himself, it was also simply for the Caid's own greater erotic excitement.

Emma felt the handcuffs being removed from her wrists. Then first one and then the other was held by the post, a metal strip inserted to prevent her wrists from being broken by the hammer, and then each manacle was closed tightly around each wrist by three rivets. She heard the clink of the chains as her second wrist was manacled. Horrified she realised that her wrists were now permanently chained.

Again, the blacksmith smiled as he checked his handiwork. Looking at the helpless chained creature, he could certainly understand why the Caid found the sight of a chained young woman so arousing. Doubtless, he thought, the Caid also found the rattle of a girl's chains in his bed highly stimulating. The eunuchs had told him that all the Caid's concubines were kept permanently chained for his pleasure – even those who were the mothers of his daughters. Not until a girl had first been selected to bear his progeny, and had then presented her Master with a son that had lived for three months, would the chains be removed. Even then the collar and the actual wrist manacles would remain riveted on the girl as a constant reminder of her true station in life.

The blacksmith also checked the enlarged 'purity' link in the middle of the chain. This was designed to allow the Caid's eunuchs to padlock the centre of the chain to the ring on the front of a girl's collar at night or during the harem afternoon siesta. The girl could then just about reach down to touch her nipples, it was true, but no lower. She was forced to keep herself pure for her Master and prevented from secretly indulging in what the Caid and his eunuchs would regard as wanton unfaithfulness.

It was also the normal harem way of ensuring that even the most reluctant girl was driven by frustration, into becoming positively eager for the embrance of her, perhaps hated, Master. He wondered how long it would be before this proud European woman would be panting for the Caid's touch.

The ring at the back of the collar, he knew, was often used for padlocking, in a similar way, a girl's wrist chain behind her neck. This was the usual procedure for the first few occasions when a girl was summoned to the Caid's bed, especially if she had not entered the harem voluntarily, but had been kidnapped or was the wife of a man who had tried to rebel against the Caid. It made sure that the girl was completely helpless and unable to harm him. Doubtless, it would not be long before this white woman found herself with her wrists chained behind her neck as she lay in the Caid's bed, awaiting his arrival.

The blacksmith now turned his attention to fitting Emma with a nose ring. These were now fashionable amongst rich harem owners who found that, like manacles, they had a powerful psychological effect on their women at a time when otherwise they might get carried away by the ideas of women's rights that were now being imported from the West.

He fastened little clips onto each of the girl's nostrils and asked the eunuchs to pull them up, whilse keeping the girl's hood down as far as possible so that she would not see what was being done. Then with one hand he removed a red hot needle from a little brazier and with the other he held her nostril steady.

Suddenly there was a scream as he drove the needle through the septum of Emma's nose. The pain was over in a few seconds, but then she felt something being threaded through her nose. It was quite painful. Whatever it was seemed to be supporting something large and heavy that she could feel touching her face and chin. She felt more heat near her face and felt it spreading to the thing in her nose. Then she heard horrible laughter as she felt her nose being touched.

The hood was removed from her head, and the shroud pulled back. Her wrists were still locked by the chain to the ring at the back of her collar. The eunuchs laughingly pointed to a mirror.

Emma gave a gasp of horror. Hanging from her nose was a large brass ring that circled her mouth and came down to the point of her chin. It reminded her of the big rings she had seen in the noses of pigs and bulls. It made her look and feel like an animal.

Then she saw the chain and wrist manacles and the wide iron collar riveted round her neck. She saw the big ring on the front of the collar and she saw the Caïd's crest and the Arabic writing engraved on it. They made her feel even more like an animal. She thought of the unfortunate girls who had joined her under Ursula's lunch table, and who had had their heads kept shaved by their cruel Mistresses. They had lost their human look. So too, she felt, with her collar, her chained manacles and above all her nose ring, she had almost lost hers.

The worst part about it, she saw, was that just as the collar and manacles had been permanently closed with rivets, so the ends of the nose ring had been permanently brazed together.

At least, she thought, as she gazed in horror into the mirror, the part of the ring that actually went through her nose was much smaller in diameter than the massive ring that hung down to her chin.

Once again the blacksmith stood back and looked at his handiwork. It was perfect. The Caid would be pleased and give him a large present. He knew that the Caid insisted on all his concubines being ringed in this way. It not only excited him, but also played a significant role in keeping his women docile and submissive.

As with the wrist manacles, only the mothers of the Caid's sons were allowed to have their nose rings removed. The Caid had almost as much enjoyment having his eunuchs show the aggrieved husband or father of one of his women the man's wife or daughter, now wearing his nose-ring, collar and manacles as a sign of her new status – just as later he might enjoy watching his eunuchs part the girl's robes to disclose to the humiliated man a prettily protruding tummy.

Emma was now hustled from the room. Outside was a windowless van. The back door was opened. Inside was a low cage. Inside the cage, kneeling on straw, was a very pretty black girl. She was gripping the bars of the cage. Round her neck a black iron collar had been riveted. Her wrists were joined by two lengths of light chain. A big brass ring hung from her nose. Just like me, thought Emma despairingly.

One of the eunuchs unlocked a sliding door in the front of the cage. Emma, now as naked as the day she was born, except for her collar, wrist manacles and nose ring, was pushed inside. The eunuch gripped the two women by the hair. His colleague snapped a short length of chain onto the front of each girl's collar and locked the fastening. The two girls were now closely locked together inside the cage. Having no common language they could only look at each other – like chained animals.

Emma had read that cages had been traditionally used in Morocco to transport rebels and valuable slaves, now she was seeing the modern version.

Emma saw that the black girl, overcome with the pain and emotion she had suffered, had wetted the straw in the corner of the little cage. Equally overcome herself, she backed into the corner, pulling the black girl by their neck chain, and did likewise. She heard laughter from the front of the van. The eunuchs had been watching her through a little one-way mirror in the driving cab of the van. Emma blushed with shame.

The chain linking the two girls was only a couple of feet long. The cage they were in was only six feet square. It was usually used for transporting prize rams to inseminate the Caid's flocks. Now it was being used to transport different animals but also ones which belonged to the Caid.

The van drove off. The girls, bumping about as they lay huddled on the straw of the tiny cage, could not see out. After a time, the van stopped. For a short time nothing happened. Then there was the sound of voices: a deep man's voice, a boy's voice and the falsetto voices of the two eunuchs.

The van door was flung open. The two girls, each gripping the bars of the cage, blinked in the sunlight. There standing in front of them was the imposing figure of the Caid. He was accompanied by a young boy, dressed like him, and evidently his son. They were talking in Arabic. The Caid was pointing to Emma and to the black girl. He pointed to Emma's nose ring. The boy laughed. Evidently the Caid was showing his son his latest acquisitions and telling him that even white women must be kept subdued, if a man is to get maximum pleasure out of them.

The Caid reached into the cage with one hand, and gripped Emma by the hair, holding her close to the bars. With his other hand he felt her breasts. He invited his son to do the same. Emma felt two small podgy little hands gripping her nipples. She felt degraded beyond all belief. She was just an animal being shown off to her owner's young son.

The Caid forced her head right back. With his other hand he parted her knees. Emma could not now look down, but she realised that her new terrifying Master was showing her hairless body lips to the young boy and inviting him to feel them. Soon his podgy fingers were busy too. To her utter shame, Emma felt herself responding. She heard the Caid laugh and clap the boy encouragingly on the back. Then the process was repeated with the black girl.

The door was then shut again and the van set off on what was to be a twelve-hour journey across mountains and desert, broken for a few hours during the night whilst the eunuchs and their guard slept, after thrusting a couple of bananas and a bowl of water through the bars of the cage.

For Emma, caged like an animal and chained like one to another girl with whom she could not talk, it was an horrific journey. She had always thought of Ursula as being ruthless and cruel, and of men as being basically soft under their macho veneer. But she was now in the power of a man whose sheer callousness and natural cruelty made Ursula seem like a saint. Similarly she had always regarded the Dragon and Rafaela as being implacable servants of Ursula. But these eunuchs had shown themselves to be far more pitiless servants of the Caid, gloating in the pain and humiliation they inflicted on his behalf.

If this was how the Caid had her treated now, before he even got her into his harem, how would he treat her once she was in his complete power, locked up in his harem under the surveillance of those terrifying eunuchs?

And would he really keep his promise to return her to Ursula after a few weeks?

It was a frightened and nervous Emma who lay curled

up with her companion in the tiny cage as the van bounced and swayed through the countryside which she could not see, and who sobbed herself to sleep during the short stop in the middle of the night.

Never in all her life had she felt so scared of anyone as she now felt of the Caid. Never had she felt so alone, and so uncertain of what was going to happen to her.

15

In the harem of the Caid

It was light when they reached their destination.

If Emma had been able to see out of the cage in which she was chained inside the bumping van, she would have been astonished by the sight that would have greeted her.

Cragged mountains, bare of any vegetation reached upwards on either side of the fertile valley. Halfway up one mountainside was the rambling maze of the Caid's castle or kasbah with its innumerable castellated towers and high walls. It dominated the valley which was watered by a typical North African oued, or dried up water course. When it rained this turned into a raging torrent as the water poured down the sides of the mountains. Numerous large plantations of date palms, almond trees and olive trees marked the twisting course of the oued. On either side of it was rich pasture and arable land.

Every few miles there was a group of twenty or thirty houses built of dried mud. Innumerable flocks of hardy sheep grazed the pasture land and good crops grew on the arable land.

This valley was the heartland of the Caid's own tribe and the origin of his power and wealth. The valley had become even richer with the building of a large reservoir.

The French colonisers had largely relied on selected tribal leaders for the pacification of the country. When French troops were withdrawn back to France at the outbreak of the First World War, the Caid's great grandfather, like many other tribal chieftains, had been given virtual carte-blanche to do what he liked in his region, provided it remained quiet.

Between the wars his grandfather had thrown in his luck with *T'hami el Glaoui*, the all powerful Pasha of Marrakesh, and the virtual ruler of Morocco, who had also left him to run his region virtually as he liked. After the Second World War, his father had switched allegiance to the Sultan just in time before the fall of *El Glaoui*.

Now he himself ran his region in the name of the Sultan, free to do almost what he liked.

The results of all this had been dramatic: the complete subjugation of the surrounding tribes and the implementation of a state of complete servitude to the ruling Caid, and his family.

For centuries the innumerable tribes had all been rivals. They had bickered and fought, taken each other's women and decapitated each other's men, or thrown them into the dark underground dungeons that lay beneath each kasbah. But the Caid's family had been given sufficient modern weapons and resources to really dominate their neighbours – and all in the name of the state!

The surrounding tribes were made destitute by taxation imposed by the Caid and his armed retainers. Cultivated lands left vacant by ruined tribesmen were worked by black slaves, bought solely for this purpose by the Caid, or by his khalifas, or lieutenants, who were invariably members of his family.

This may all sound incredibly oppressive, but in fact the Caid and his father and grandfather had merely been acting in the tradition of their country. Cruelty, torture and oppression had always been regarded as signs of strength. Mercy was evidence of weakness. No man could rule and show pity.

So it was that tax collectors were used by the Caid and his khalifas to enforce their demand for more and more money. When there was no more money left the wretched villagers were forced to pledge their unripe crops, their almond trees still in flower, their lambs still unborn, or to give their prettiest daughters as concubines to the Caid or his local khalifa, whose harems grew rapidly in size.

To accommodate these girls, even the most junior members of the Caid's family built large and imposing residences – the Tighremt, or tall castellated palaces of the rich. But none rivalled the kasbah of the Caid himself in size and grandeur.

The girls would be sent to the Caid's kasbah for a personal inspection by him. Those who particularly caught his eye were put into his harem. To emphasise her new status, any girl seized by the Caid in lieu of payment of taxes would immediately, like Emma, have an iron collar riveted round her neck, have her wrists manacled and chained, and have the Caid's distinctive big brass ring put through her nose. This latter had been the particular distinguishing mark of the Caid's own personal female slaves and concubines long before it had become fashionable amongst other harem owners.

To establish the Caid's authority over the girl's father, these operations were usually carried out in front of him – to make him realise that his daughter was now just one of the Caid's creatures. The slightest sign of objection was punished by the seizure of the man's wife. She would then be stripped and flogged before being thrown to the Caid's brutal guards, whilst the man would be consigned to the Caid's dungeons.

Even in his own tribe, any girl who caught the Caid's eye, or that of his agents, was liable to be sent to the kasbah, where she too would be collared, chained and nose-ringed, partly to ensure her own submissiveness and partly for the Caid's greater pleasure. There was no question of refusal by the girl's parents and indeed it was considered a great honour to have a daughter in the Caid's harem.

But once the doors of the harem closed behind a new acquisition, she knew that she would never again leave the women's quarters of her Master, or ever again see any other man face to face except her Master.

From then on she was a woman of the harem, her life bounded by its jealousies, and rivalries, under the watchful discipline of black eunuchs; where even petty squabbles and minor household breakages risked being reported to the Caid for his personal judgement and punishment;

where conversation would be limited by the listening eunuchs to the endless sexual gossip of her fellow concubines regarding the sexual prowess of their Master; and where her own sexual life would be limited to her necessarily infrequent turn in her Master's bed and, if the eunuchs' supervision ever slackened, in the passionate, but very occasional, solace of her own sex.

Her collar, chains and nose-ring would remain on her forever, unless she was lucky enough to present her Master with a son who lived. But even in this case the collar and nose-ring would remain as a constant reminder of her status.

If all this sounds incredibly cruel, then it must be remembered that such things had been normal here for centuries and were still accepted as part of the way of life of rich and powerful men in a culture where traditionally women had few rights and privileges. So the Caid was left in peace in his remote castle, virtually able to treat his women as he liked . . .

But of all this, Emma was blissfully unaware, as the van containing her cage stopped outside the harem entrance of the Caid's kasbah. But, nevertheless, it does illustrate the barbaric background of the man who was now her Master. The contrast between him and the very sophisticated and artistic woman who had previously been her Mistress could hardly have been greater.

Thus it was that when the van stopped, and the rear doors were opened, making Emma blink in the sudden bright sunlight, the eunuch unlocked the cage door, reached into the cage and unlocked the chain linking Emma's collar to that of the black girl. Then using the chain as a dog lead, and indicating to Emma that she should remain on all fours, he pulled her out of the cage and down into the sandy soil.

It was Emma's last brief moment in the outside world before the big strong harem door opened and closed behind her as she crawled through it.

The Caid liked a girl to enter his harem naked and on her knees.

Meanwhile the van had driven off to take its other female passenger to one of the Caid's henchmen as a present, and out of this story.

However, for both girls a new chapter in their lives was now opening.

Two days later, the Caid's large Mercedes was approaching his castle. The Caid was seated in the back with his young son, whilst his pretty white pageboy or personal attendant, Karl, was seated alongside the chauffeur.

Karl had been in the Caid's service for a couple of years. His brilliant blue eyes and blond hair had attracted the attention of a gang of kidnappers whilst he and his Swedish parents had been holidaying in North Africa. It had not been difficult for them to lure the boy away and bustle him into a van. His distraught parents had never seen him again. The boy had been taken to a small private clinic where, along with half a dozen other European boys, he had been taught Arabic – and cut. It was a simple operation, but being done before puberty it was enough to ensure that the boy's manhood would never become erect, that his voice would never break, that his chin would remain beardless and that his skin would remain as soft as that of any girl.

When judged to be sufficiently submissive and trained in the arts that wealthy Moors expected from their pageboys, he was paraded in front of the Caid who bought him, or rather, since slavery no longer exists officially, signed the papers making the boy his indentured servant.

The boy had been firmly told that there was no future for him, now that he had been castrated, back in Europe, and had accepted his new role as the Caid's loyal personal attendant.

The Caid kept the boy in permanent attendance on him, and the boy's beauty and Nordic appearance increased the Caid's own standing. Only the most important men had castrated white boys as their personal attendants, and the Caid had refused many offers for the boy.

Since the boy had been made sexually harmless, the Caid

had no qualms about taking the boy with him into his harem, or even of having him in attendance when he was enjoying one or more of his women.

But it was not Karl that the Caid had on his mind during the drive across the mountains. He was looking forward to enjoying the English girl he had so artfully borrowed from that European lesbian.

He had kept his word and had spoken to the chief of police about ensuring that she and her women friends were not disturbed by any Moslem fundamentalists.

Indeed he felt that he had found a future regular supply of nubile young European girls whose Mistresses would be willing, albeit perhaps reluctantly, to send one of their girls for a spell in his harem, in return for his protection.

He had never previously bothered to have European women in his harem – he had felt that they were too expensive to acquire, and too delicate, ill-disciplined and difficult to dispose of when their charms faded. However, the idea of borrowing already submissive girls from the harems of European women made it all much easier.

This English girl would now have spent two days in his harem, being put through the standard induction procedures by his eunuchs. She would have been wormed and thoroughly purged with castor oil. She would have learned to relieve herself, humiliatingly, into a bowl held by a eunuch – so that her wastes and health could be kept carefully checked.

She would have been given her new harem name, Naima, and her harem number, seventeen. She would have been given the two formal beatings, one on her buttocks and the other on the soles of her feet, that were administered to all new girls by the eunuchs to instil a proper sense of fear and discipline.

Her rear entry would have been stretched just enough to make penetration easy. She would have started her mainly liquid diet, with nothing more solid than yogurt, so as to ensure that she remained clean internally.

She would have learnt to eat and drink through her nose-ring without spilling anything. She would have learnt to keep her big brass nose-ring highly polished, together with her iron collar and manacles.

She would have been taught how to make up in the heavy Arab way that he liked to see on his girls, especially around their eyes. She would have learnt to dress in the standard uniform harem dress that he liked to see all his harem girls wearing, each dressed absolutely identically to her companions.

As she was already adept at dancing in the Arab style, she would have quickly learnt to take her place amongst his other dancing girls; displaying her body and her sensuality just like them. She would have begun to learn to live with her hands permanently chained and to use her clinking chains as an erotic and provocative ornament. Finally, of course, she would have learnt that at night and during siesta, she, like the other girls, would have her wrist chain fastened to the ring on the front of her collar – so as to prevent her from getting at the more interesting parts of her body, whose use was strictly reserved for the Caid alone.

He had realised that language would be a problem. None of his eunuchs spoke English and few spoke more than a few words of French. He had therefore given orders that she was to be attached to Zuriba, his Lebanese Christian girl, who spoke a little English. He would take them both together. They should make an interesting pair. Zuriba's sister, Murina, was pregnant, having been allowed to try and get her foot on the ladder that might eventually lead to promotion to odalisque.

It would also be amusing, he had decided, to see what this English girl had learnt in the harem of a woman. He had therefore also given instructions that she and Zuriba were to be instructed in putting on a little exhibition for his private enjoyment. The eunuchs enjoyed training girls to put on such exhibitions of unnatural love. It would be exciting to see a blonde English woman having to degrade herself in this way. If she proved adept, it would be amusing to have them both, suitably masked, perform their little show when he entertained the neighbouring Caids.

The car reached the crest that overlooked the green valley. The long reservoir stretched from the edge of his castle for several kilometres up the valley. He smiled to himself. As well as dramatically improving the fertility of the valley, it also provided him, and several of the neighbouring Caids, with a new type of sport – a sport that required a large number of women, something that they were not short of! Perhaps it might later be amusing to use his new English plaything as well. He gave a sinister laugh.

He turned to his young son. It was time he had his own women. Perhaps the English girl would be ideal for this too?

She certainly looked like having a busy time in his harem before she was returned to her Mistress – if she ever was. Perhaps he might decide to keep her! Again he laughed.

16

A harem inspection parade

Emma, or concubine Number 17 as she was now called, knelt back on her heels on a little sheepskin rug on the shiny marble floor of the main harem room. She was facing the dais with its throne-like Moorish sofa on which the Caid would soon be sitting as his concubines were formally paraded in front of him when he returned after an absence of several days. Above the dais was a grill through which the Caid, unseen, might already be looking at them.

The atmosphere in the harem was tense. On some previous similar parades, the Caid, in a fit of temper, had ordered all the women to be flogged. On others, however, he had been friendly and charming, inviting the girls in turn to come and sit on his knees or at his feet whilst he examined them. He was, like many men, unpredictable and liable to take out on his women his frustrations over business or political matters.

Emma only partly understood all this, but it was enough to make her understand the other girls' tension and to share their extreme nervousness. Indeed, she was trembling with fear and trepidation as she kept her eyes fixed on the back of the Berber girl kneeling in front of her.

The women were aligned in four rows with seven women in each row. Thus, seen from the front, the women were aligned in seven dead straight lines, each of four women.

Emma was third from the right in the second row.

The eunuchs had taken care to ensure that each row and each line of girls was perfectly aligned. It was certainly all very different from Ursula's relatively friendly little harem, reflected Emma ruefully.

All six of the Caid's big eunuchs were now on duty awaiting his arrival. They were eager to show him how beautiful and well-disciplined were the girls whom the Caid had entrusted to them.

Each eunuch wore a gleaming white turban which contrasted with their coal-black faces and their gleaming naked torsos and their bright red baggy Moorish trousers.

They were big and powerful-looking with mean bloodshot eyes. The head eunuch held a long thin silver tipped cane as his badge of office as he stood proudly by the dais his quick eyes glancing over the lines of frightened women. The other eunuchs held short-handled whips, their well-oiled black leather leashes coiled in their hands. They stood round the sides of the room, the whites of their eyes shining as they, too, carefully watched the women kneeling on the floor.

The eunuchs had spent two hours getting the girls ready for this moment. First, each girl had to be purged, washed and then douched from both behind and in front. Then, each had to be supervised as she made up and dressed so as to ensure that she was looking beautiful; her eyes huge with belladonna and outlined with kohl; her cheeks heavily rouged; and her lips, nipples and body lips carefully painted.

They also had to make sure that each woman had her hair done identically under her little jewelled cap from which hung the two long white silk scarves that were fastened to each of their little manacled wrists. Perhaps most important of all they had to ensure that all the girls, even-those heavily pregnant, were identically dressed. Each wore a little silver beaded bolero, that disclosed her naked breasts and painted nipples. Each also wore long transparent blue, silk harem trousers, cut away in front between her legs, to display her hairless and carefully outlined body lips, and of course the swelling bellies of those who were pregnant. From behind, the cutaway trousers showed off each girls' pretty little backside and also, on closer examination, the little silver plunger that served to both stretch and protect their rear entrances.

Emma had now been wearing the plunger for over a day. It was a strange feeling. It also made her realise just what her fate was likely to be when the Caid sent for her. She remembered having heard that Arabs enjoyed penetrating a woman there. She remembered Henry's 'little predilection', but that had seemed mild compared with what now apparently confronted her. How awful men were, she thought. Ursula was right!

As befitted mere concubines, the girls were all barefooted, their little feet heavily ornamented with henna – like their hands – and their ankles clinking with shining anklets.

Each girl held her manacled hands up level with her shoulders, the heavy chain linking her wrists, hanging in a pretty curve below her breasts with the large central link exactly level with her navel – something the eunuchs had carefully checked.

On Emma's left knelt the Lebanese Christian girl, Zuriba. She was, of course, dressed and painted identically to Emma. But her soft belly showed the stretch marks of a recent pregnancy and her heavy white breasts showed the pronounced blue veins and prominent nipples of a woman producing milk. She too kept quite still and silent, but out of the corner of her eye she was watching lest Emma made some little mistake in the elaborate ritual of a formal harem inspection by their Master. As the only girl who could make herself understood to Emma, she had had to instruct Emma, with the threat of a flogging should Emma make the slightest mistake. The chief eunuch noticed with satisfaction that her heavy breasts, like Emma's smaller ones, were rising and falling rapidly with her anxiety. The Caid liked, he knew, to see women trembling with fear in his presence.

Emma had been intrigued when Zuriba had told her how all the concubines were longing to be promoted to the rank of odalisque.

Odalisques, Zuriba had explained wistfully, had certain privileges that mere concubines did not enjoy. For a start, although odalisques still had to wear their collars, the degrading nose-rings and wrist chains were removed. Perhaps even more important, they could only be beaten by the eunuchs on the order of the Caid. But this privilege had its limitations since during the frequent short absences of the Caid, his wives were left in charge of the harem. They would enjoy seeing one of the hated 'half wives' writhing under a eunuch's cane.

But to be promoted to the rank of odalisque, a girl first had to persuade the eunuchs to let her conceive. Normally they made certain that none of the Caid's concubines became mothers. But she then had to produce a healthy boy. If she had a girl, or if the boy died, then she would not be promoted.

If, however, she produced a boy and he lived, then the Caid might reward her by allowing her to become an odalisque.

But anyway in her case, Zuriba had said softly, it was all for nothing since she had only borne a daughter – and that did not count. She had to continue her life as a concubine and was not even allowed to see her daughter. The eunuchs had, however, kept her producing milk for the Caid's personal enjoyment. Indeed, Emma had been shocked to see that several of the girls were in milk – a state that apparently appealed to the cruel Caid.

On Emma's right knelt Zuriba's younger sister who did not speak any English. She was already pregnant. In Europe a pregnant woman is not thought of as being desirable, but in the Arab world, Zuriba had explained, it is considered to be a natural and desirable state for a girl – and the younger the better. It was clearly a state that the Caid enjoyed in his young concubines.

Emma had found it all very terrifying. Supposing the Caid decided that it would be amusing to have his new English concubine try to become an odalisque? Would he then keep her or return her to Ursula? How could she ever face John's family if, on her return to England, she gave birth to a little half-Arab baby? No wonder she was trembling as she awaited the arrival of the Caid – the man who now had power of life and death over her.

She had asked Zuriba how she and her sister, Murina,

had come to be in the Caid's harem. Zuriba had told her that they had been the daughters of a rich Lebanese of good family. Her father and mother had been killed during the fighting in Beirut. An aunt, thinking to save them, had agreed to send the two girls out under the auspices of what she had thought had been a charity for refugees. However, they had been taken not to a nice boarding school in France, but to North Africa. There, they found themselves in a slave dealer's establishment, operating under the guise of a domestic agency. Here they had been seen by the Caid, who after having them more closely inspected by two of his eunuchs had acquired them as indentured servants. It was, Zuriba said, as simple as that.

Emma had listened horrified as Zuriba had said that. Presumably, Emma was in the same boat – an indentured servant for as long as the Caid decided he wanted to keep her. Not knowing what to say, she had nodded in agreement. Perhaps, indeed, she had thought, that was exactly what she was.

Zuriba was a pretty girl with long auburn hair and white skin of the kind so often found in Christian societies in the Near East. Nevertheless, Emma had been appalled when two eunuchs had taken Zuriba and herself into a separate little room off the harem. A tape recorder was playing Arab music. Shyly Zuriba had told her that the eunuchs were going to teach them to put on a little exhibition to music, for their Master's entertainment. As the eunuchs barked out a succession of strange orders, punctuated by sharp cracks of their whips, Zuriba would whisperingly try to translate them.

Soon Emma realised just what sort of exhibition they would be putting on for the Caid. Before long, the panting girls were writhing stark naked in each other's arms. But every movement had to be made to the music and only as and when the whip was cracked. The eunuchs would give a sharp order. Zuriba would hesitatingly tell Emma what they were to do. Then they would have to wait until the whip cracked before doing it – and do it immediately and passionately, or else they got the whip themselves.

They had to repeat their little exhibition over and over again, waiting for the short staccato orders of the eunuchs and then the crack of the whip before making any move. Both girls were panting with desire, but the clever eunuchs always pulled them back before there was any question of relief.

Soon the orders were reduced and the two girls performed their little exhibition largely to the music and to the crack of the eunuchs' whips.

It was, Emma realised, not to be an exhibition of two young girls doing what came naturally, but rather an exhibition by two trained animals responding to the specific and harsh orders of a eunuch and executed to the crack of his whip on the one hand and the music on the other. It must be very exciting to watch, Emma realised shamefacedly, and the fact that two girls were performing to the orders of a eunuch must make it all the more so, with no movements being allowed that had not been expressly ordered and practised.

It was all a long way, Emma thought, from learning to satisfy Ursula. Neither she nor Zuriba were allowed to be interested in satisfying either themselves or each other. They were simply putting on a highly erotic show, to order, to music, and for the amusement of a watching man. Their own feelings were of no account.

Emma's thoughts were suddenly interrupted.

There was the noise of a door being unlocked and a remarkably good-looking boy stepped into the room by the side of the sofa on the dais. With his long blond hair and soft beardless skin, he might have been a girl, except for his height, thought Emma. The youth held the door open and bowed. The chief eunuch clapped his hands. The four rows of waiting girls knelt up, clasped their hands behind their necks and parted their knees in a gesture of utter submissiveness. They were females in the presence of a male.

The chief eunuch clapped his hands again. The well-trained lines of girls, including Emma, strained their heads back, their eyes fixed on the elaborately carved ceiling.

They were now unable to watch the Caid enter and take his seat on the sofa. Emma could not help blushing at the thought of what she was displaying to this almost unknown and terrifying man.

There was another clap of the hands and the girls, their knees wide apart and their erect bodies strained backwards, began to wriggle their bellies to and fro, in the erotic way they had been taught by the eunuchs. Emma had, of course, been made to practise all this, but she felt deeply humiliated at having to do it in front of a watching man. She could feel her little body lips moving as her belly wriggled forwards and backwards. It was too degrading. And how about the pregnant girls? Out of the corner of her eye she could see Murina making the same movements. She was shocked.

Again the chief eunuch clapped his hands. This time with a rattle from their chained wrists, twenty-eight beautiful young women, keeping their backs perfectly straight, lowered their foreheads to the floor, their chained arms stretched out in front of them, and their hair flung forward across the cold shining marble.

It was, Emma realised, a picture of utter female abasement. The abasement of young females to a much older and more powerful male. Never had Emma felt so humbled, and so servile in the presence of a man, a man she scarcely knew and with whom she had no common language. It was so utterly degrading and yet, as her increasingly moist loins kept telling her, it was also unbelievably exciting. Against her will, her natural female instincts, strengthened by her feeling of utter helplessness, were taking over control of her body.

Emma heard the voices. The Caid was talking to his chief eunuch – discussing his silently waiting women as a man might discuss his horses with his stud groom. Emma longed to look up momentarily to see this terrifying man who was now her Master. But she did not dare do so. Her forehead remained as if glued to the floor.

She heard heavy footsteps. The Caid was descending the steps that led down from the dais. He was coming to inspect his women. To choose women for his pleasure! To her shame, Emma felt her loins become even more moist. She could smell her own arousal. It was so embarrassing!

The chief eunuch clapped his hands again. The girls, keeping their heads and chained hands on the marble floor, parted their knees again and raised their buttocks high for the Caid's inspection.

The eunuchs who had been lining the walls now moved in amongst the lines of kneeling women ready to hold them quite still for the Caid's inspection.

The heavy footsteps were coming closer. She must have caught the Caid's eye with her blonde hair, she thought. She heard the footsteps pause by Zuriba. She longed to have a quick look at what was going on, but did not dare to do so. She heard Zuriba give a little moan. She heard the Caid asking a question in a deep gruff voice. She could not understand what he was saying. She heard one of the eunuchs reply and then a high pitched European-sounding voice.

Was that, she wondered, the voice of the blond youth who had entered the room before the Caid. The thought that a European youth might be looking at her from behind, made her feel even more humiliated. She thought about his high-pitched girlish voice. Was he a eunuch? A white eunuch? She had heard that some rich Arabs liked youths, but to have a boy castrated merely for his amusement seemed unbelievably cruel.

Then she remembered her own terrifying treatment in the hands of the Caid, and the fear of him shown by the other girls in his harem. No, she thought, if a man was sufficiently cruel to keep girls helpless in his harem, in the old traditional way, then she should not be surprised if he had a white boy castrated for his personal service, again in the old traditional way in which good-looking captured Christian youths had been treated for centuries.

She heard the voice of the Caid right behind her. She blushed with shame at the thought of what he was seeing. She realised that he was giving an order. Suddenly, she felt hands on her buttocks, holding them even wider apart.

Instinctively she knew they were the black hands of two of the eunuchs.

She wanted to jump up in protest, to cry out. But the memory of those two awful beatings, one on her bottom and the other, unbelievably, on the soles of her feet, were still with her. She made herself keep quiet still. She blushed again at the thought of what the Caid would now be looking at.

She heard the Caid give another order. More hands gripped her, holding her up by her belly and hips. She was now held quite helplessly. Desperately she wondered what was going to happen.

There was a long pause.

She felt the awful plunger being slowly removed. She gave a little moan. It sounded just like the moan that she had heard Zuriba give a few minutes before. She remembered that the eunuchs had inserted a little plunger into her too.

She heard the Caid give yet another order. She felt a little grease being applied. She felt a finger probing as if testing her tightness. Was it the Caid? She did not dare look round to see. She tried to pull away, but was held firmly. She heard herself give another little moan. The finger was withdrawn – apparently satisfied with what it had discovered.

She felt another hand replace the plunger. Appalled, she heard the Caid talking to the chief eunuch behind her. Obviously he was discussing her. It was too awful. She felt she could have died of shame.

She felt the hands release her. She heard the Caid and his party moving on to Murina.

Surely, she thought, he would not subject the poor little creature to the same sort of examination, bearing in mind her state. But soon Murina was moaning just like she had been. Out of the corner of her eye she saw the grey speckled beard of the Caid as he bent down over Murina. One hand was behind her buttocks, doubtless probing just as he had apparently probed her. The other was holding the young girl's prettily swollen tummy. The Caid gave a little laugh. Evidently he was pleased by what he had found.

The Caid moved away to the row behind them, leaving the three ashamed young women kneeling abjectly on the floor, too frightened to dare break position, and keeping their heads still down, their knees still parted, and their buttocks still raised.

Then a few minutes later the Caid and his party moved forward to the row in front of Emma. Not daring to raise her head, Emma could only see the bottom of the Caid's robe and his white Moorish slippers. She saw how he paused by one or two of the trembling little white bottoms. She saw how, when he did so, the eunuchs held the girl helpless for his inspection – just as they had held her. Once again she was made to feel that she was part of an utterly degrading performance, and yet one which clearly excited the women forced to take part in it.

Indeed the smell of female arousal was now almost overpowering.

The awful thing was that she, too, had found it exciting being forced to display herself to a powerful and ruthlessly dominating man. So clearly did the other women. It seemed to satisfy something buried deep in her consciousness – like her desire to please and serve a strong minded man – or woman.

17

Forced to please the Caid

The Caid walked back to the dais followed dutifully by his pretty white pageboy. He sat down again on the sofa. His pageboy stood behind him waving a large fan over his head.

At a sharp word of command from the chief eunuch, the women all gracefully stood up. They raised their chained hands above their heads, the backs of their hands touching. The chains linking their manacled wrists hung down level with their foreheads.

Like the other girls, Emma stood quite still, expectantly, a picture of grace and beauty. But with her shiny collar, the heavy chain linking her wrists and the large and demeaning nose-ring, she, again like the other girls, also made an erotic picture of subdued femininity.

Suddenly the room was filled with Arab music. As one, the women began to dance. The eunuchs had made Emma rehearse this several times. Shyly, she too began to sway erotically to the sensuous music. She could feel her bare breasts swinging and bouncing clear of her pretty little fringed bolero. With legs parted she swung her lower belly forwards and backwards and then round and round – just as she had been taught in the dancing classes in Ursula's harem and as the other girls were now doing. However, she now felt ashamed at having to do so with her body lips utterly exposed.

'Look at the Master!' hissed Zuriba.

Emma had been too embarrassed to do so, but now she forced herself to look at the terrifying man in whose power she was and to whom she was having to display her sensuality.

Timidly she raised her eyes. To her surprise, the Caid was looking directly at her, and smiling encouragingly. She forced herself to smile back – smiling at this awful man at whose command she had been so degradingly chained, collared and nose-ringed. Treated indeed as if she were some animal, and all merely for his amusement.

She saw his eyes drop to her exposed breasts and then drop further to her equally exposed body lips. She blushed with shame. She saw his eyes glisten with desire. She felt utterly helpless. Helpless in the presence of a powerful and commanding man; it was an exciting feeling.

She saw him suddenly point to her and Zuriba. One of the eunuchs stepped forward. He snapped a dog lead onto the ring on the front of Zuriba's collar. He snapped another onto Emma's collar. He barked an order.

Zuriba fell to her hands and knees. 'Down!' she whispered to Emma. 'Get down.'

The eunuch raised his whip.

Hastily Emma too fell to her knees alongside Zuriba. The eunuch gave their leads a tug and led them, crawling between the still swaying women, up to the dais. The two women crawled up the marble steps behind the man.

Emma saw Zuriba take one of the Caid's feet in her manacled hands. Humbly she started to lick the sole of his slipper. It was, Emma thought, a gesture of utter servility and abasement. Zuriba nodded to Emma to do the same. She hesitated. The eunuch raised his whip again. Hastily Emma followed suit. The sole of the slipper was dusty and tasted horrible, but she did not dare show her disgust.

Satisfied with the women's submissiveness, the eunuch respectfully bowed to the Caid, handed him the two chains, and backed away. The Caid snapped his fingers imperiously. Zuriba stopped licking his slipper. She moved up to his side. She knelt up and started to kiss his ringed hand, her eyes fixed adoringly on him. Emma found herself following suit on his other side.

The sumptuousness of the Caid's robe highlighted her own half-nakedness, making her feel even more embarrassed. Her embarrassment was made even greater by the realisation that her head was only inches away from the Caid's manhood, and that it would probably be responding, hidden under his robe, to the erotic sight of a couple of dozen half-naked women, dancing purely for his pleasure.

The Caid paid no attention to Emma and Zuriba as he watched the remaining women begin an intricate dance in which they mimed the desire for their Master. Occasionally, however, he would absent-mindedly stroke the neck, cheek or back of one of the girls kneeling like pet dogs at his feet.

Finding herself, for the first time, so close to the Caid, Emma's emotions were at breaking point. On the one hand she hated this dreadful and much older man who had had such awful things done to her, and who even now was treating her like a little dog. On the other hand, she had to admit that she found it exciting. She could not help licking his hand, just like Zuriba, and looking up at him, if not with adoration, certainly wih respect. The respect of a young female for a much older and successful male.

She looked at his grey speckled, short, pointed black beard and sensuous lips. She looked at his glittering eyes. She could not help wondering about his probably erect manhood – only a few inches away from her face, under the silken robe. He was, she thought, a man who would not stand any nonsense from a young woman; a man who was used to having young women obey his every whim.

This Arab Caid, she found to her dismay, made her feel submissive and humble – just as she used to feel in the presence of Henry. But at least Henry was a civilised man. Whereas the Caid was a tribal leader – a fact that made her ashamed of her feelings.

Could she ever fall in love with such a man? she wondered. Not unless he was the only man she was ever allowed to see, she laughed to herself. But then, she thought, he was indeed the only man whom she, or any of the beautiful and passionate young women locked up in his harem, were allowed to see or talk to. Deprived, like them, of the company of exciting young men, and prevented by the eunuchs from enjoying the alternative delights of lesbianism, the Caid would indeed be the centre of her whole life. The idea made her shudder, though she was not sure whether it was from revulsion or from excitement.

She looked at the girls dancing in front of the Caid. They were all displaying themselves shamelessly and adoringly as they tried to catch their Master's eye. Just like me, she thought as she bent again to lick the Caid's hand, and I've only been in the harem for two days!

Suddenly the Caid snapped his fingers in an impatient gesture. To Emma's horror, Zuriba lowered her head under the Caid's long robe. Emma saw her head moving up and down under the robe. Appalled, she realised what Zuriba was being made to do. She saw that the Caid was still watching the dancers – apparently oblivious of Zuriba's frantic attentions.

Then suddenly he kicked Zuriba away. He gave Emma's chain a tug and snapped his fingers again. His meaning was only too clear to Emma. No! No! she thought, I just can't do that to a man I hardly know, even if I am in his power.

But her hesitation had been noticed by the watching eunuchs. She heard footsteps running up the steps of the dais. Suddenly she felt a flash of fire across her almost-bare back. Her screams of pain were drowned by the music. The Caid did not even bother to look down. She felt her neck being gripped by a strong eunuch. Her head was thrust down under the Caid's robe. Simultaneously she felt another flash of fire, this time across her now exposed little bottom.

Still she hesitated. Twice more the whip descended. Hastily she now raised her head in the darkness under the Caid's voluminous robe. She was overwhelmed by a strong male smell. She felt something hard against her cheek. She felt the whip tapping warningly against her bottom. Quickly she began to do what she had seen Zuriba do.

As her head rose up and down, just as Zuriba's had done, she wondered whether the Caid was again ignoring the little personal attentions he had ordered, and was still concentrating on watching the dancing women. She could feel his already large manhood becoming yet larger. Was it, she wondered, as a result of her efforts, or the result of a particularly lascivious part of the dance.

Driven by the sharp little taps of the whip, Emma applied herself diligently to her task. Never, she thought, would she have dreamt a few months ago that she, a simple housewife in England, would become the sexual slave, first of a rich and dominating woman, and then of a rich and even more dominating Arab tribal chieftain.

None of her friends would ever believe what had happened to her, should she ever get back to England to tell the tale.

Kneeling in the darkness under the Caid's robe, Emma thought back on the last two days. If her arrival in Ursula's harem had been a surprise, her arrival in the Caid's had by contrast been a terrifying shock.

Ursula had just five girls, watched over by the Dragon and Miss Marbar. The Caid had some thirty young concubines watched over by half a dozen eunuchs. And this did not include his three wives and several odalisques – promoted from the ranks of the concubines after giving birth to a son for the Caid, and now excused some of the harem discipline.

Emma had noticed that successfully presenting the Caid with a son resulted in the uncomfortable wrist chains being eventually struck off, but did not excuse the woman from still permanently carrying the Caid's nose-ring as an outward sign of her inferior status.

Only the three wives themselves, veritable goddesses in the eyes of the concubines, and even regarded as far superior by the odalisques, were excused the demeaning nose-rings.

A girl who produced only a daughter for the Caid remained a mere chained and nose-ringed concubine.

Only if a girl succeeded in persuading the Caid to make her one of his wives could she really raise her status; and the position of wife was reserved for the daughters of other Caids!

The Caid's own daughters by his concubines were removed at birth and given to one of his wives to rear. They would later be valuable commodities with which to forge useful family alliances. The fact that they were the progeny of mere concubines would not be disclosed and the girl herself would never know her real mother.

But it was the presence of the burly eunuchs and the way they enjoyed controlling and supervising the girls at all times, even in their most private moments, that had most shocked Emma. She had also found it unbelievably embarrassing. It had been embarrassing enough being supervised by the Dragon in Ursula's harem. To be even more closely watched over by these huge great eunuchs was too shameful for words.

No wonder, Emma thought, that unlike Ursula, the Caid did not bother to put chastity belts onto his women to keep them pure, for the eunuchs regarded keeping the girls in their care completely pure as their most important task. The girls were never left unsupervised, even at night, and Emma soon found that she was given no opportunity to secretly play with herself – or with another of the girls. Life in the harem of the Caid was as excitingly frustrating as life in Ursula's!

Emma was particularly terrified of the huge fat chief eunuch with his piggish eyes and his glistening half-naked torso.

As she had learnt the first time he had effortlessly picked her up and carried her into the bathroom to be wormed and dosed as a newly acquired concubine, he was immensely strong.

She just could not believe what was happening when he forced the horrible castor oil down her throat and had then just waited for it to have its devastating effect.

Then had come the dreadful insertion of the stretching plug, as Zuriba had euphemistically called it. The realisation of its true purpose, and of the reason why she and the other girls were all kept on a virtually liquid diet, had come as a terrible shock.

The uncomfortable presence of the plug reminded her constantly of what her body was being prepared for. It was yet another terrifying thought that she could not get out of her mind.

She would lie awake at night, longing to ease the plug or take it out. But she had not dared to touch it, knowing that the eunuch on duty in the dormitory would check that it was still in place several times during the night, his little whip at the ready. It was just too awful being treated in such a degrading way by these hideous brutes!

Similarly, she simply could not believe it when later, the awful chief eunuch had suddenly come to where she was sitting with Zuriba, picked her up again like a doll, and carried her off to be given her 'introductory' thrashing with his long whippy cane.

If the idea of this beating was to make a new girl utterly submissive and obedient, and to put any idea of revolt right out of her head, then it had certainly succeeded in her case, Emma thought ruefully.

She had felt a little better about it afterwards when she had noticed that all of the girls, even the odalisques with their superior airs, eyed his cane, and the whips of the other eunuchs, with constant nervousness. At least she was not the only one terrified of the chief eunuch's cane!

Emma had even noticed how one of the Caid's gorgeously dressed wives, a vastly superior personage, before whom all the concubines and odalisques had to kneel as she passed, had also looked nervously at the chief eunuch's cane.

Zuriba had told her that although the eunuchs could not thrash the Caid's wives without permission, nevertheless they were constantly seeking to impose their authority over the wives by reporting them to the Caid for some minor misdemeanour – a report that often resulted in the Caid ordering the wife to be thrashed by the chief eunuch himself in front of him, or, if she was lucky, in the privacy of her own apartments in the harem.

The mere concubines, of course, could be beaten by the eunuchs for impertinence or disobedience without reference to the Caid. But even so, as Zuriba had explained to Emma, the eunuchs would often report a girl to the Caid for merely dropping a glass, or for not putting sufficient rouge onto her cheeks or nipples, knowing that it greatly amused the Caid to watch the face of a terrified girl as she stood in front of him whilst he ordered her to be thrashed – quite apart from the pleasure he also had later watching the punishment being carried out.

It all sounded terrifying, Emma thought. Clearly the cane and the whip played a key everyday role in the harem. She was used to Ursula's strict discipline, but this was far worse. The Dragon had not been a patch on those awful huge eunuchs.

But she noticed how the girls all seemed to take it in their stride. Despite the constant fear of the cane, they seemed to be a happy lot, spending the days laughing and giggling together.

The Caid's harem was, of course, much bigger than the relatively small one attached to Ursula's villa. Whereas the centre of Ursula's harem had seemed to be the modern open-air swimming pool on the patio, here the centre seemed to be the baths – a huge vault-like room with an inside swimming pool.

Watched over by the eunuchs, and constantly handicapped by their wrist chains, the young women swam naked, lay on the marble benches to be massaged by servant girls or just sat around laughing and talking. The main topics of conversation were invariably the sexual prowess of the Caid, or whether he would himself beat the last girl whom he had sentenced to be thrashed for some minor misdemeanour.

A beating was not considered to be so awful, Zuriba had explained, if it was administered by the Caid himself. Who knows, she had laughed, there was always the chance that he might find the little squirming bottom so attractive that he would order its owner to be sent to his bed!

Emma had learned that there was a strict code of behaviour in the baths. The girls had to be very careful not to make the eunuchs suspect that they were touching themselves or each other. The punishment for this was so awful that Zuriba would not even tell Emma what it was.

'We must keep ourselves pure for our Master,' Zuriba had whispered earnestly to Emma.

Emma also learned that if one of the wives came into the baths, then all the concubines and odalisques had to quickly scramble out of the pool so that she could have it to herself. Invariably the last girl out would be ordered to be beaten by the wife.

A wife could at any time order a eunuch to give a concubine three strokes of the whip for 'impertinence', but only one stroke to an odalisque. But they would often make up for the limited number of strokes by ordering them to be given on a girl's belly, or across her thighs.

Emma had seen the telltale marks of the cane on the bottoms of several of the girls. She also saw the girls sniggering at the marks on one of the wives, whom the Caid had apparently ordered to be beaten. Clearly the girls were delighted to see that one of the hated wives had been given her come-uppance.

The girls were deliberately kept unaware of whether or not the Caid was away. Their eyes kept flashing provocatively up towards the wooden lattice screen on the balcony that looked down into the baths and behind which the Caid might at any time be sitting unseen. They would shamelessly flaunt their bodies up at the screen, just as they would spend hours painting intricate designs onto their hands and feet and on their faces, to catch the Caid's attention.

The eunuchs had ordered the servant girls to do the same to Emma.

Later, looking in the mirror, Emma had been shocked by the picture of sheer eroticism that she saw staring back at her: a girl with huge painted eyes; a big shiny nose-ring; rouged cheeks; painted lips and a fascinating pattern of black dots on her forehead, going down her nose and repeated on her chin. It made her look, she thought, just like the native Arab girls.

The girls all slept on the floor of the large dormitory room on roll-up mattresses, under the constant watchful eye, once again, of one of the eunuchs.

A permanently illuminated portrait of the Caid, looking particularly manful and commanding, looked down on the girls. It was the last thing they saw before falling asleep and the first thing they saw on awakening. It ensured that even their dreams were dominated by images of their Master.

Psychologically, Emma realised, it was all very clever, particularly since no drawings or photographs of other men were allowed in the harem, and since the listening eunuchs made sure that no other man was ever talked about.

As Zuriba had sadly told her, when a girl entered the Caid's harem, she had to forget all about her former life. Above all, if she had been married or engaged, she had to forget her husband or lover. She now just had to think only about the Caid, about how to attract his attention and then about how to keep it by giving him much more pleasure than any of the other girls.

'The eunuchs are ruthless about getting rid of a girl who the Caid is no longer interested in,' whispered Zuriba.

'But what happens to them?' Emma had asked.

'We don't know. They just disappear and are never seen again. All the girls disappear sooner or later. It's very frightening.'

'How awful!' Emma had said.

'Don't you see? That's why we are all so desperate to bear the Caid a son and so become an odalisque. They may still have to wear those humiliating nose-rings, but whilst their son is still alive at least they are safe. There's even a special harem in one of the Caid's other castles in which he keeps his retired odalisques, his divorced wives and elderly female relatives. It may be dull there, but at least you are alive!'

'But is it really so difficult to get pregnant by the Caid?' Emma had asked. 'He seems to have a rather randy reputation!'

'Yes, that's all very true, but the eunuchs keep us on the pill,' Zuriba had replied. 'Don't you realise what the pills that the eunuchs make you take every day are for?'

'Oh!' Emma had cried, not knowing whether to be

shocked at not knowing what the eunuchs were doing with her body, or relieved to learn that she would not conceive.

'Anyway the Caid often prefers to take his pleasure with his women in the same way as he does with a boy,' laughed Zuriba. 'And they don't get pregnant that way!'

Emma had blushed at the thought of the uncomfortable plug that the chief eunuch was making her wear so as to get her ready to please the Caid in his preferred way.

'So you have to be specially selected to try and bear a son for the Caid,' Zuriba had continued. 'The eunuchs only allow two girls to try at a time. Two a year.'

'But that's barbaric,' cried Emma.

'But it's also the first step towards being promoted to odalisque,' replied Zuriba. 'But if it's a girl, like mine was, then it's all been for nothing. You never get a second chance.'

'But your sister . . .' asked Emma, remembering noticing that she was pregnant.

'She's now having her chance,' replied Zuriba with a laugh. 'If she's lucky she'll have a little boy. And then if he lives, she'll be an odalisque!'

'But she looks so young,' said Emma.

'Yes she is, but the Caid likes seeing a young girl carrying a baby,' explained Zuriba. 'And the eunuchs like to start breeding early from a girl. They say that being pregnant is the natural state for a girl and one that brings out her beauty and so makes her more likely to catch her Master's eyes.'

'My God!' Emma cried.

She had wanted to ask Zuriba lots more questions, but it had been just at that moment that the huge chief eunuch had arrived. Without a word of explanation, he had picked Emma up, thrown her over his shoulder, and had taken her off for that terrible 'introductory' beating.

Suddenly Emma's thoughts, as she applied herself to pleasing her terrifying Master, were rudely shattered as he abruptly kicked her away.

Emma blinked in the sudden bright light. She saw that the other girls, except for Zuriba, had gone.

The Caid gave an order. One of the eunuchs took Zuriba's collar chain from the Caid. He unfastened it from the ring in front of her collar and snapped it onto the ring at the back. Another eunuch did the same with Emma's lead.

The two girls were led down to a mat at the foot of the steps below the dais on which the Caid was sitting. They were now kneeling on all-fours, facing each other. Each was held from behind by a eunuch holding a chain fastened to the back of her collar. Just like dogs being set at each other, thought Emma, or with their big brass nose-rings, perhaps more like pigs.

The Caid flicked his fingers. Appalled, Emma saw the pretty white pageboy kneel down in front of his Master and put his head under his robe – where Emma's had been just moments before.

Suddenly the music changed. Horrified, Emma recognised it. It was the music to which the eunuchs had trained her to perform with Zuriba.

She realised that they were going to have to put on their little exhibition in front of the Caid, whilst a boy pleasured him.

Even more shameful, whereas they had rehearsed their act unfettered except for their wrist manacles, now they were going to have to do it grovelling on all-fours on a mat at the feet of the Caid, whilst each was held by her neck by one of the eunuchs. The eunuchs were going to control them completely, pulling them back if things were moving too fast, and driving them on with their dog whips if they should slacken.

It was all too humiliating for words, Emma thought. She just couldn't go through with it all, she couldn't!

She was certainly used to lesbianism, thanks to Ursula. But to have to do it as previously instructed, to music, and with each woman held by her collar like a dog by a burly man armed with a dog whip, was just too awful for words.

It was all a horrible sham, an act to be put on to amuse a cruel and vicious man.

All real lesbianism was completely forbidden in the

harem. She and Zuriba were to put on a display of passionate love and affection that the eunuchs would never allow them to show to each other in real life in the harem. And the chains on their collars would allow the dreadful eunuchs to pull them back from each other if it looked as though they might be reaching a climax.

She would not go through with it. She simply couldn't.

But any idea of resisting the eunuchs was abruptly driven out of her mind by a slash across her buttocks from the dog whip of the eunuch holding her chain. She gave a little cry. She heard Zuriba give a similar little cry.

Timidly and shyly, under the approving smile of the chief eunuch and the cruel gaze of the Caid, the two women reached out for each other, their movements made awkward by their wrist chains which clinked as they touched. Each was thrusting her pointed little tongue through her big brass ring that hung down from her nose.

There was another little clinking noise as their rings touched . . .

18

A mere concubine

Two weeks had passed. Emma had lost count of the days. Each day had seemed so like the others in the harem.

Each day had been spent largely lying in the baths, or sitting on the big leather cushions in the main harem room, wondering whether the Caid was still in the castle and when he was going to send for her again. The eunuchs, she had learned, made a point of keeping all the girls guessing about both these key matters, in order to keep them on their toes.

There had been days in which the girls had to listen whilst the latest girl to be summoned to the Caid's bed gave a graphic and doubtless, greatly exaggerated, account of what had happened. This made all the other girls madly jealous, and so was insisted on by the eunuchs as part of the standard harem routine. They also insisted on Zuriba translating the most lurid parts of the girls' accounts for Emma's benefit, and were delighted when, as a result, she too started to show signs of jealousy.

There were also days in which Emma and the other girls were kept constantly wondering if the Caid was even at that very moment secretly observing them from behind one of the lattice screens that enabled him to look down, unseen, into the baths, the dormitory and the main harem room.

There was also the endless battle between the vicious eunuchs, ready at the slighest provocation to use their whips to punish what they decided was 'impertinence' or 'lack of respect', or 'disobedience' or 'dumb insolence', and the half-naked young women, protected only by their wits.

There was no appeal when a grinning eunuch, slowly

uncoiling his short whip, silently beckoned a protesting girl forward with his finger; indicated with his hand the number of strokes she was going to receive; and told her to bend over. It was an experience that Emma found terrifying. It was also one that might be repeated at any instant, depending on the temper and mood of the eunuch on duty. Certainly fear of the eunuchs' whips ensured that the level of discipline in the harem was very high indeed, with the girls desperately running to obey their orders or slightest gesture.

Emma had by now begun to get used to the chain permanently riveted round her wrists. But the big brass nose-ring was quite different. Never, never, she thought, would she get used to that. Never, never, she decided whenever she looked in the mirror, would she get over the degradation of having to wear it permanently as a sign that, as one of the Caid's women, she now had the same status as one of his animals. Indeed, she thought, it made her look like a pig!

She also found it difficult to accept having to wear the uncomfortable little insert, at first all the time and then later, like many of the other girls, just at night. She had, however, been glad that the eunuchs had stretched her when the Caid had taken her there as if she had been a boy. It had been a terrifying experience, but at least it had not been painful as it might have been without the insert.

They had also, of course, been days of not seeing or hearing any man other than the Caid. The eunuchs were certainly frightening, but they were not men. Being allowed to see only the Caid, was already having the intended effect of making her regard him no longer as merely a cruel, grizzled swine of a man, but rather as her Master, the man to whom she must devote her whole being.

Every day she would grip the bars of the one window in the harem that allowed the women to catch a glimpse of the outside world: a distant view of the fertile valley, of the blue waters of the long reservoir, of the arid looking rocky mountains, and of the road that wound over them to the outside world, and to freedom. Freedom! There would be no freedom for any of the Caid's women, she knew. And precious little for any woman in this strict Moslem country.

Frequently the Caid would suddenly order his concubines to be paraded for his inspection. They would rush off to make themselves as beautiful as possible, before lining up on a little low platform under the eyes of the eunuchs. Then minutes later the Caid would enter the harem. The women would have to show respect for their Master by dropping to their knees and making a humble obeisance with their foreheads touching the floor.

Then at a word of command from the chief eunuch, the women would rise and stand on the edge of the platform with their chained wrists clasped behind their necks, their heads up, and their eyes looking straight ahead above the Caid's head. The women would stand rigidly at attention. But their nose-rings and breasts would tremble deliciously as the Caid slowly made his way down the line, accompanied by the chief eunuch, proudly pointing out each girl's best points with his cane.

As the Caid passed each girl, a eunuch, standing on the low platform behind them, would give the next girl in line the signal with a tap of his dog whip on her buttocks to separate her legs, bend her knees and thrust her tongue through her nose ring. The Caid would reach up to feel a breast or thigh, or pause to comment approvingly to the chief eunuch on a pouting pregnant belly or on the design a girl had painted on her chin.

It was all, Emma found, unbelievably humiliating and yet, perhaps even more humiliating was the fact that she could not help herself from becoming wet with excitement as the Caid came closer and closer.

Sometimes, the girls would instead be ordered to parade in front of a screen, behind which the Caid was presumably sitting. Each girl would then have to step up on a little stool and display herself to the eunuch's orders.

Frequently, the Caid would order the women to dance for his delight, with Emma now playing a leading role.

Three times now Emma had been chosen for the Caid's

bed. On the first occasion, Zuriba had also been summoned, ready to interpret the Caid's orders. The two girls had been positioned by the eunuchs, kneeling on all-fours side by side on the Caid's bed, their well-oiled little inserts prominently displayed and inviting removal. Emma had felt terrified as she knelt there in silence, waiting for the Caid to arrive and take her.

To her horror, the Caid had indeed removed both their little inserts, and used them both like a boy, much to her shame and then to her discomfort. However, it must have been an experience that the Caid at any rate found enjoyable, since he had repeated it only a few days later.

On this second occasion, however, it was not Zuriba who knelt alongside the trembling Emma, proffering her bottom for deep penetration, and ready by her example to show Emma what she should do to please the Caid or to translate his more erotic demands, but the pretty Swedish pageboy, Karl.

Once she had got over her initial shock at having to work with a boy to please the Caid, Emma found it an enjoyable experience. She had been surprised by the softness of the youth's skin, and again shocked when she noticed the explanation. Where the boys testicles should have been, there was . . . nothing!

On both these occasions, Emma had found to her surprise that, partly thanks to the African eunuchs' careful stretching, this type of penetration had been quite exciting, once the initial pain and shock was over. But, frustratingly, the Caid always seemed to switch his attentions back to Zuriba or Karl just when her arousal was reaching its height.

Indeed, it had at first seemed to Emma that giving his partner pleasure was something that simply did not concern the Caid. She was surprised, remembering the graphic descriptions of delight that she had heard from the other girls.

Then suddenly, on her third visit to the Caid's bed, he had brought her to the very summit of ecstasy. Never, she thought, had any man shown such expertise. Never had she felt so fulfilled, not even with Ursula. Never had she come to regard a man in the way she now did the Caid, not even Henry. She could not now stop herself from feeling that the Caid, her Master, was simply the most wonderful man in the world! She was prepared to forgive him all his cruelty simply to feel his hands again on her body.

Like the other concubines, she now spent all day dreaming of this wonderful man. The constant sight of the illuminated portrait of the Caid in the dormitory ensured that at night she also dreamt only of him.

The eunuchs noticed with pleasure that her natural resentment at her fate disappeared and was replaced by a submissiveness that they felt was surprising in a white woman.

Simultaneously, her irritation as Zuriba translated the other girls' stories of how the Caid had also brought them to the peaks of ecstasy, changed to feelings of blind jealousy. The Caid's new white woman, the eunuchs told each other with delight, was now just another concubine, as desperately eager to catch the Caid's eye as the rest of them.

But despite all this, and indeed partly because of the frustrated state in which she was deliberately kept, Emma was also finding herself becoming more and more emotionally involved with the beautiful Zuriba.

The Caid had found their lesbian exhibition, carefully choreographed as it had been by the clever eunuchs, quite fascinating. The sight of two white women, one of them an English woman, held back on leads like dogs by coal-black eunuchs, as they kissed, stroked and aroused each other to music, was really very erotic. He had warmly congratulated his chief eunuch for having trained the two women so well. He had their little exhibition performed in front of him again and again as an hors d'oeuvre, prior to using other concubines for his more serious pleasures – much to the frustrated rage of Emma and Zuriba.

As a result of having to put on their shows so frequently, they had become more and more expert, not only at making their exhibition more exciting to watch, but also at exciting each other. The eunuchs who held the chains attached to the backs of their collars had to be quicker to pull the two girls back so as to prevent them from really reaching a climax.

The effect of all this on the two young women had been devastating. Deprived as they were of the company of young men, kept usually frustrated by their Master, and constantly bringing each other to the very edge of pleasure before being pulled back by the awful eunuchs, they found themselves frequently rebelling, despite their normal submissiveness, against the strict harem rules forbidding secret lesbianism and masturbation. The Caid might want both to be performed in front of him for his entertainment, but for a woman to obtain pleasure secretly by herself or with another woman behind his back, was tantamount, the eunuchs warned her, to adultery. And the punishment for this by a woman in this country could be death.

The two young women, found themselves reaching out for each other, whenever they thought that the normally watching eunuchs had turned their backs. In the baths they vied with each other to grope secretly for each other under the water before the eunuchs noticed, or to massage each other in an apparently innocent way before the suspicious eunuchs intervened. In the main harem room, they would try and sit on neighbouring cushions and at night in the dormitory they would wait in vain for the eunuch on duty all night to fall asleep himself.

Emma scarcely knew which was worse: being made madly excited by the Caid himself and then kept frustrated whilst he amused himself with other girls; or being constantly made by the eunuchs to play with Zuriba in front of the Caid but never allowed to reach a climax. Both were deeply humiliating.

The cunning and experienced eunuchs, of course, were fully aware of the feelings that had been aroused in both girls. They enjoyed the feeling of power that came from preventing the girls from making love to each other except in the presence of their Master, just as they also enjoyed the power that their whips gave to them.

Indeed, three times, Emma had felt either the cane of the

chief black eunuch or the whips of his assistants. On the first occasion she had childishly put her tongue out at the back of a retreating eunuch who had just admonished her for letting her hair fall out of place. One of his colleagues had noticed her gesture of defiance.

This had cost her six strokes of the eunuch's dog whip across the palms of her hands, like a naughty schoolgirl – a feeling that was accentuated when Zuriba translated to her that the eunuch was going to punish her for 'gross impertinence'.

The second occasion had been after the Caid had taken her for the first time. Still sore and shocked, she had received six strokes of the chief eunuch's cane on her buttocks 'to encourage her', as Zuriba had translated, 'to keep her back arched back and her bottom thrust up more when the Caid honoured her from behind'.

This beating had certainly had the effect of making her concentrate like mad on maintaining a perfect position throughout on the next occasion, the one when the Caid had alternately mounted her and his pageboy.

The last occasion had been when, deeply embarrassed by always having to relieve herself into a bowl held by a eunuch, she had tried to slip, unseen, into the harem's luxurious loos which were reserved for the exclusive use of the Caid's wives and odalisques. To her great embarrassment that had resulted in her being taken in front of the Caid himself, with Zuriba again acting as interpreter.

The Caid had ordered her to be given six strokes of the chief eunuch's cane for 'gross disobedience of harem rules'. To Emma's even greater embarrassment he had also ordered her to be given a large dose of castor oil to drive home to her the enormity of trying to avoid the eunuchs' bowl.

He had also said that the caning was to be carried out in front of him. At first Emma had thought that this might make the beating seem almost worthwhile, especially when she was taken to his bedroom to be punished. But to her dismay she saw, as she was told to bend over by the chief eunuch, that the Caid already had a girl on either side of him in his bed, as he lay watching her punishment – and that their hands were already busy pleasing him beneath the bedclothes.

She felt deeply humiliated when she was ordered to crawl out of the bedroom behind the chief eunuch, her buttocks on fire, having been used, once again, merely to act as the hors d'oeuvre for a feast to which she had not been invited to stay.

Never again, she resolved, would she ever break that particular harem rule, no matter how degrading it might be for an educated European woman.

19

The Caid's young son

Emma was sitting chatting to Zuriba on one of the brightly-coloured leather cushions in the main harem room.

Both girls were looking very beautiful. Both were dressed in the standard harem dress of little bejewelled cap, a stiff little bolero that left exposed both their nipples and most of their backs, and long silk transparent trousers. These were slung low on their hips so as to leave the belly bare and cut away in front to expose the hairless body lips. The girls were kept barefooted. Like the other concubines they made an erotic sight.

'Damn this wretched thing,' murmured Emma trying in vain to brush aside her big and carefully polished nose-ring. 'I'll never get used to it. It's there the whole time, always in the way, and always making me feel like some animal.'

Zuriba looked around nervously. Talk like that could get them both a thrashing for 'impudence' from a listening eunuch. She was relieved when she saw which eunuch was on duty, watching the girls in the main harem room. His bloodshot eyes ceaselessly swept over the women in his charge. He tapped a dog whip against the palm of his hand. He looked a frightening figure. But Zuriba smiled. She knew that he was one of the eunuchs who did not understand a word of English!

'That's the effect these horrible nose-rings are supposed to have on us,' she replied. 'The eunuchs say they are to make us more submissive.'

'I'm afraid mine certainly succeeds in doing that,' said Emma sadly.

'But that chastity belt, that your Mistress made you wear, sounds even worse,' laughed Zuriba quietly, looking round again to make sure that no other eunuchs had come into the room.

She had already taken the opportunity to ask Emma about her life before she was put into the Caid's harem, and had been fascinated to learn all about Emma's husband, about Henry and especially about Ursula.

The concubines were strictly forbidden by the eunuchs to talk about any man other than their Master, the Caid. Zuriba knew that she was running a great risk, but felt safe provided one of the eunuchs who understood a few words of English did not come into the room and overhear them.

She knew that, with lesbianism regarded in the male dominated Moslem world as being almost on a par with adultery, she was also running a great risk in asking Emma about Ursula. Any talk that the eunuchs might construe as being about lesbianism could result in a highly embarrassing, and subsequently extremely painful, interview in the study of the Caid himself.

'I thought that Henry and Ursula were strict enough,' said Emma wistfully after a pause. 'But I must admit that neither were a patch on the Caid and his terrifying eunuchs. Still, the rest of you seem to be happy enough here in this harem . . . and I must admit that I'm also finding that in some strange way it all seems to meet my own deep-felt longings. It's as if we women have some instinctive desire to be treated as the chattel of a strong and powerful man.'

'Well, like you,' said Zuriba, 'I was brought up in a Christian community where men respect women. I was engaged, before he was killed in the fighting, to a charming and handsome young man, Michael, who . . .'

The words froze on her lips as she saw that the chief eunuch himself was coming towards them, his cane, the badge of his office, gripped in his hand. Petrified lest he had been alerted to their forbidden conversation, the two girls watched him open-mouthed. They were mesmerised with fear as he slowly approached.

The other concubines in the room were also anxiously watching him. The sudden arrival in the harem of the chief eunuch himself was an alarming matter. Was one of them going to be beaten? Each girl was desperately thinking back on whether she might have been caught out breaking one of the many petty harem rules, or having inadvertently given offence to the eunuchs.

The huge eunuch stopped and pointed with his cane at Emma.

'Come here!' he ordered in Arabic with a gesture of his hands that Emma could not fail to understand.

Quivering with fear Emma quickly stood up and ran over to him.

'Inspection!' he ordered sharply. It was a word she had learned to understand and obey. Hastily she raised her chained wrists and clasped them behind her neck.

He looked her up and down carefully. Emma was trembling lest the heavy make-up on her eyes and cheeks, or the paint on her lips and nipples might be smudged, or her hair might be ruffled. It was a strict harem rule that the girls must look beautifully groomed at all times, since the Caid might at any moment decide to come in and look at his women in the harem itself, or inspect them in secret from behind one of the lattice screens.

Apparently satisfied, he gave another harsh order which Emma now understood only too well: 'Open!'

Blushing crimson, she opened her mouth and thrust her tongue out through her nose ring. Simultaneously, she parted her legs wide, bent her knees, and thrust her hips forward.

The huge eunuch thrust a black finger into her mouth. He ran it over her teeth as if testing that there were no rough edges. Then he sat down to examine similarly her body lips. Emma did not dare look down as she felt her lips being pulled apart and the probing black finger was inserted.

Then apparently satisfied again he gave another order.

'Turn round for inspection!'

Feeling deeply humiliated, Emma quickly turned round,

keeping her legs still wide apart, her head up and her hands clasped behind her neck. But she now also thrust her bottom back towards the seated eunuch.

She felt his hands on her buttocks. Ashamed, she felt him checking that, thanks to the horrible insert she was still made to wear at night, she would be ready to accommodate the Caid's manhood there. She still hated it though, it seemed so degrading.

Then she heard him call out to the eunuch on duty. She saw the latter look in his little book and then call out a reply. Shocked, she realised the chief eunuch was checking that she was now empty. Indeed, earlier on she had successfully placed her meagre little daily offering, the results of the strict liquid diet, into a bowl held by a closely watching eunuch, who had then examined, weighed and recorded it. It was a humiliating daily harem routine that she would never get used to.

Then the chief eunuch stood up. Without saying a word, he clipped a leather lead onto the ring on the front of her collar. He turned away and gave the lead a tug. Emma trotted obediently behind him, her hands still clasped behind her neck and wondering what on earth was happening. Was she going to be punished? she wondered. But, if so, why the careful and degrading intimate inspection? Or had the Caid sent for her?

Her heart was pounding as the big eunuch led her into a room. There were several other eunuchs there. On a trolley stood a cage and inside the cage was a creature that looked like a young dwarf. She had heard that such creatures were popular as playthings amongst the rich in Arab countries – rather like they used to be in medieval courts in Europe.

Emma saw that the cage was being wrapped up in coloured paper as if the dwarf was to be a present. When the cage was completely covered, a pretty ribbon was fastened round it, making it look even more like a present.

Another eunuch pushed forward a trolley with another cage on it. Before she could say a word, a rubber ball with a strap through it was thrust into her mouth. The strap was fastened tight round her neck with the buckle hidden inside the ball. Her hands were roughly raised and she felt the chain linking her wrists being fastened to the ring on the back of her collar. She could not now unfasten the gag.

Suddenly she was lifted up. Her silken trousers were slipped down and taken off, leaving her wearing just her cap and the bolero – apart from her metal collar, her heavy chains and, of course, her nose-ring.

Then she was unceremoniously put into the empty second cage.

The lead clipped onto the front of her collar was fastened tightly to one of the bars of the cage, holding her kneeling up prettily.

Again the chief eunuch gave a grunt of approval.

Quickly her cage was wrapped in coloured paper and tied up with a ribbon, just like that of the dwarf. She could not see out. She felt very frightened. Tightly gagged as she was, she could only make a whimpering noise. She could hear the equally frightened dwarf making a similar noise.

There was a long pause. She could hear people coming and going. Then she felt the trolley, on which her cage rested, being pushed along down long corridors.

Suddenly she heard excited voices. She heard the raised voice of a boy. She heard the distinctive voice of the Caid. There seemed to be some sort of a party going on. Then she heard them singing what sounded like an Arabic version of 'Happy Birthday to you!', followed by the sound of the paper round the dwarf's cage being torn off.

She heard the voice of the boy becoming very excited, as if he had been given the dwarf as a present. The boy, Emma realised, must be the Caid's son. This must be a birthday party for him. My God, she thought, am I too going to be given by the Caid to his son as a present!

She remembered the gossip in the harem that the Caid was going away for a few days and would then be taking his son back to school. Emma's horrified brain was racing. Was the Caid giving her to his young son to enjoy before going back to school? Was she, a young married English woman going to be given as a toy to a young Arab boy?

She heard the noise of excited young fingers untying the ribbon round her cage. This was followed by the ripping noise of the wrapping paper being impatiently torn back.

Emma blinked in the sudden bright light. She seemed to be in a small courtyard of the palace, a private patio surrounded by a small suite of rooms. She saw toys, train sets, plastic miniature tanks and cars, toy guns, swords and whips – all the paraphernalia of a spoilt child.

There right in front of her was the excited face of the same young boy to whom the Caid had shown her off, naked in the cage inside the van that had brought her here to the Caid's harem. She remembered with shame how the Caid had encouraged the boy to feel her breasts through the bars of that cage and then to feel her body lips.

This time the proudly smiling Caid, standing behind the boy, did not have to encourage the boy at all. Immediately he thrust his hands through the bars of the cage and with a squeal of delight began to feel his new and exciting present. Chained and gagged as she was, there was nothing that Emma could do to stop the boy. She glanced up at the Caid, but he was clearly delighted to see how his son's masculinity was beginning to show itself in the way the boy was twisting her nipples and eagerly parting her hairless body lips.

The boy turned away from Emma back towards his other present: the little dwarf. He stroked and patted the dwarf and then turned back to Emma again, stroking and patting her in just the same way. The boy was evidently equally delighted with both presents.

Then the Caid gave an order. A shroud was dropped over the dwarf's cage, and then another over Emma's. She was now in darkness. She heard the voices of the Caid and his son going away, presumably to continue the party elsewhere. There was a long silence. She heard the dwarf give a little whimper. She had heard that dwarfs were often muted by their Masters. Was this one mute? Was a whimper the only noise he could make? Had his tongue been slit to make him less human and more like a pet animal?

She found herself answering his whimper with another.

* * *

Several days later, Emma was again in the same cage on the same patio. The dwarf, however, had been taken out of his cage, but was still chained to it, like a dog chained to his kennel. He was now busy sniffing at the bars of Emma's cage and she felt like a bitch on heat being protected from unwanted attentions. With her chained hands again fastened to the ring at the back of her collar she was unable to push him away.

Horrified, she watched him cock his leg against the bars of her cage. It seemed to typify the animal-like way she had to live ever since she had been given to the Caid's son to enjoy as a going-back-to-school present, whilst the Caid was away for a couple of days.

The boy's mother, the Caid's second wife, a very grand lady dressed in a magnificent silk brocade caftan had come to inspect her son's new toy. She had Emma and the dwarf taken out of their cages, and then had shown her son how to make both little animals sit up and beg for lumps of sugar or to scuttle into the corner both chasing the same piece of chocolate – something he had subsequently much enjoyed, making them do it in front of his younger brothers and friends.

It had been one such friend who had suggested a new game. First, the dwarf was put back into his cage. Then with their toy whips, they made the shame-faced Emma play with herself in front of them. When they were satisfied that she was thoroughly aroused and smelling like a bitch on heat, they held her down on all-fours like a dog, over a high, stiff leather cushion in front of the dwarf's cage.

She was forced to offer herself helpless to the now equally aroused mute dwarf, who was making whining noises and slavering at the mouth as he threw himself against the bars of his cage in his eagerness to get at her.

They kept her like that for a couple of minutes and then let the dwarf out of his cage. He bounded towards Emma growling. Terrified and deeply ashamed, Emma tried to get up and run away. But the boys held her down.

Holding the dwarf back by his lead, they encouraged him to lick her from behind. Eagerly the dwarf applied his long tongue. Horrified, Emma found herself becoming even more aroused, for it was a sensational feeling. The boys laughed cruelly as, to her even greater shame, she found that she simply could not help parting her thighs and thrusting her buttocks back towards the dwarf.

The boys began to encourage the dwarf to mount her, standing upright between her parted knees.

Never had she felt so ashamed. With their whips, the awful boys had made her bark like a dog to show her rising excitement. They had made her bark again and again as first the dwarf penetrated her and then brought her to a juddering climax as she felt the dwarf's seed shooting up inside her. She now felt more ashamed than ever.

It was at that moment that the boy's mother had stormed into the patio, screaming blue murder at her son and his friends. She had pulled the dwarf off Emma, ordered the other boys out of the patio and then, after ordering the still shaking Emma to be washed out, had encouraged her son to take her to bed.

With her chained wrists still fastened behind her neck, she had been quite helpless as the boy played and experimented with her body as he became more and more excited himself. It had been the boy's mother who had presided over the first time that the boy had been allowed to take a woman – and a real European woman too. That, his mother had told him, would really be something to boast about at school!

Emma had been put back in her cage on the patio whilst the boy rested, but constantly during the next two days, he had pulled her out for his private amusement. The boy might have been young but he still imposed his masculinity onto Emma, and he also soon showed that he was very adept at using the whip.

His command of the English language may have been limited to such simple phrases as 'pretty girl!' and 'kiss me!' However, it also included sufficient of the cruder expressions used to describe lovemaking to ensure that Emma was in no doubt as to what he wanted her to do. Nor did she dare to refuse to carry out any of his humiliating orders.

Indeed it was an exhausted, as well as a terrified and

thoroughly degraded, Emma who with relief saw the returned Caid enter the patio with his chief eunuch to take her back to the harem.

But first she had to listen, gripping the bars of her cage, to the Caid jovially questioning his son in Arabic, pointing at her and doubtlessly asking what use he had made of his present. She also had to listen, ashamed and unable to understand, as the boy pointed to her and laughingly seemed to be boasting to his delighted father of all his exploits with Emma.

That night, the boy having apparently left to go back to school, the Caid sent for Emma. With Zuriba translating he made her recall all that had happened. He laughed uproariously at Emma's tremulous account of her encounter with the dwarf – even sending for the little creature and then making poor Emma re-enact every aspect, down to barking her excitement as the dwarf again penetrated her and, to her utter shame and the Caid's delight, made her climax yet again.

But this only served to arouse his own libido. He ordered his eunuchs to wash Emma out and to put her into his bed. Her chained hands, he instructed, were to be fastened again behind her neck, just as they had been in the boy's bed.

Then later the Caid himself re-enacted on the helpless Emma the same scene that his young son had carried out. It was a sport which he found so enjoyable that he not only repeated it there and then, but resolved to repeat the experience on subsequent nights, after first having the eunuchs make Emma put on her degrading, and yet frustrating, little exhibition with Zuriba.

It was indeed an exhausted and silent Emma who tottered back into the harem the following morning – only to be greeted with jealous looks from her fellow concubines.

20

Caught red-handed!

'Hurry, darling, hurry,' whispered Zuriba in a conspiratorial tone. Her English was strongly accented, but fluent.

'Why? What do you mean?' asked Emma, surprised.

The two girls were sitting on adjacent leather cushions in the big harem room.

'Don't you see?' replied Zuriba impatiently. 'I've found just the place. Let's go there quickly while the eunuch on duty is taking my sister to the bathroom. She's promised she'll pretend to faint there, and say she's having a miscarriage! That'll bring the chief eunuch running, for the Caid has enjoyed having her mated and he'll be furious if anything now spoils his fun. So there'll be such a scene going on that no one will notice we've slipped away. Come on, darling, hurry! We may not get another chance to be alone together for ages.'

Emma hesitated for a moment. She looked around carefully to make sure that it was true that, for once, they were not being watched by any of the eunuchs.

'Yes, let's go quickly,' she said, getting up hurriedly.

'Hang on, darling. We mustn't risk being seen going out of the room together,' said Zuriba. 'I'll just walk casually in a moment to the dormitory as if I'd left something there, and then I'll slip into the corridor. You meet me there in two minutes time. My sister, Murina, will be starting her little act just about then. So we won't be seen and then I'll show you the little door that I found behind an empty chest of drawers. It leads to an empty forgotten room. It must have been a rest room once for the eunuchs. We'll make it our secret love nest!'

'You are a sly one,' laughed Emma again in a whisper. 'Planning all this and never saying a word to me!'

'I didn't dare. One of the eunuchs might have heard me, and anyway you'd have been so excited that the eunuchs would have suspected something. Anyway I'm off now. See you there in two minutes time.'

She got up slowly and strolled over towards the dormitory, leaving Emma in a state of turmoil.

How many times had she longed just for a few minutes alone with Zuriba! How she had despaired of such an opportunity ever arising in this closely watched harem! And now it was really going to happen!

Ever since the Caid had come back, after giving her to his son to play with for a few days, he had amused himself more and more often by having Emma and Zuriba perform their little lesbian act together in front of him, but always with a eunuch holding each of them by a lead fastened to the back of their collars, to pull them back in time whenever they looked like reaching a climax. And to drive them on with their dog whips if they showed any sign of flagging.

It might have been a delightfully erotic spectacle for the Caid, thought Emma, watching two educated young Christian women being made to behave in front of him in such a shameful way merely for his amusement. But for us two girls, not only has it been horribly degrading, but also madly frustrating.

Indeed, to have to embrace each other passionately, sometimes several times a day, in the normally strictly supervised atmosphere of the harem, in front of the cruel Caid, was bad enough, Emma kept telling herself. But to have to bring each other repeatedly to the point of release, and then to be pulled back by the neck by two grinning eunuchs was too much. It was driving them both crazy!

Watched particularly closely by the eunuchs, they would sit around all day, looking at each other, and longing to fling themselves wildly into each other's arms. But all they would dare to do was occasionally to touch hands, or perhaps exchange a chaste little kiss under the approving eyes of the supervising eunuch.

Indeed, the eunuchs liked to see women showing a little innocent girlish affection towards each other. The inevitable frustration that resulted, the eunuchs calculated, would make the women realise more than ever that they were utterly dependent on catching the Caid's eye if they were to have any chance of enjoying sexual relief. This in turn made the women more submissive and humble towards the Caid – much to his delight and hence to the enrichment of the eunuch's pockets.

But, of course, any attempt at anything more serious was stamped on immediately by the eunuchs.

The Caid, as Emma had learned, sometimes enjoyed keeping a woman he had chosen for his bed, uncertain as to whether she was going to be sent away the following morning still hopelessly frustrated, or whether he was going to use his great experience to bring her to the heights of passion. This terrible uncertainty made the girls all the more eager to please the Caid, but in no way did it reduce Emma's desire to find relief at last in the soft arms of the beautiful Zuriba.

There were no clocks or watches in the harem just as there were no calendars or books. Such things were only for the eunuchs. The Caid liked to keep his women uneducated, ignorant, and preferably illiterate. He enjoyed keeping a harem of frustrated young creatures with the bodies of grown up women, but with the minds of adoring and submissive little girls.

So the agitated Emma was reduced to counting desperately on her fingers the seconds before she was due to get up and join Zuriba. She was also praying that the eunuch would not come back in the meantime.

Just as she was standing up, she heard a cry from the bathroom. Murina had started her feigned sickness! As the other girls all looked towards the bathroom in alarm, Emma quietly slipped out of the room.

So far so good, she thought.

However, she would not have been so complacent, and nor indeed would Zuriba, had she noticed the vague figure of the chief eunuch silently surveying the room from behind the lattice screen that was normally used by the Caid to watch, unnoticed, his pretty young creatures at play.

The screen was, however, also used from time to time by the chief eunuch for the very purpose of checking on just how affectionate certain pairs of girls were getting. In particular, at the present time his considerable experience in handling and supervising young women was making him keep a discreet but close eye on Emma and Zuriba. With their superior education, they were moreover a disruptive influence in the harem. He would not be sorry to see them go.

But in the corridor, Emma, blissfully unaware that they had been observed, was thrilled to see Zuriba awaiting her, a delicate little finger raised warningly to her lips. She was half-naked in her harem dress, just as Emma was herself. She looked entrancing, her eyes dancing with excitement and anticipation, just like those of Emma. Zuriba beckoned Emma and led her down the little used corridor to where a large chest of drawers was propped up against the wall. Emma looked at it in dismay. They would never manage to move it – or anyway not quietly. However, just as Zuriba had said, it turned out to be empty and quite light. And there behind it was indeed a little door, just as Zuriba had described!

Zuriba led the way into the little room. It was comfortably furnished with thick Turkish rugs, several ottomans and a large bed. Such luxury, Emma realised, bore out what Zuriba had said about it having been used as a rest room for the eunuchs. No such luxury was wasted on the Caid's concubines, she thought bitterly.

Zuriba put her chained arms round Emma's waist.

Emma's hands were on Zuriba's large breasts.

They began to make love passionately, their lithe little bodies rubbing against each other. Breathlessly, they fell together onto the bed.

Soon, they found themselves doing for real what they had so often had to do for show. This time, as each girl's head disappeared between the other's legs, there were no chain leads attached to their collars against which they had to strain and which might at any moment painfully jerk their heads back.

Nor, of course, were there any little dog whips insistently driving them to greater efforts. Indeed there was no need for such encouragement and before long the two young women were panting with mutual desire and both were about to reach the heights of ecstasy for which they had waited for so long.

Suddenly there was a swishing noise as the chief eunuch, his eyes blazing with anger, brought his cane down first across the back of Emma and then of Zuriba, as he screamed an order to them both to get up at once.

Appalled at having been caught in the act of making love to each other, and at the enormity of their offence in the eyes of both the eunuchs and the Caid, both girls jumped up and stood by the bed looking down sheepishly at the floor.

Seeking supporting corroboration for the evidence he would soon be giving to the Caid, the chief eunuch gave an order. Immediately, the young apprentice eunuch with him put his hand down between Emma's legs. He was holding a piece of silk white cloth. After a moment he stood up, looked at the cloth, smelt it, nodded grimly to the chief eunuch and handed it to him. Then, with another piece of silk cloth, he did the same to Zuriba.

Emma was appalled at the sheer sordidness of it all.

'Out!' ordered the furious chief eunuch. 'Run!'

The two girls rushed back to the harem room.

The other girls, each now sitting silently and demurely on her leather cushion, looked at them open-mouthed. The now angry-looking eunuch on duty waved them to the leather cushions on opposite sides of the room. They were not going to be allowed, Emma realised, to talk to one another – and the other girls spoke no English.

What was going to happen to them, she wondered, anxiously biting her lips.

Then she saw Murina, Zuriba's much younger sister. She was bending over a high cushion in the middle of the room. Her harem trousers were down round her ankles. Her swollen little belly and her now rapidly developing little breasts hung down prettily from her little teenage body.

It was a sight that had often given the Caid much pleasure as he sat watching from behind the screen. He had been entranced at the way the young teenager's immature little breasts had begun to swell quite delightfully in preparation for her forthcoming lactation. It would be a lactation that the eunuchs would prolong for as long as possible, for the milk of a young girl was particularly sweet, and much enjoyed by the sensuous Caid.

She was looking over her shoulder with terrified eyes at the huge figure of the chief eunuch who was slowly coming towards her, his long whippy cane raised.

Clearly Murina's ruse and her diversionary role in the whole affair had been exposed.

There was complete silence in the harem.

The chief eunuch called out: 'Twenty!'

Murina gave a litle sob of disbelief. There was a gasp from Zuriba. The other girls held their breath. Twenty strokes of the cane! And to a girl who was pregnant. Not that this, they knew, would make any difference.

Twenty strokes of the cane! Even Emma understood that. It was more than she had ever seen administered to any girl since she had been in the harem. If Murina, who had not after all been involved in any lesbianism, was to get twenty strokes, then what sort of punishment was in store for Zuriba and herself?

It took over twenty minutes for the beating to be completed. The young girl was allowed to jump about after each stroke, trying to ease the pain with her manacled hands. Then she was made to run round the room in front of the silently watching girls and to kiss the cane before bending over for the next stroke, for which the huge eunuch kept her waiting for a different length of time for each stroke.

It was a spectacle that struck fear into the heart of every girl who was watching – as it was intended to do.

Not only had Murina tried to distract the duty eunuch whilst her sister and Emma indulged in strictly forbidden love, but also she had tried to take advantage of a very basic harem rule: that a girl must always be accompanied by a eunuch when she went to relieve herself in the bathroom. But at the same time Emma and Zuriba had deliberately broken another basic rule: that girls must at all times be under the surveillance of a eunuch.

Clearly this constant surveillance could easily be put in jeopardy when only one eunuch was on duty, by girls pretending they urgently needed to go to the bathroom. This was something that the chief eunuch was determined not to tolerate.

So poor Murina had been punished for this, as well as for being involved in covering up something that was regarded by the eunuchs, and by the Caid himself, as only slightly less serious than helping a girl to make a secret assignment with a strange man. Hence the chief eunuch's decision to make an example of Murina, as well as reporting her sister and Emma to the Caid.

Two hours later, Emma and Zuriba were standing nervously in the Caid's study. They were standing at attention in front of the desk, behind which an angry looking Caid was sitting in a modern swivel chair. Both girls were stark naked. Both were too embarrassed to look the Caid in the eye.

Lying on the desk were two white silk cloths – the proof that the girls had taken pleasure from each other – pleasure which they were only permitted to receive from the Caid himself. They had both deceived the Caid. To all intents and purposes they had both committed adultery, and by the Moslem sharia law, a man has the right to kill a woman of his household who dishonours it by committing adultery.

The Caid had listened to what Emma had presumed was the chief eunuch's description of what he had seen in the little room. Then the eunuch had produced the white silk cloths. The Caid's fury had been terrible. He asked no questions of the two women, nor were they given any chance to speak, since by sharia law, the evidence of a woman is of little or no account unless it is corroborated by a man.

Then there was a long silence whilst the Caid decided what to do with the two young women.

Clearly an example must be made of them, or else other concubines might be tempted to follow their example. Moreover, they must be removed from the harem, where they would clearly be a bad influence. If they had been ugly or if he had been bored with them, then he would quite happily have had them sent to the brothel he maintained in another part of the castle for the benefit of his guards.

But these two girls were too desirable for that, and in any case he had given his word to return one of them to her Mistress. Indeed the English girl was so attractive, that it was only the fact that he had given his word to return her, that had prevented him from having a son by her. She would have looked delightful in an interesting state. Deprived of that particular pleasure he had been wondering what to do with her next. Now this had happened.

As he turned the problem over in his mind, he remembered his thoughts as he had driven over the pass several weeks before and he had looked down into the valley and admired the sight of the long blue reservoir.

Of course! That was the answer.

The Caid gave his short and concise instructions to the chief eunuch. The latter was smiling as he listened to the Caid. But Emma, who did not understand a word of what was being said, was extremely alarmed to see that the Caid's words had the effect of making Zuriba shake with fear.

She longed to ask Zuriba to explain what was happening, but she had no chance to do so. Both girls were marched by a posse of eunuchs out of the Caid's study and into a courtyard.

There, leather hoods were slipped over their heads. Each had two little breathing holes opposite the nostrils. Terrified, Emma found she could breathe quite easily, but she could see nothing and was in complete darkness. Moreover, the hood muffled any attempt to speak. She felt the hood being fastened with a strap round her neck. She heard a click as the strap was fastened by a little padlock.

She put her chained hands up to feel the hood. It was thick and stiff. She felt the little padlock that kept it fastened round her neck. She realised that there was nothing she could do to remove it.

She was quite helpless. She could see nothing. She couldn't talk properly. Her hands were manacled together. She was stark naked.

She felt a long shroud being put over her. She was, she realised being veiled so that she could be taken out of the castle. Then her arms were gripped together through the shroud and she was frogmarched forward. She had no idea where they were going. She could hear Zuriba stumbling behind her. She tried to call out to her, to ask what was happening, but her words were muzzled by the thick leather hood. She felt herself being taken along winding corridors. She heard a door being closed. Moments later she was unceremoniously lifted up and dumped into what she realised must be the back of the truck. The truck drove off, bumping over the stone track.

After what seemed ages, the truck stopped.

Emma now heard men's voices. Where were they, she wondered anxiously. Was this where she was going to be executed? Was her life to end in some remote desert gully? And all merely because she had been found making love to another girl! What a fool she had been to agree to meet Zuriba in secret!

Suddenly she was pulled out of the truck. Again, her arm was gripped and she was frogmarched forward. She felt the enveloping shroud being removed. She was now stark naked again in front of these unknown men. She blushed under the hood. Was she now, she wondered, going to be shot?

She felt herelf again being marched forward. She seemed to be going up some sort of plank. Then she seemed to be standing in something that seemed to be rocking slightly. She heard the whispers of women. Women! Where on earth was she?

She was made to sit down on what seemed to be a hard wooden bench. Her chained hands were pulled forward. She could hear the big link in the middle of her wrist chain being locked to something. She groped around. Her hands gripped something that felt like a heavy wooden pole.

She was left alone, unable to see or speak and with her hands fastened in front of her. She heard a woman's whispered voice immediately behind her, and another in front of her. There was a rattle of chains and a barked order. She heard the crack of a whip. She flinched in fear. There was another crack followed by a woman's cry.

Then she heard footsteps approaching. She felt the strap of the thick leather hood being unlocked. Suddenly the hood was pulled off her head. She was no longer in darkness. She looked around her. Then she screamed in sheer disbelief.

21

Galley slave

Emma saw that she was seated on a rowing bench in a long slender wooden galley. The heavy pole which her hands were gripping was the loom of a long oar. The large centre link of her wrist chain had been padlocked to an iron staple on the oar. Horrified she realised that she was now chained to her oar, just like the galley slaves of yore. But they had been men, usually fit young men, not delicate young women. This was awful!

In front of her was the naked back of another young woman. There were whip marks across it. She was silently reaching forward with the loom of her oar, as if awaiting the order to start rowing.

Emma felt something hard touch her own back. She looked round. A beautiful Arab woman, stark naked except for a metal collar, big brass nose ring and wrist manacles, all identical to her own, was sitting behind her. Her wrists, like those of Emma, were chained to her oar. Emma was appalled to see the marks of the whip across the woman's delicate but firm breasts.

She too was reaching forward with her oar, the loom of which was pressing against Emma's back. Emma realised that the only way to avoid being hit by the oar of the woman behind her was to reach forward herself, with her own oar.

On one side of the wooden thwart on which she was seated was the wooden side of the galley with a little porthole through which the oar protruded. The side of the galley rose up above the level of the head. This hid her, she realised, from prying eyes, but also made it difficult for her to see out. She could only see the blade of her oar through the little gaps in the porthole on either side of the oar itself.

In this way, she also realised, the female galley slaves would not be distracted by what might be going on outside the galley. They had to keep their eyes on the back of the woman in front of them, and concentrate on pulling their oars in perfect time to the beat of the drum.

Female galley slaves! The expression raced round her brain. Was this the state to which she had been reduced? Was this the Caid's punishment? Was this why Zuriba had looked so frightened when the Caid announced his sentence on the two of them? But what was the purpose of the galley? Merely for the punishment of naughty or disobedient concubines? Hardly!

Emma remembered what Zuriba had said about girls disappearing from a harem and not being seen again. Was this where they were sent? To start a new life as a galley slave?

But were the galley slaves kept permanently chained to their oars day and night? If so, how did they eat with their hands chained to their oars? And how did they . . .? After the horror in the harem of having to perform into a bowl held by a eunuch, Emma was prepared for anything, but even so!

Emma looked around her. On her other side was a little platform, or catwalk, which ran down the centre of the galley. On the other side of the catwalk was another thwart on which a woman was also seated. She, too, was chained to an oar – on the other side of the galley.

Emma saw that she was a pretty girl. She was smiling at her, as if to welcome her as a fellow galley slave. She too was reaching forward with the loom of the oar to which her wrists were chained. She too wore the distinctive collar and nose ring of the Caid.

Shocked, Emma saw that she carried the marks of the whip across her shoulders and thighs.

There were ten oars on either side of the long slender galley, with a young woman chained to each oar. The larger women seemed to be seated aft and the more slender ones, like herself, were seated forward in the galley. Some of the women were black, but all were tanned by the sun – tanned all over. Emma recognised Zuriba's still white back. She was chained to an oar just ahead of her on the opposite side of the catwalk.

Right aft of the galley was a little raised poop covered by a light roof to give shelter against the sun and rain. There was no shelter for the women galley slaves, she realised. On the poop was a ship's wheel, presumably for steering the vessel, and several comfortable divans, presumably for the Caid and his guests. She saw the galley's Arab coxswain standing there, his eye to the shore, presumably keeping an eye out for the arrival of the Caid.

Beneath the raised poop, at the level of the thwarts, were two cages, presumably to carry spare women for the oars. Emma saw two nose-rings flash from behind the bars of the cages. They must be, she thought, the two women who had been moved to make room for Zuriba and herself.

Also at the foot of the poop was a naked little boy sitting by a drum, ready to give the beat to the women, varying the speed of the beautifully made galley in accordance with the orders of the man at the wheel.

But it was the man who had pulled the hood off her head, and who was now standing on the catwalk, leaning over her, who really caught her attention. Later she was to learn that he was the whip-master, in complete charge of the female galley slaves.

As she looked up at him in some alarm, she saw that he was big, bald and brutal looking. He was naked except for a bulging loin cloth, the sight of which made her cower in horror and in shame at her own nakedness in front of this evidently very virile man. In his hand he held a short black leather whip, the sight of which made Emma cower again, this time in fear as she remembered all the whip marks she had seen on the other women's unprotected backs and thighs.

The whip-master bent down. He separated Emma's chained wrists so that they were the same distance apart as her shoulders as she held her oar forward, her arms stiffly outstretched. With her hands well separated, she realised, she would be able to pull her oar more effectively. Then he slipped a pair of gloves onto her hands and slipped a little piece of carpet under her buttocks. Clearly, both were to guard against blisters until her skin had toughened. Emma glanced up at him in gratitude. She wanted to thank him, to ask him a thousand questions. But he put a finger to his lips. Clearly, the galley slaves were not allowed to talk on board. They were just there to pull their oars!

Then the whip-master produced a length of light chain. He locked one end to the ring on the front of Emma's collar and the other to the ring on the back of the collar of the woman seated in front of her. In the centre of the light chain was a bottle screw which allowed the chain to be shortened or lengthened slightly.

Then he locked a similar length of chain to the back of Emma's collar and onto the front of the collar of the woman behind her. He adjusted the two bottle screws so that the chains were taut.

Emma's neck was now tightly held. She saw that the women on both sides of the galley were all linked like her, forming two separate chain gangs. She would, she realised, now have to sway to and fro, and therefore row, in perfect time with the other women. It was a very ingenious way of making the women all row together.

The craft appeared to be moored by the stern to some sort of jetty, Emma thought. She could see several other galleys.

The crew of the nearest seemed to be standing up, as if for inspection by a swarthy man dressed in Arab robes who was presumably the galley's owner.

The galley seemed to be manned by women with shaven heads. Their completely bald heads gave them a strangely animal-like look – just like the girls of the Italian woman who had visited Ursula's studio, Emma thought. There must, she decided, be something very erotic about keeping a woman's head shaved and polished.

Emma thought about the other galleys. Did they belong to other Caids or rich Arabs? Did they each mark their own galley slaves in a distinctive manner? Is that why the women in the other galley had their heads shaved whilst those in this galley wore the distinctive nose-ring of the Caid?

But why, Emma asked herself in some bewilderment, why did these men have these galleys? Just for amusement? For the erotic feeling of power that came from making twenty beautiful young women strain at their oars under the whip of a black whip-master?

But did they perhaps also race their galleys? If horse racing was the sport of kings, was galley racing with female galley slaves, on a remote reservoir, the sport of rich and bored Caids and their friends?

Was the acquisition of sufficient pretty women to act as galley slaves cheap and easy here? Was keeping and feeding them similarly cheap and easy?

Was this the ultimate erotic sport, a secret and highly sensuous pursuit?

But if they did race these galleys, surely it woud be a handicap to have a pregnant woman amongst the galley slaves? Handicap? That must be the explanation, she thought.

Emma knew that the Caid enjoyed mating some of the girls in his harem with his guards and also enjoyed watching the subsequent enforced maternity. He would also, presumably, equally enjoy breeding from women in his galley. After all, Emma thought, it was really just an extension of his harem.

So presumably he and his cruel friends might have some handicap system for their races which would make it worthwhile to keep a proportion of the galley slaves pregnant. Perhaps, she thought with a shiver of apprehension, to make it more worthwhile the handicap would increase with each month of pregnancy for each pregnant galley slave. Perhaps the handicap would continue for a year after the girl gave birth, making it even more worthwhile to breed from one's galley slaves.

My God, she thought, will he want to breed from me?

She thought of the frightening whip-master. He certainly

seemed to be in complete charge of all the galley slaves. Just as the eunuchs had been responsible for producing well trained and submissive girls for the Caid's bed, was the whip-master responsible for producing a team of fit female galley slaves for the Caid's racing galley?

Did the owners wager huge sums, she wondered, on the outcome of their races? Did the whip-master have a vested interest in the fitness of the women in his charge by sharing in the prize money? Certainly the wretched women wouldn't! Any more than a winning horse shares in the prize money, Emma thought bitterly.

Suddenly there was an air of excitement in the galley. The whip-master shouted an order. Holding the looms of their oars level with their bellies, the women all stood up and respectfully lowered their eyes. The Caid was coming on board!

Out of the corner of her eye, Emma saw this terrifying man, this man who had sentenced her to this terrible fate, sit down in comfort on the poop. He looked down onto the rowing deck in front of him. There was a cruel smile on his face. Clearly he was enjoying the sight of twenty naked young women all chained to the oars of his galley.

The Caid gave a nod to the whip-master. He called out an order to the boy at the drum. He took the wheel from the coxswain.

Simultaneously, the whip-master gave an order. The women all sat down again on their benches. They reached right forward with their oars. Emma found her neck first jerked forward by the chain leading to the woman in front of her, and then back by the chain at the back of her neck.

Emma saw that the Caid was now looking down alternately at her and at Zuriba. The cruel smile on his lips was even more accentuated.

There was a warning roll of the drum and the first of a slow regular beat. In perfect time together, the women on both sides of the galley swayed back, each straining to pull her oar through the water, each terrified lest the whip-master might think she was not putting her back into her work and give her a cut across her naked back with his whip.

Emma found herself being pulled first backwards and

then forwards by her neck at an increasing rate as the drum rate increased.

Emma soon learned that although her oar was heavy she could go through the motions of rowing without having to really strain at her oar. She did not, however, deceive the whip-master, standing behind her where she could not see him. Suddenly there was a crack of his whip just behind her and then another crack as he brought his whip down across her back so that the tip flicked round and caught her bare breast. She cried out, but instantly she also started to really strain at her oar. Now she knew the meaning of the expression 'put your back into it!'

She would do anything, she told herself, to avoid another stroke of the whip like that!

She glanced up at the poop. The Caid was looking at her and laughing. The swine! The utter and unspeakable swine!

She could not meet his stare. As she lowered her eyes, she felt herself to her shame becoming excited by him. It was as if she, as a mere female, was yet again responding in some primaeval or instinctive way to the presence of a powerful and dominant male.

For the next two hours the Caid exercised his team of pretty little galley slaves.

A clever trainer of race horses will exercise them alternatively at the walk, at the trot, at the canter, at the gallop and then at the trot again. So too, the Caid exercised his female galley slaves at a frequently changing pace.

The drum boy would beat out the pace for slow speed ahead. Suddenly this would be followed by a change to the quicker pace of half speed ahead. Then, just as the women were beginning to tire, however, the beat would change to a burst at full speed ahead, with the whip-master cracking his whip menacingly, and the sweat pouring down the naked bodies of the straining women before the drum reverted to half speed again.

Then, so as to keep them on their toes, the Caid would order full speed astern, with the women desperately straining to bring the galley to an emergency halt.

The Caid was not merely getting his women slaves fit for the start of the racing season. He was also trying them out under realistic conditions.

Galley races were not often held over short distances. They were usually long drawn out affairs, lasting perhaps an hour or even more. Such races were intended partly to really test the stamina of the female galley slaves. But they were also intended to test the skill of their owners in conserving the flagging energy of his slaves and in outmanoeuvring his rivals.

In horse racing, a clever jockey might keep his horse back and then suddenly use his whip to drive his horse forward to overtake his rivals at just the critical moment when they are beginning to tire. So, too, in galley racing the Caid regarded himself as an expert in judging just how much more his exhausted women could be flogged into straining at their oars without finally collapsing.

He would rein back to rest them for a few minutes of rowing at a relatively slow beat. Then suddenly he would decide to put on the pressure, increase the rate of the drumbeat dramatically, instruct his whip-master to use the whip, and then shoot past an unsuspecting rival.

Similarly he was also an expert at conserving just sufficient of his women's energy to enable him to make a last minute high-speed dash for the winning line, with his whip-master driving the already exhausted galley slaves into producing new unexpected reserves of stamina as they toiled at their oars in response to an increasingly fast drum.

He would be furious with his whip-master if the women were not all in a state of utter collapse as the race ended.

It was a cruel sport. It was the element of cruelty that accounted for its popularity amongst the Caids and some other rich Arabs.

Whilst the women galley slaves were being put through their paces by the cruel and demanding Caid, the drum boy would periodically be sent to water them: each sweating girl having to hold up her chin, and open her mouth as she rowed, so that the boy could pour water into her mouth.

After one particularly hard spell at full speed, the Caid handed over the helm to his Arab coxswain and came down from the poop. Then accompanied by his whip-master he came down the catwalk to inspect his galley slaves.

Whilst the drum kept up a relaxed but brisk beat, the two men worked their way slowly down the catwalk, examining and discussing each of the women in turn, like a successful racehorse owner examining and discussing his string of race horses with his trainer.

Each woman being examined would continue to strain at her oar, terrified by the near presence of both her dreaded owner and his equally dreaded whip-master. Similarly, she would keep her eyes fixed on the back of the woman in front of her, as the men felt her arm and shoulder muscles, felt her belly carefully if she was pregnant, and judged whether the hang of her breasts was impeding her efficiency at the oar. Emma had noticed how firm the women's breasts were – presumably, she thought, rowing was very good for the pectoral muscles!

When the Caid came level with her, she could not help glancing piteously up at him. He was furious at this and turned to give an order to the whip-master. Horrified, Emma recognised the Arab word for 'impertinence' – it was a word she had heard so often in the Caid's harem.

The whip-master nodded with a smile. He stood back and brought his whip down under her outstretched arms. The whip caught right across her belly, just as she was raising it at the end of a stroke. She could not help giving a little cry of pain. She did not dare move her eyes again from the exact middle of the back of the woman seated in front of her as the Caid ran his hand across her belly. Emma was aghast. However, she would have been relieved had she known that the Caid was simply regretting that there was not time, before he had promised to return her, to enjoy watching her belly swell prettily as it carried perhaps a pair of kicking babies.

At last the Caid turned his back on Emma and putting his hand down began to examine the heavily pregnant pretty galley slave seated on the opposite side of the catwalk to Emma.

During races, each galley was allowed to carry two spare galley slaves. To prevent any cheating however, by having the spare women double bank one of the oars, it was a strict rule that until one of the spare women was used to replace a specific galley slave, she had to be kept locked up in a cage – hence the two cages that Emma had seen below the poop.

Thus, the rapid replacement of a particularly exhausted slave also needed frequent practice. Indeed, Emma was greatly relieved when one of the women in the cages at the foot of the poop was dragged out by the whip-master and used to replace her for a short period.

She was delighted when the metal door of the cage clanged shut behind her. Every muscle in her body was aching, and she was covered with the marks of the whip-master's whip. She looked up at the Caid with increasing hatred. But, she realised, it was a hatred also mixed with increased respect for him as a man, a real man, a man who had no qualms whatsoever in using his women purely for his own entertainment and sport.

Her delight at being put into the cage, apparently to rest, was short lived. She soon learned that she was merely being taught the drill for replacing a galley slave. A few minutes later, she was dragged out and chained again to her heavy oar.

She was just in time to take part in some practice emergency turns when, as if to avoid a collision, or to round a buoy quickly, the oars on one side of the fast-moving craft would be ordered to hold water. This made the long thin galley spin round much quicker than it would normally under the control of the rudder.

It was, however, a manoeuvre that called for considerable effort from the unfortunate galley slaves.

The Caid then pointed at two women who had caught his eye during his inspection. The women in the cages were dragged out again and chained to the oars of the other two women. Emma sensed that the rest of the slaves were very jealous of the two chosen women. They were made to crawl humbly along the catwalk and up onto the poop.

Then in front of the other women, they were made to kiss the Caid's shoes lovingly and put their hands under his robe.

The Caid now ordered full speed again. Whilst he enjoyed the sight of the other women all straining at their oars under the whip of his whip-master, he was being pleasured by two little creatures kneeling under his robe.

Although she knew now only too well that she must keep her eyes straight ahead, fixed on the naked back of the woman in front of her, like the other galley slaves, she simply could not help risking the whip and glancing up at the Caid.

He was, she had to admit, a magnificent figure of a man as he stood at the wheel, his legs astride, whilst at his feet, four little feet and two little naked bottoms peeked out from beneath his robe.

She wished her little bottom was one of them!

Would he choose her next time? she wondered. The very thought made her feel ashamedly excited again.

22

The slave pens

The exercise period was over. The Caid disembarked into a small boat to return to his castle – and to the delights of his harem.

The galley was now taken by the coxswain back to a remote island in the middle of the reservoir where the galleys were moored when not in use and where the galley slaves were kept.

After some complex manoeuvres, the galley was moored stern on, to a wharf on the little island. The two chain gangs, one each side of the vessel, were now unfastened from their oars.

Then at a word of command from the whip-master, the naked women, still chained by the neck to form two chain gangs, formed up silently on the catwalk. They were joined by the two women who had been let out of their cages again. Another word of command, accompanied as usual by a terrifying crack of the whip, and the women ran down the gangplank and formed up again on the wharf under the interested eye of several other rival whip-masters.

Their own whip-master, keen to show off his mastery over his female galley slaves to his peers, then called out another word of command. Twenty-two women obediently assumed a squatting position with their chained hands placed on the top of their heads. There was a pause and then another barked word of command. There was a sudden sound of running water as twenty-two women let their wastes run away into the sand.

After several hours in the galley, Emma was as anxious as the rest to spend a penny. But to have to do it like this, to the order of a man and watched by several more, was too humiliating for words.

The two chain gangs then ran off, their knees rising in perfect time with each other as the whip-master called out the step, his whip cracking as he ran alongside the women.

It was one of his rules that whatever the galley slaves did: eating, running, drinking, urinating, marching or defecating, all had to be done in perfect unison and to his order. In this way he helped to ensure that the female galley slaves ceased to think of themselves as individual women, or even as women at all since no human speech was allowed, but rather as a team of performing animals controlled at all times by their whip-master.

Similarly he took great care to ensure that the women's energies were strictly conserved for their efforts at the oar, and not dissipated by any sexual relief or activities.

It was therefore a standard rule that unless a girl's wrists were fastened to her oar, or to a restraining chain in the galley slave's cage, then they were at all times to be placed on the top of her head – where he could see them!

Just at that moment Emma heard the noise of a departing helicopter. It must be a wealthy galley owner departing, she thought. She had wondered how they got to the island, for few lived by the side of the reservoir, like the Caid. No wonder they had succeeded in keeping the existence of the galley slaves so secret! Private helicopters would certainly make it much easier for busy men to visit the island.

They ran past a beautiful white building – the clubhouse where visiting owners could stay in comfort, attended by one or two of their prettier galley slaves.

They ran on towards a long, simple, open-sided building. It looked rather like a cattle shed. Outside were neat piles of unused straw and dung pits for dirty straw.

But it was what was under the roof of the building that caught Emma's eye: a row of iron cages. And, inside each cage, was a chained group of women just like themselves. A chain gang of galley slaves from another owner's galley.

As they doubled past the low line of cages, each with its row of silently watching women, Emma recognised in one cage the team she had seen earlier standing up in the galley – all with their heads shaved and polished. Another group all had a distinctive mark tattooed on their foreheads, and yet another had a crest apparently branded on their naked bellies.

Like the ringed noses of the Caid's women, these distinctive emblems were intended to make the women all feel a sense of identity and of belonging to their owner's team. They were also intended to curb any sense of individuality. The whip-master's job was to produce a well-trained team, used to working together, not a set of different individuals.

Emma saw a group of black workmen emptying a dung pit into a handcart. Later she would learn that the rotted-down human wastes were used as valuable manure on this isolated island, and especially in the kitchen garden that served the clubhouse of the galley owners and the quarters of the whip-masters and crew.

The two chain gangs were finally ordered by their whip-master to halt in front of the two cages. Each already contained several naked women. They were collared, manacled and wore the Caid's big brass nose-rings. Evidently they were spare girls who had been left behind that day.

All in all, Emma realised, the Caid kept about thirty female galley slaves in training to ensure that his galley could be raced at all times. Choosing the exact crew for each different race was a complex matter and one that took up much of the time of the Caid and his whip-master.

With the women still standing with their hands on their heads, the whip-master now hosed them all down to wash off the sweat and to clean them up. He liked his team of galley slaves to take pride in their appearance, whilst insisting, of course, that they all looked alike as much as possible.

They were, for instance, allowed to use the same shade of lipstick, from a stock kept in the cages. Similarly they had to comb their long hair in the same way with a parting down the middle and the hair twisted into an attractive chignon at the back of the neck so as to keep it out of their eyes as they toiled and sweated at their oars.

The starboard chain containing Emma was now put into one cage and the port chain, including Zuriba, into the other. Emma sighed. Doubtless they had been separated on purpose.

Even in the cage, the women were careful to keep their hands on their heads and did not talk. As they were still chained to each other by the neck, movement was restricted. Indeed to all intents and purposes, each girl only got to know the girl on either side of her on the chain gang, the girls who rowed immediately in front and behind her in the galley, and the head girls of each chain gang, who being the biggest and strongest were seated on the stroke thwarts right aft, next to the drum.

Each head girl was responsible to the whip-master for discipline in her chain gang, something which she had to enforce with the flat of her hand, or occasionally with her fist. Like the other girls, she was not allowed to talk, however, and indeed one of her main tasks was to enforce the no talking rule when the women were locked in their cages.

Their main task, of course, was to keep a sharp lookout at night in the cage lest any girl, unable to use her hands to give herself relief, might try to obtain it by rubbing herself against another galley slave or even, in her desperation, against a bundle of straw.

The head girls were allowed the privilege by the whip-master of being permitted to give themselves relief once every two weeks – provided no race was imminent. They had to do this under the orders of the whip-master and facing the cage in which the rest of the chain gang were lined up, jealously watching.

This privilege made the position of head girl a much sought after one. Once a week, any girl could challenge her head girl to a fight in front of the Caid. There were no rounds and no rules. The fight continued until one girl gave in.

To discourage frivolous challenges, if a challenger lost the fight then she would later be thrashed by the whip-master in front of the remainder of the chain gang. If, however, the head girl was beaten, then the winner became the new head girl and exchanged places on the chain gang with the former head girl. Usually a head girl beat off her challengers and remained in her prestigious position on the stroke thwart right aft. She also of course then retained the jealously guarded right to give herself relief once every two weeks.

An open truck now drove up from the beautiful white clubhouse that Emma had noticed earlier. It stopped in front of the two cages containing the Caid's galley slaves.

In the back of the truck were several large metal rubbish bins. The driver and his mate unloaded the bins. Emma saw that the two girls on either side of her were licking their lips in anticipation. She did not understand why.

Right in front of the cage, resting on the sand, was a low metal cattle trough, running the whole length of the cage. It was polished and empty.

Emma now saw that the rubbish bins were full of scraps of food of the type normally used to feed pigs: potato peelings, bits of oranges, apple cores, pieces of bread, lumps of meat and coffee grains. Another bin was full of bones with bits of raw meat and fat still sticking to them, rather like the bones that one might give to a dog.

Clearly, these were the scraps left over from the magnificent meals enjoyed by the owners and their guests in the clubhouse restaurant.

Emma looked at the nauseous mess with revulsion, even though it had been a long day and she was feeling hungry. They had been given a little water to drink in the galley, and some glucose energy tablets, but nothing else. Presumably, she thought, this was because the only toilet facilities on board the galley appeared to be those below the poop and they were clearly reserved for the use of the Caid, the coxswain, the whip-master and the drummer boy. Certainly the galley slaves could not use them.

That was why, Emma realised, the whip-master had allowed the girls to empty themselves onto the sand as soon as they were all ashore.

To Emma's surprise the workmen now emptied their

rubbish bins into the metal troughs just outside the cage. They added a sackful of bran and poured on water. They stirred up the mess with a stick. The whip-master came to look at it and nodded in approval.

He was responsible for feeding the Caid's women galley slaves. The more he could feed them on scraps, the more money went into his pocket. But, in any case, the scraps were full of energy-giving protein, and the women did very well on them.

The workmen threw the empty bins into the back of the truck and drove off.

The whip-master now blew a whistle. The whole line of women, facing the bars on the front of the cage, fell to their knees, pulling Emma down with them by her collar chains.

There was a long pause. Then the whip-master pulled a lever and a slot along the bottom of the bars on the front of the cage was lifted up. Again there was a long pause, whilst the line of women became more and more restive.

Then the whip-master gave another blast on his whistle. The women, now kneeling on hands and knees like animals, thrust their heads through the raised section at the bottom of the cage. Without daring to use their hands, which were still flat on the floor of the cage, the women eagerly began to gobble up the food in the trough in front of them, and with their teeth to fight over the more succulent bones which they tried to bring into the cage to chew later.

Emma hesitated. She was certainly hungry, and the thought of eating some solid food again after just being on a liquid diet, was exciting. But it looked so repulsive with all the bits and pieces floating in a sort of wet bran mash.

She was also shocked at the animal-like behaviour of the women. They were like pigs at the trough. They were fighting over the bones like dogs.

Suddenly Emma's head was pushed down into the trough by the whip-master.

'Eat! Eat quickly!' screamed the whip-master, holding her head down in the food.

Emma understood that order all right! Hastily she

started to gobble and guzzle, whilst the whip-master looked on. It would be a lesson she would not quickly forget, she thought, as she desperately swallowed and swallowed.

At last the trough in front of her was empty. The whip-master released her head. She saw that the whole trough was now empty and that the other women were licking it clean. Not wanting to anger the frightening whip-master any more, Emma too began to lick and lick until the trough in front of her shone too.

The whip-master now blew his whistle again. The women all withdrew their heads into the cage. Several were now holding succulent bones in their hands or hiding them under the straw so that their neighbours on the chain gang would not steal them.

The raised slot was lowered and locked into place.

There was another blast of the whistle. The women all knelt up again, holding their manacled wrists up to the bars of the cage. The whip-master threaded a long chain through the loop in each woman's wrist chain. He locked each end of the long chain to a ring at either side of the cage.

The women's arms were now all held by the long chain up against the bars of the cage. There was another blast of the whistle, and the women all lay down on the clean straw, their arms held away from their bodies by the long restraining chain. They were all very tired after their exhausting training session with the Caid. They began to fall asleep.

Some of the women quietly pulled out their bones from under the straw with their teeth and began to chew on them.

The whip-master looked carefully down the line of women lying on the straw. It was beginning to get dark. He switched on the cage light. This would enable anyone outside to see what was going on in the cage. He and the other whip-masters took it in turn to patrol the line of cages. But certainly in his cage, the long restraining chain really made it impossible for a girl to play with herself.

He laughed to himself as he remembered playing a little

prank on another whip-master the night before a big race. The galley owner concerned was very unpopular. He had wagered a large sum of money on winning the long-distance race for which he had specially bought and trained some new women.

The Caid's whip-master had offered to patrol the cages in the middle of the night. He had quietly unlocked the long restraining chain in the cage holding the galley slaves of the unpopular owner. The frustrated girls had eagerly seized this unexpected opportunity. Soon the cage resounded to little cries of female ecstasy.

Before leaving a few hours later, he had fastened the restraining chain again so that no one had ever known how he had nobbled the specially trained girls.

Next day he had smiled as he saw that the unpopular owner's girls all had rings under their eyes. Sure enough, although their galley had got off to a flying start and took the lead, it soon began to drop back, as the galley slaves unexpectedly began to tire.

He had heard the angry owner shouting at his bewildered whip-master, demanding to know why his galley slaves were performing so badly, and screaming at him to whip the sluts into action. But it was all in vain. By the end of the race the women had been frequently chastised by their whip-master's whip, but the galley had come in last!

Carefully the whip-master checked the padlocks on his own long chain. They were brand new and only he had the key.

There was no chance of the women being allowed to get at themselves or at each other! Not even that new European woman that the Caid had sent to the galley as a punishment for misbehaviour in his harem.

He could go off and have his dinner and a comfortable bed in the whip-master's comfortable quarters. There was a pretty slave waiting for him too. He could relax and enjoy himself.

Back in the cage, Emma was in despair.

How she hated the horrible Caid who had so cruelly condemned her to the life of a galley slave. How dare he treat a delicate English woman like this!

But once again, she could not also help half-admiring a man who was so strong and utterly self-confident, and who treated his women merely as animals to be exploited, or toys to be played with.

He might rely on eunuchs to run his harem, and on his whip-master to run his galley, but the driving force was his. What a truly magnificent man he was – and what a cruel bastard.

Just as she had become aroused in the galley by merely looking up at him, now she could not stop herself becoming wet with excitement at merely thinking about him. She felt very ashamed.

She tried to put her hands down to her body, but, of course, the restraining chain prevented her.

'Damn!' she muttered to herself. 'Damnation!'

23

Home!

The days passed slowly for the Caid's galley slaves. Each morning they were given a light feed and then at the whip-master's command they emptied themselves onto the straw at the back of the cage.

The whip-master would then unfasten from the chain gang the spare women he did not require for that morning's exercise. They were then chained by their manacled wrists to the bars of the cage to prevent them from taking advantage of the absence of the whip-master, and of their own head girl, to play with themselves.

Since the Caid attached great importance to making his women galley slaves think of themselves more as dumb animals than as intelligent human beings, they were also gagged to prevent them from breaking his strict rule that the galley slaves must not be allowed to talk to each other at any time.

The two chain gangs were then doubled down to the wharf and onto their galley to be chained to their oars. If the Caid was not away on public or private business, then he would often come on board during the morning exercise period. If he was away, then the Arab coxswain would take charge.

When he did come on board, Emma found herself frequently being chosen to crawl up the catwalk, lick his shoes humbly and then put her head under his robe to give him pleasure. It was, of course, something at which she had had plenty of practice in his harem. Each time she was called on to perform, her feelings of respect for the Caid grew. She felt she was worshipping a magnificent male creature and that she was unworthy of his attention.

Usually, the galley slaves would be exercised twice a day, sometimes three times!

No explanation was, of course, given to the women about what was happening; they were mere animals to be whipped into pulling their oars to the best of their ability. Nevertheless, Emma sensed there was a growing feeling of excitement in the galley. The women, including herself, were being made stronger and stronger. They were beginning to pull their oars for longer and longer in time with an increasingly fast drumbeat.

Clearly, they were being worked up for something. The whip-master was taking increasing care in the feeding of each of the women and in her wastes. The Caid was paying more attention to examining each of his galley slaves as she strained at her oar.

The women's positions on their chain gang was frequently varied, as was the choice of who was left behind chained to the bars of the cage. It was as if the Caid and his whip-master were experimenting in getting an optimum mix of galley slaves for a particular purpose.

Just what that purpose was became clear one morning when the galleys all lined up, a gun was fired and they were off. Deliberately, of course, the women galley slaves had been kept completely ignorant of the length of the race. The decision as to when they should conserve their energies, and when to give their all, was not to be theirs but that of their master, the Caid – aided by the whip of his whip-master.

Indeed, thanks to the high sides of the galley, the women had little idea of how they were doing during the race. Perhaps this was just as well, for they were leading for much of the time and might therefore have been tempted to take it easy.

As it was, the Caid by judiciously setting off at a fast speed that tired the less well-trained crews of the other galleys, then easing back to conserve the energies of his own flagging crew, and finally flogging them into one final burst right up to the finishing line, was able to win the large prize.

That night the Caid, slightly inebriated from celebrating his win, came to the cages of his exhausted and well-whipped galley slaves. As a special treat he ordered the two chain gangs to be released from their restraining chains for the night. There would be no other important race for another two weeks. He felt that he could afford to let the women excite each other and then give each other relief that they had been denied for so long.

However, he gave strict instructions that there was not to be a complete relaxation of discipline. The girls were to remain chained to each other by the neck and no talking was to be allowed.

Emma found herself reacting passionately to the touch of the two girls on either side of her on the chain although she had never been allowed to even exchange names with them, and although her back was still smarting from all the strokes of the whip-master's whip that she had earned during the race . . .

Her only regret during that long night of love was that the beautiful Zuriba, still fastened to the other chain, was not alongside her.

Next morning, to her surprise, she was unfastened from her chain by the brutal-looking Arab whip-master. She was hooded and gagged, just as she had been when first brought to the galley. She was put in some sort of craft and taken to the mainland. There she was lifted up and put into what seemed to be the boot of a car.

The subsequent journey seemed to last for hours, indeed it might have been days for all that she knew. Periodically she was taken out by unseen male hands and allowed to relieve herself, squatting on the road. Periodically, the hood was slightly lifted and she was given something to drink and to chew on. For much of the time she slept, curled up on a rug in the boot and exhausted by the combination on the race itself and the celebratory night that followed.

Emma heard the car stop. She did not pay much attention for it had stopped several times, apparently for the driver and guards to eat or to fill up with petrol. But this time she heard the noise of a gate being opened.

Then suddenly she heard the distinctive voice of Miss Marbar, the Dragon's assistant harem mistress. The Caid had sent her back to Ursula, just as he had promised!

Moments later she was lifted out of the boot. She felt Miss Marbar's hands covering her with a cloak of some sort. She was gripped by the arm and taken away. With the hood still covering her head she could not see where she was going.

At last the hood was unstrapped and removed.

Emma found herself standing in Ursula's studio in her villa. But it looked deserted. There was no sign of any new pictures being painted and much of the furniture was covered by dust sheets.

Miss Marbar silently led the way into the harem quarters. The door which had previously always been kept locked by its electronic lock was wide open. Emma looked around for Karen and the other girls. There was no sign of anyone. The harem seemed deserted.

'But what's happened? Where is everyone? Where is the Mistress? Where are the girls?' stammered Emma in astonishment.

'First you have hot bath,' replied Miss Marbar.

Brushing aside all questions, she took Emma to the harem bathroom and put her into a piping hot bath. The sheer joy of a bath again after her life in the galley and on the chain gang made Emma feel a new woman. It was indeed hard to believe that only a few hours, or was it days before, she had been living the appalling life of a galley slave.

Emma just lay and soaked. But soon her curiosity got the better of her.

'Oh, come on, Miss,' she cried. 'What's going on? Where is everyone?'

'Mistress she go back England suddenly,' replied Miss Marbar. 'She not come back here for six months – maybe one year. She shut up house.'

'Gone back to England for a year?' Emma queried, very surprised. 'Are you sure? But what's happened to the girls?'

Miss Marbar laughed. 'I quite sure. I just keep eye on house until she comes back. And girls . . . Mistress lent them to her friends.'

'Lent!' cried Emma in astonishment. 'Why lent?'

'Mistress say not safe take girls back to England. They talk to newspapers. Get Mistress into trouble! Mistress say they must stay here. And she not want sell girls to rich Arabs. Mistress too kind. So she lend to friends until she come back.'

'But what friends?' asked Emma, beginning to feel alarmed.

'Well, Mary, she go to Mistress's rich Arab lady friend. The one who has the Austrian mother and daughter and the Scandinavian girl.'

'But she was the one who . . . who . . . liked to . . .' stammered Emma, remembering her horror at hearing the Arab woman boast of how she liked to breed from her girls.

'How awful!' gasped Emma, thinking of Mary's slim little teenage figure and remembering how innocent Mary was. She had never seen a naked man and didn't properly understand the facts of life. She wouldn't really understand what was happening to her. And doubtless her new Mistress would keep her isolated so that no one else could tell her either.

Emma paused for a moment. 'But what about the others?' she asked.

'Monique, she go to Italian lady. She got bald head now just like her new Mistress's other girls. She also got harem number written on skull and on belly just like others. New Mistress like feel bald head between legs and she like girls just have numbers not names. Monique look very pretty with bald head!'

Miss Marbar laughed, whilst Emma just stood open-mouthed, remembering the sight of the shaven-headed girls of the Italian woman.

'And what about Daphne?' asked Emma at last. Daphne had been her particular friend.

'She gone back to same Saudi Princess where she was before Mistress got her. Princess want her for her young son again. Now he have his toy back again! But Mistress will still take her back again when she return. She not jealous of little boy!'

Emma thought back to her terrible experience with the Caid's young son. How awful for Daphne! These spoilt young Arab boys could be incredibly cruel to a white woman.

'And Karen gone to same Caid as you come from.'

'What?' cried Emma in sheer disbelief.

'Caid tell Mistress he want another girl to take your place. Mistress send Karen. Few weeks ago. Caid say he keep her until Mistress return and send new girl. Poor Karen! You not see her in harem?'

Emma shook her head. Karen must have arrived after she had been sent to the galley. No wonder the Caid seemed to spend so much of his time in the harem! Would she also end up as a galley slave in the Caid's galley? Poor Karen indeed!

'But what about me?' Emma now asked desperately. The words poured out. She was almost hysterical. 'Am I going to be sent to one of the Mistress's friends too? Which one? Oh, do tell me which one, please! Oh, please let it not be the rich Arab lady. Please! I don't want to be used for . . . The Mistress promised my husband I would be back by the time he returned to England. Oh, my God!'

'Don't you worry. Mistress arrange you now go back.'

Miss Marbar pulled an envelope out from her dress.

'Mistress leave ticket and passport with me and letter to immigration saying she agree you may leave Morocco. You booked on flight this evening. You go home. Mistress contact you when she wants to see you again. She give me money to give you. Three months wages. I think you earn that! Now I get you dressed for flight.'

Sitting in the plane that night, Emma thought about all that had happened since she had flown into Morocco four months before.

She remembered her astonishment at finding that Ursula had a real live harem of girls and that she was one of them.

She remembered the terrible jealousy between the girls as they vied for Ursula's attention. She remembered only too well all that had happened in the Caid's harem and in the galley.

She looked round the happily chattering tourists in the aircraft cabin. None of them would have believed her if she had said that she had been a Caid's galley slave, chained to an oar just like the galley slaves of several hundred years ago.

These people had absolutely no idea of the existence of the secret world to which she had been taken by the Caid. They had no idea of the existence of the secret world in Morocco of Ursula and her friends with their secret harems of young girls. They would, indeed, scarcely believe what she could tell them about the secret world back in England where Ursula and her lesbian women friends dominated and controlled young women. At least, however, she was not now having to wear a chastity belt!

The fact was that what had happened to her in both England and Morocco, since she first met Ursula, was quite unbelievable.

What would happen to the lovely Zuriba, she wondered as the plane levelled off after take-off. In a couple of hours she would be back in England. Already memories of Morocco were fading – although the marks of the whipmaster's whip on her back would take a little time to disappear completely.

What was going to happen to her when she got back to England?

What had made Ursula abandon her villa in Morocco, and her harem of pretty young girls, at least for the time being?

Had Ursula also abandoned her? Or did Ursula have some new plan in mind for her?

PART IV

BACK IN ENGLAND

24

Ursula re-appears

Emma had been back from Morocco, staying in her home in the country for a month without hearing a word from Ursula. She had immediately rung Ursula's house as soon as she arrived, longing to hear what was going on – and longing, of course, to tell Ursula all about her extraordinary adventures with the Caid.

But there was no reply. The same thing happened the next day and the next. Nonplussed, Emma went up to London and went round to Ursula's house. It was shut up. Ursula and her entire secret world seemed to have completely disappeared.

No longer locked into Ursula's dreaded chastity belt she was free to excite herself and even occasionally to enjoy making love to her husband – for John had now come back from his long trip to the Pacific. He was full of stories of remote tropical islands, of beautiful underwater reefs and extraordinary fish. He was so bound up with his own adventures that he hardly remembered to ask Emma how she had got on – merely assuming that Emma had as usual been acting as Ursula's personal assistant and helping her with selling and displaying her pictures.

In fact Emma was delighted that he did not press her to tell him all that had happened to her. How, she wondered, could she ever tell him about Ursula's secret harem of girls or about her own experiences in the harem of the Caid, never mind his racing galley.

Emma had slipped into her old way of life, the lazy rather dull life of the wife of a scientist who lived in the country. She was busy in their rather neglected garden. She went for long walks. She looked in on many of her women friends. She could not, however, confide in any of them. None of them would have believed a word of the stories she could have told them about her adventures in Morocco. She was even beginning to wonder herself if they really had all happened.

She had paid into her bank the large cheque that Miss Marbar had given her on Ursula's behalf just before she had left Morocco. She had already spent much of it on buying a really very expensive dress, the first such dress she had ever had.

She was also delighted to find that Ursula's monthly credits were still being paid into her bank account and even more delighted that the restrictions Ursula had placed on her not being able to sign cheques not countersigned by her had been removed. She was now, she felt, a lady of leisure.

Emma kept thinking back, of course, on all the extraordinary things that had happened to her since she first met Ursula and had been introduced to the secret world of strong dominant women and their young women followers and admirers. It had all been so exciting, perhaps too exciting at times, but certainly life without Ursula now seemed dull and dreary.

Most people would have imagined, Emma thought, that her terrifying experiences in London, in Paris, and certainly in Morocco, would have cured her for ever of her passionate masochistic longing to be completely dominated by a strong-minded man, or woman. But, she realised, they had not.

Indeed, if anything, they had strengthened her secret longings because, despite being so terrifying, they had also been so intensely exciting. Moreover, they had shown her that such longings need not be just fantasies but could be lived out in the real world.

The fact was that despite all the awful things that Ursula had done to her, Emma was missing her and her commanding ways more and more. Ursula was the only person who had understood her longings and her need to be commanded and dominated. Except for Henry, of course.

She wondered what she should do. If Ursula had apparently disappeared, anyway for the time being, then why should she not start making love to her husband again? This had previously been stopped by Ursula who had arranged for a lady doctor friend of hers to write to John, who in any case was not the most demanding of husbands, to say that Emma was not strong enough for a normal sexual life.

Even more to the point, she thought, why should she not contact Henry again?

Indeed why not, Emma asked herself. He was a most exciting man! It had only really been fear of Ursula's cane that had made her stop seeing him. And then later, of course, being put by Ursula into a chastity belt. But she wasn't wearing one now, she laughed. What was she waiting for?

Emma went towards the telephone to ring him.

Then Nemesis! Just as Emma reached for the phone, it rang. It was Ursula!

Emma felt a sudden thrill. Whatever Ursula and her secret world might now have in store for her, she felt, at least it would be exciting again. No longer would she complain that life was dull and dreary!

As usual, Ursula wasted no time in pleasantries. She scarcely bothered to ask Emma about her experiences with the Caid, or how she was, simply saying that Miss Marbar had told her that she was fit and well.

She gave no explanation as to where she had been. She was at her most mysterious. She simply assumed that Emma was now ready and available again.

Apparently, she had even telephoned John at his office and he had agreed that, as far as he was concerned, Emma was still free to work for Ursula, and help her with her exhibitions or anything else. He was sure that Emma would jump at the chance of doing so.

'Jump at the chance of what?' said Emma almost hysterically, furious at the way Ursula and John had discussed her future behind her back as if her own views were of no account. She wasn't some silly little empty-headed girl! She was an intelligent woman!

She certainly wasn't jumping at the chance of being sent back to Morocco to be locked up in Ursula's harem again, or to be lent to a cruel and vicious Caid! Nor to being sent back to the terrifying school in France for the young attendants of older lesbian women! Nor to being put back into a chastity belt again!

Desperately she asked: 'What will happen to me?'

'Whatever I decide, little Emma. Surely you've learnt that by now? And that's what you find so exciting, isn't it, little Emma, isn't it?'

'Yes,' said Emma in a sad little voice.

'Yes what?' The tone was icy.

Emma swallowed. 'Yes, Mistress!'

'That's better, my girl!' came Ursula's voice. 'Now listen carefully. I want you to help at an exhibition of my pictures in Norwich . . .' Detailed instructions followed. Emma was to go directly to the art gallery the following day and make herself useful. Ursula had booked rooms at a luxury hotel out in the country.

'Oh! And I shall have a friend with me,' added Ursula in a casual voice.

'A friend!' exclaimed Emma, alarmed. Visions of the huge repulsive Helga, of the cruel Francoise, of the snooty Mrs Guggenheim from Texas and of all those terrifying friends of Ursula in Morocco with their private harems of helpless girls, passed through Emma's mind. 'Who do you mean? Who?'

'Never you mind!' said Ursula.

'But I jolly well do mind,' said Emma assertively. 'I just don't want to see any of your dreadful friends.'

There was a long pause down the line. Emma could hardly believe that she had really spoken in such a disrespectful way to Ursula. A whole month in her own house, off Ursula's leash, had certainly gone to her head, she realised. She now expected one of Ursula's wild rages, for she knew only too well that Ursula would not tolerate any such impudence from one of her girls.

Then suddenly Emma heard a soft purring voice, something that was unusual for Ursula.

'Oh Emma, I think you'll like her, all right!'

Emma's mind raced. Who was 'her'? she asked. Did she know her? How old was she? Was she blonde or brunette? Where did she come from?

But Ursula was being very coy. 'You'll find all that out when you meet her at the exhibition.' With that she put the phone down.

Emma tried to ring back. There was so much more that she wanted to know. Where had Ursula been? What was going on in Morocco? What plans did Ursula now have for her? And who was this mysterious woman?

But just where could she reach Ursula?

Emma tried reaching Ursula's house. But the phone was answered by Rafaela, Ursula's housekeeper, now apparently back again. She showed no sign of recognising Emma and ignored her friendly questions.

'Madam is out for the evening,' was all she said, before she too put the phone down.

Emma had instructions to arrive well before the official opening of the exhibition at 3 o'clock so that she could be introduced to everyone. However, she ran into fog and by the time she got there, the opening ceremonies had already taken place.

Emma had not seen Ursula for nearly three months, not since Ursula had handed her over to the Caid's eunuchs. Emma was therefore both thrilled and frightened to see her again. But Ursula showed no sign of affection, nor of wanting to know what had happened to her in the Caid's castle. She was just too busy with potential buyers of her pictures and angry with Emma for having arrived late.

She was also very dismissive when Emma asked her where her friend was.

'She's circulating and being helpful. It's about time that you did the same,' was the only reply that Emma got to her friendly query.

There were about fifty people at the exhibition with a slight majority of men. Some of the women were very young, a few in their fifties, and the rest around thirty.

Feeling rather wounded by Ursula's cold reception after such a long absence, Emma looked around curiously, wondering which could be Ursula's friend. Might she be one of the youngest? Ursula enjoyed young women, she knew. She remembered young Mary in Ursula's harem in Morocco. Or perhaps she was one of the older women, someone of Ursula's own age who shared her taste for younger women?

Then, just as Emma was pondering the answer, a stunning redhead with fantastically beautiful and striking features glided up to her.

'Are you Emma?' she asked. She had a slight foreign accent. She might have been Italian or South America. 'I'm Celestia!'

Celestia! What an extraordinary name! What an extraordinarily attractive young woman! Emma wondered if she was dreaming. Was this gorgeous creature really talking to her?

'Ursula has told me all about you.' The young woman's voice was the most seductive that Emma had ever heard. Emma looked at her again. Celestia was slim, chic and oozing with glamour and sex appeal.

Emma felt seduced at once, even though women did not normally appeal to her. Emma was fascinated by the younger woman's huge eyes. She was also astonished that the girl was so obviously attracted to her. What can she see in me, thought Emma.

'Ursula has told me what fun you are!' she said.

Emma was nonplussed. One could never be sure what Ursula might say.

Celestia moved on, but with a wink and said: 'See you in the hotel tonight.'

25

Emma and Celestia

Two hours later, Emma had just finished unpacking in the comfortable old hotel and was getting into her bath when there was a knock on her door. Emma ignored it, but a minute later her phone rang.

'Emma! It's Celestia – like to join me for a drink?'

Emma said she was in the bath but Celestia insisted. 'Do come when you're ready. I have a double room, number nine.'

Neither of them had mentioned Ursula. Lying in her hot bath, Emma wondered if Celestia was sharing a room with Ursula, and what she would find out when she went there.

She decided to make herself look really glamorous and so instead of rushing, she took about an hour to get ready – putting up her hair and ironing her new and very expensive dress.

She knocked on Celestia's door. There was silence.

Emma began to feel slightly nervous. Where was Ursula? She had not contacted Emma since they had arrived at the hotel, which was strange.

Suddenly the door was opened – by Ursula!

'What do you want, you little bitch? How dare you come here just to see Celestia.'

'But she invited me!'

'Did she? Well, now that you're here, you'd better come and look at your deceiving little friend,' Ursula screamed and to Emma's astonishment she dragged her into Celestia's room.

At first Emma could not see Celestia. She wondered if she had been tricked, set up for something she did not understand.

Then suddenly Ursula pulled back the bedclothes of the big double bed. Emma was aghast. There was the gorgeous Celestia, naked, gagged and tied spread-eagled across the bed. Her eyes, her huge beautiful eyes, were looking at Emma piteously.

Ursula began to mock her. 'Celestia has misbehaved and you know what happens to naughty girls, don't you, Emma?'

Emma was too stunned to speak. She was also terrified at Ursula's remarks. What did Ursula mean by misbehaving? Had Ursula overheard Celestia when she had rung Emma? Was she therefore also implicated?

Or had she caught Celestia playing with herself? Both were regarded by Ursula as being unfaithful to her. She remembered with a shudder how Ursula and her friend, Jennifer, had punished her when she had stupidly boasted of deceiving Ursula with another girl. She also remembered the thrashing Ursula had given her once when she had found her playing with herself.

Presumably she had interrupted Ursula just as she had been about to punish Celestia. But Ursula's anger also seemed to be directed now at her as well. It was all very frightening.

Despite her fear of what might happen to her, Emma simply could not take her eyes off Celestia. Tied down, gagged and naked, she looked more gorgeous than ever. Emma felt that she wanted Celestia more than anything in the world. It was an animal feeling; the result of seeing her exquisite little naked body tied helpless, her legs wrenched apart, her mouth strained by the gag.

But quickly she put such thoughts aside. Such lovely creatures, she knew of old, were not for the likes of her! Celestia was Ursula's private property, just like Emma herself. She would certainly not be allowed to touch her!

Indeed, Emma thought, she herself was now in serious trouble, having been caught by Ursula red-handed coming into Celestia's room. Ursula would never let her get off scot-free, she realised. She would be punished along with Celestia. She could already feel the pain and humiliation of Ursula's cane.

Then Emma had a sudden flash of inspiration. She knew that Ursula was always very vain about her pictures. Emma had only to say that she knew a buyer or that she had just read a review of her work, and immediately Ursula would switch her sexual drive onto her art.

'Oh, Ursula,' said Emma, 'I've been meaning to ask you. Do you know that Exhibition Number Eight was reviewed in Gallery Update?'

Ursula could hardly believe it. This was wonderful and exciting news – if it was true! 'How do you know?' she asked suspiciously.

'Because I have a copy of it in my room,' replied Emma, trying to keep her voice normal. 'If you come with me, I'll show you it.'

'Yes! Yes!' cried Ursula, all thoughts of punishing Celestia and Emma now being brushed aside. Eagerly she followed Emma back to her room.

Emma did in fact have a copy of the magazine, and she had noticed something about Ursula's exhibition. Emma showed her the article. Ursula wanted to digest it in peace in her own room.

Laughing, Emma snatched the article away again and said that Ursula could only have it if she left her alone with Celestia for half an hour. She said she wanted to show Celestia something and have a little chat, which was, she lied, the reason why she had come to Celestia's room.

'So can I now go back to Celestia?' Emma asked still holding the magazine away from Ursula.

'Oh very well,' said Ursula irritably as Emma now handed the article to her. 'But only for fifteen minutes and then as soon as I've properly read the article, I shall come to see that you are both behaving yourself.'

Emma could hardly believe her luck. She slipped back into Celestia's room, her groin wet with excitement. Celestia's eyes were now bulging. Her lovely breasts were soft and ripe. She could hardly be more than about twenty-one, thought Emma admiring her body. A body still unspoiled by childbirth.

Emma rushed over and untied the bonds. She took out

the horrible gag. Then she tiptoed to the door that led to the adjoining room in which Ursula was avidly reading the article, and very quietly turned the key. Then she repeated the process with the main door onto the corridor.

Celestia and Emma just looked at each other in silence.

Emma found that all her inhibitions were disappearing fast. So used to being herself always the little girl of an older woman or man, she was hesitant at what to do now that she was alone with a younger woman.

Celestia had the advantage of being already naked. Quickly she lifted up Emma's dress. As flesh met flesh, any hang-up that Emma might have had about being slightly older disappeared. They wanted each other and nothing else mattered.

They felt one another like two naughty schoolgirls exploring each other's bodies. They laughed at Ursula banging on the door and demanding to know what they were up to. It was fun! It reminded Emma of being back at her convent when the nuns had tried to interrupt a little petting party in the gymnasium.

Celestia was also loving it. The more angry and threatening Ursula became, the more it made the two passionate young women long to ravage one another. At first they just exchanged hesitant little touches. Then their fingers became more active. Emma parted Celestia's beauty lips and put some cold cream in there. She was indeed gorgeous, thought Emma.

How sad it was, they whispered to each other, that Ursula had all her little playthings in her room next door.

Suddenly Ursula yelled from behind the locked door that she would tell Celestia's husband of how she had misbehaved with another woman.

'Husband!' cried Emma in despair. 'Do you really have a husband? You're so young!'

Celestia nodded. She was now very frightened. Before Emma could stop her, she had let Ursula into the room.

Ursula strode slowly into the room. To Emma's horror she was now carrying her cane. She looked furious, but she contained her anger. She looked around. She saw the now dishevelled bed. She saw Emma cowering on the bed, her dress up around her shoulders. She saw the marks of Emma's lipstick on Celestia's body.

Then she spoke slowly and clearly.

'So, you little tarts. You thought you were being clever, did you? I will not have you both behaving in this disgusting way behind my back. You should be ashamed of yourselves. You dirty little bitches!'

Emma and Celestia both lowered their eyes in shame.

'You will now each get eight strokes of the cane. I want complete silence. The strokes will be given two at a time to each of you in turn, starting with Celestia. You will not speak. If I hear one word from either of you disobedient little tarts then you will both get two more strokes.'

She paused. The two girls were staring at her, open mouthed in horror like rabbits hypnotised by a stoat.

'Now, when I say "Move!" you will both quickly kneel down on either side of the bed, facing each other with your bottoms raised for the cane. Emma! You will pull your dress up to bare your bottom. You will each watch me as I beat your little friend. You will both also look at each other and reach forward to hold each other's hand. In this way not only will each of you see your little friend getting her punishment, but you will also feel her reaction as well.'

She turned and pulled up each girl's head in turn by her hair, looking them in the eye as they cowered in fear, Emma still on the bed and Celestia in the corner of the room. Both looked scared stiff. Satisfied, she went on speaking, slowly and deliberately.

'And every time the cane comes down, just remember that you belong to me; that I am your Mistress, that you are merely my sluts; that as such you exist only to give me pleasure; that I do not allow my sluts to play with each other behind my back, and if they do then they both get thrashed, just as you're both going to be thrashed now.'

Again Ursula paused as if to give time for what she had said to sink into the minds of the horrified young women.

'Now . . . Move!'

Emma and Celestia rushed to obey their terrifying Mistress. As Emma reached forward to grip Celestia's hands she thought how extraordinary it was that two young married women should both be so obediently submitting to being beaten by Ursula. What an extraordinary hold she had over them!

Then, as they looked horrified at each other in silence, Emma wondered how Celestia fitted into Ursula's life. She had never mentioned her before. Somehow she knew that they would be seeing a lot of each other in future.

Emma saw Celestia grit her teeth. She saw Ursula, standing behind Celestia, tap her bottom several times with the cane. Then mesmerised by the sight, she saw her raise it high into the air.

There was a swishing noise and Celestia gripped Emma's hands urgently as the stroke was applied. There was a long pause. Then the next stroke fell.

Looking at Celestia's face as she was being chastised, Emma felt her heart strings being tugged. She looked so soft and appealing, so helpless and lovely. Emma longed to comfort her, to put her arms round her and hold her.

But then looking up at Ursula, she saw the expression of delight on her face as she brought the cane down. She saw the way her eyes glittered as she looked at the weal that her stroke had left. What a swine, what an utter swine Ursula was to beat such a delightful little creature and to make Emma witness it so closely.

But such thoughts were quickly interrupted as still in complete silence, Ursula moved round the bed to stand behind Emma. Petrified, and deeply humiliated at being beaten in front of this beautiful younger woman, Emma in turn gritted her teeth. She simply must not cry out!

She jumped nervously as she felt the exploratory taps on her bottom and on the back of her thighs. Then she too jerked madly with each of the two strokes and gripped Celestia's hands tightly.

She felt an almost savage hatred for Ursula. But she also remembered Ursula's remarks about them merely being her sluts and existing only to please her. How stupid she had been to go blundering into Celestia's room without first asking Ursula's permission. How stupid she had been to think that she and Celestia could really get away with making love by merely locking the doors.

There was a long pause as Ursula nonchalantly walked round the room, swishing the cane and bringing it down heavily on cushions and chairs. Enjoying the sight of the two kneeling young women giving little shivers of fear with each stroke.

Then it was time for Celestia's next two strokes, and then Emma's.

There was a long gap between each stroke. So much so that Emma kept thinking that Ursula must have relented and decided that they had been sufficiently punished. But then, each time, the next stroke was suddenly and ferociously applied.

Celestia seemed to be submitting to her beating with surprising obedience and stoicism, but Emma was in a rage. Four strokes to go! Four! Another two lots of two! She simply could not stand it. Moreover, she felt that Ursula had gone beyond the bound of acceptable behaviour in treating them in such a humiliating way and in making them kneel down in this way to be beaten in front of each other.

Driven almost mad by fear, pain and resentment, Emma did a stupid thing. Just as Ursula went round to give Celestia her next two strokes, she jumped up and threw the nearest thing she could find, a book, at her.

Celestia watched, shocked, as Ursula grasped Emma by the hair and threw her to the floor. Emma retaliated by rushing into the room in which several of Ursula's painting were on display. She picked up a paint jug containing a special mixture of colours.

'If you don't let Celestia and I alone, I'll throw this at you or at one of your precious paintings,' Emma screamed.

Without bothering to reply and whilst Celestia was yelling 'Stop this! It's not worth it!' Ursula suddenly rushed forward and seized the paint jug and threw it at Emma, ruining her new dress.

For Emma, this was the final straw.

She looked in horror at her ruined dress and rushed from the room, crying that she never wanted to see Ursula again, that they were finished and that she would never again help or do anything for her.

She banged the door behind her and then stood listening for a moment. She heard the swish of the cane and the dull thud as it landed on Celestia's soft little bottom. Ursula was carrying on with her punishment! It was again the last straw! She rushed back to her own room, tears running down her face.

Sobbing she looked at the remains of her new dress. It was completely ruined. It could never be dry cleaned. It had been very expensive, the only really expensive dress she had ever bought. It had cost her nearly all the cheque that the black nanny had given her in Morocco to make up for all her dreadful experiences there. And now there was nothing left to show for it at all!

Disgusted and shocked at Ursula's behaviour she got into bed, lying on her tummy to ease the pain from the beating, and fell asleep, still crying.

Emma did not know how long she had slept, but suddenly she was woken by what seemed to be a little tap on the door. She looked at her watch. It was twelve-thirty. She listened. There was a definite tap.

'Can I come in? Can I come in?' came a little whisper.

Emma knew it was not Ursula's voice. She would never speak in such a begging way. It must be Celestia! She rushed over and opened the door.

There stood Celestia looking magnificent in a pure white negligée. She looked about sixteen; all sweetness and light. After the horrors of the scene with Ursula, Emma could not have been more delighted. It was like suddenly finding a box of marshmallows, she laughed.

Celestia had been terrified of Ursula who had threatened to give her another thrashing in the morning. Unexpectedly she had managed to slip away to the safety of Emma's room. They flung themselves into each other's arms sobbing with relief.

Through their nightdresses, they stroked each other's weals in a little gesture of mutual sympathy and understanding. Celestia had been given her full eight strokes, even though Emma had stormed out after only four.

Anxious to forget their fear of Ursula, they decided to act like naughty little schoolgirls in a dormitory – girls who had just come from being caned in the headmistress's study. Celestia got into Emma's bed and they put the light out just as if they were back in school.

They would be very quiet, they told each other, in case the other girls might hear them and run and tell the terrible headmistress!

They played with each other for what seemed hours, kissing and touching each other, until they were brought to the very heights and then fell asleep in utter ecstasy – only to be woken the next morning at nine, not by a maid, but by Ursula!

Not content with just banging on the door, she rang to say that the manager would be charging them, as she certainly was not going to pay for them, unless they begged her forgiveness and submitted to her punishment.

It was a very expensive hotel. Neither of the two young women could really afford to pay. But they felt that it would be worth it to show Ursula that they were not dependent on her money.

So when Ursula rang for the third time to say that the manager was coming up if they did not report to her room immediately, they rudely told her to send him up and that they would pay for the room themselves.

That sign of independence infuriated Ursula. 'All right, you can damn well pay for your own rooms, and you can find your own way home. You're not coming home with me!' she screamed down the phone.

So Celestia and Emma had a very expensive lesson in the cost of throwing over the traces. But they put a brave face on it, and so like naughty schoolgirls who had been expelled from school, they made their way to the station, laughing at what had happened.

Then, as each was wondering when they would see each

other again, and whether they would dare do so behind Ursula's back, they made their separate ways; Emma back to Norwich where she had left her car, and Celestia back to her home in the country.

Back at home, Emma was utterly confused. Had she really broken with Ursula? Was it really worth doing so over a girl? Would Ursula ever forgive her? And if she did what punishment would she first exact? At the same time, Emma had to admit that she was longing to see the unbelievably lovely Celestia again. Oh, how difficult life was!

She heard nothing from Ursula, and she could not bring herself to ring her, fearing either a terrible scene or an equally terrible snub. Nor could she quite bring herself to ring Celestia.

Then a few days later, she was rung up by some friends in the country, asking John and her to go to tea next weekend. They understood that she knew the artist, Miss de Freville, who was probably going to be staying with them.

Emma's heart missed a beat. What should she say? Was this a coincidence or was it Ursula's way of re-establishing contact in a pleasant way?

Then, lying, she said that John would not be able to come, but that she would love to do so. It would be rather fun to see Ursula's reaction to her in a different setting – amongst her own friends, particularly since relations had cooled since their last awful row.

Emma rehearsed the meeting over and over again in her mind. She decided that she would be distant and aloof to Ursula, as if she was no longer interested in her.

Emma arrived at four-thirty. It was a lovely house and there were quite a few people staying, mainly husbands and wives from London. Out of the corner of her eye she saw Ursula . . . and then who else? Celestia!

Emma was thrilled to the marrow to see Celestia again. But she could not show her feelings because of Ursula's presence. She found herself making polite conversation to both of them, as if they only just knew each other. It was so frustrating!

Then just as Emma was leaving, Celestia thrust a note into her hand when Ursula was not looking. Quickly Emma hid it. Obviously, she thought, she was merely regretting that they had not been able to see more of each other at the tea party.

But when she got home she was thrilled to read:

Unknown to Ursula, I have booked a room at the Angel Hotel for tomorrow. Can you come? Leave message at hotel. In haste, darling. Longing to see you, C.

Emma was overjoyed. But then she remembered that she was giving a big lunch party the next day. She would have to be there! What possible excuse, she wondered, could she give for slipping away from her own lunch party?

In desperation, Emma rang an old friend and asked her to ring her during the lunch party and beg her to come over quickly as her husband had been taken ill. Her friend wasn't happy at the idea, even when Emma pleaded with her. She wanted to know what it was all about. Emma had to promise that she wouldn't be seeing a man. Little dreaming of the truth, her friend relented.

Emma left a message at the hotel, saying that she was coming.

The lunch party went well, though Emma was on tenterhooks and constantly looking at her watch. When her friend rang at half past two, she was able to slip away without any problems.

Feeling more and more excited, she drove off and half an hour later arrived at the hotel, to be greeted with joy by Celestia.

Clever girl that she was, Celestia had brought with her two schoolgirl gym tunics. 'We'll put them on and prance about,' laughed Celestia, 'as if we were having fun with the gym mistress!'

A little later, Celestia had some drinks sent up to their room, and they sat and talked about Ursula who had returned to London for a meeting about her next exhibition, thinking that Celestia had obediently returned direct to her home.

Celestia loathed her, but being in the art world herself,

found her too useful to break away. So Ursula had a hold over her and she had to play along with whatever Ursula made her do.

'Where does she get her money?' asked Celestia. 'Her paintings would hardly maintain her high standard of living. Do you think she is being kept by someone?'

'Perhaps!' said Emma wonderingly. 'But she hates men. So what would she be kept to do? Provide girls? But to whom?'

It was all very mysterious, they agreed.

Celestia mentioned her husband, but explained him away as being a rather vague poet who was very nice and did not mind what she did, being more interested in literature than sex.

Then Celestia asked Emma about her life. Ursula had told her that she had been having an affair with a brute of a man. Was this true? Celestia asked. Emma remembered that she had been on the point of ringing Henry again when Ursula had suddenly surfaced.

'Oh yes, he's a splendid great brute of a man,' boasted Emma with a laugh. 'I just wished he lived in England so that I could see more of him. In fact I was just about to telephone him to ask if we could meet again in London, when Ursula rang and told me about the exhibition in Norwich.'

'Oh! You are lucky, Emma,' said Celestia. 'I'd love to have a really strong-willed lover who would take complete charge of me. It must be very exciting! Unfortunately my husband, is like yours, just not interested.'

Fearful lest Ursula might force Celestia to tell her anything that she said, Emma changed the subject, and suggested that they resume their little games.

It was all very exciting, pretending to be little girls again.

Both girls were thinking what fun it was making love, almost innocently, to another girl without the fear and pain that came from being in the power of an older dominating woman. It certainly did not replace making love to a man, they agreed – for neither of them was a real lesbian – but it was certainly a most agreeable change!

Finding Celestia as another of Ursula's team of submissive young women had certainly been a very exciting new experience for Emma. She just wondered when they would dare to see each other again.

Then, suddenly Emma saw that it was past seven o'clock. She had to be back at eight! Reluctantly she had to rush off, leaving Celestia looking rather sad.

Just as Emma was about to close the bedroom door and run down the corridor, Celestia called out a warning that Ursula was determined to get her revenge on them both for having so humiliated her at the hotel.

'Gosh!' called out Emma nervously through the still open door. 'Well we'll both be certainly for the high jump if she ever finds out about our fun and games together in this hotel.'

'Oh, I don't think there's any chance of that,' Celestia called out with a laugh.

26

Emma is summoned to London

A couple of days after Emma's exciting weeked with Celestia in the hotel, the telephone suddenly rang, just as Emma was sitting down to lunch in her home in the country. It was Rafaela, Ursula's rather alarming Italian housekeeper.

'You are to come up to London at once!' she said.

'But I'm busy,' said Emma petulantly, annoyed at being give such a sudden order by Ursula's servant.

'Mistress say you come at once! Mistress wishes to see you.'

Emma felt a little flush of excitement run through her. Ursula wanted her! Ursula needed her! Ursula couldn't wait! Her annoyance was replaced by a little thrill of gratitude.

'I'll catch the next train,' she said happily.

It was late afternoon when Emma rang the door bell of Ursula's house in a fashionable part of London. An unsmiling Rafaela beckoned her in. Emma's heart fell. She had been hoping to be alone with Ursula. She longed to be Ursula's favourite little girl again.

Rafaela let her in and shut the front door behind her.

Then Emma gave a cry of horror as she saw standing in the hall, grim-faced, wearing her nurse's uniform and with a dog whip in her hand . . . the Dragon!

'Oh, no! Not you!' gasped Emma.

'Oh, yes, little Emma, me!' replied the Dragon in her strong German accent. 'And from what I hear, it's just as well I am back. Follow me!'

She led the way, not upstairs to Ursula's drawing room and bedroom, but to the small, bare, maid's room that she knew so well. She smiled to herself. Evidently Ursula wanted her to play the role of her lady's maid. It was a role that she knew of old – and a very exciting one it could be!

To Emma's surprise the door was evidently locked. The Dragon produced the key from the pocket of her long black dress, unlocked the door and beckoned Emma in, before locking the door behind them. Startled by this, Emma looked round the room. Standing in the corner, her back to them and her face to the wall was a redheaded young woman. It was Celestia!

But she wasn't wearing the maid's uniform that Emma was expecting to have to put on. She was just wearing a pink satin pyjama top. Emma recognised it as one of the new sets of clothes that Ursula kept for her girls to wear when attending on her in bed, as she euphemistically called it.

Celestia's own clothes were hanging in the wardrobe. Her hands were tied behind her back, just above her delightfully naked bottom. She was trying to look at Emma out of the corner of her eye, but she did not dare to look around. Her head was thrust into the corner of the room.

Emma was mystified. What on earth was the lovely Celestia doing here? Why was she standing in the corner like a naughty child, naked below the waist?

She was about to say something to Celestia, when the Dragon took her by the arm.

'No talking! Undress!' She pointed to the bed on which a pink satin pyjama top, identical to the one that Celestia was wearing, was laid out. 'You are to put that on. Hurry! Hang all your clothes in the cupboard.'

Nervously and hesitantly Emma obeyed. Was this the lead-in to one of Ursula's delightful games, she wondered, as she felt the smooth satin on her naked flesh. But being left stark naked below the waist made her feel embarrassed and more exposed than if she had been completely nude.

'Go and stand in the other corner,' the Dragon ordered. 'Hands behind your back! Nose right into the corner!'

Emma felt her wrists being fastened behind her with a soft cord. It made her feel quite helpless and submissive. She was, indeed, now as helpless as Celestia. Was this all part of Ursula's game? She could not help feeling excited.

'The young ladies are ready, Madam,' she heard the Dragon say on the internal intercom.

'Keep them there until I tell you to bring them up,' came the harsh reply. It was, of course, Ursula.

Emma turned to smile encouragingly at Celestia. They were both going to have great fun with Ursula that evening, she felt certain.

Suddenly her hair was seized and her head thrust forward.

'I said nose to the wall!'

Emma hated being humiliatingly treated in this way by the gloating Dragon, but with her hands tied behind her back, there was nothing she could do about it.

For ten whole minutes, while the Dragon leafed through the pages of a magazine and sipped a cup of coffee, the two half-naked young women, stood silently in their corners, at opposite ends of the room, like a pair of naughty children. Both of them were longing to look round at each other, but neither dared to do so.

Ursula had sounded very angry, Emma thought, but presumably that was all part of the build-up to the game. When they had briefly met for tea at the house of Emma's friends in the country, nothing had been said about her bad behaviour at the expensive hotel near Norwich after the exhibition there. Perhaps she had forgotten about it, Emma thought hopefully.

After what seemed hours the two girls suddenly heard Ursula's voice on the intercom. 'Fräulein! Bring the sluts up.'

Emma still thought that this was the beginning of an exciting game that Ursula was planning to play with them both, and for which she had suddenly decided to summon them to London. She remembered previous similarly exciting occasions.

As both young women left their corners to follow the

Dragon out of the room and up the stairs, Emma saw that Celestia was looking terrified. She smiled reassuringly at her.

'Come on!' ordered the grim faced Dragon, gripping both girls by the arm.

Emma was still feeling fairly confident as, half-naked, their hands tied behind their backs, and their arms held by the Dragon, the two young women, feeling rather embarrassed at being dressed just in their two short little satin pyjama tops, climbed the stairs that led up to Ursula's bedroom. But they were taken aback when instead of opening the door to the bedroom, the Dragon pushed them through the door into Ursula's large study, which she also often used as a punishment room.

Emma told herself that, doubtlessly, Ursula would now come and embrace them, tell them that they were her favourite little girls, instruct the Dragon to untie their hands and let them put on the bottoms of their pyjamas.

So she was shocked to see the expression of real anger on Ursula's long angular face. Her eyes were blazing. Instead of coming and kissing them, she sat stone-faced behind her desk. Instead of wearing the negligée she usually wore when about to amuse herself with a girl, she was wearing a severe black dress that made her look more like a governess than a sophisticated woman of fashion.

But what really alarmed Emma was the sight of the two canes lying on the desk. There was, she knew, a world of difference between a cane placed ready in Ursula's bedroom for a little playful use in bed, and a cane laid out for use in cold blood in her study.

She was even more alarmed when she heard the Dragon turn the key in the door, and then come and stand menacingly behind the two trembling girls now standing nervously in front of Ursula's desk.

There was to be no escape! But escape from what? she wondered desperately.

Ursula started to read a sheaf of papers lying on her desk, ignoring the two frightened girls. Both were standing up straight with their shoulders back and their eyes fixed straight ahead. Both knew better than to look at their Mistress when she was clearly in a bad temper. Instinctively, both had pressed their thighs tight together to try and hide their nudity.

They stood there, with their hands still tied behind their backs, for several minutes in silence, each wondering what was going to happen. At last Ursula put down the report she was reading. She looked more furious than ever. She glanced at the two half-naked girls standing before her.

'You vile little sluts,' she said slowly looking them in the eye contemptuously. She looked down at their half-naked bodies. Her eyes flashed again in anger. 'Show respect to your Mistress!' she barked.

Emma did not understand what she meant. Then, out of the corner of her eye she saw Celestia part her legs wide, bend her knees, and thrust her belly forward, whilst still keeping her eyes fixed on the wall behind Ursula. At the same time she opened her mouth and put out her tongue, as if she were undergoing a medical examination.

Hastily Emma followed suit. She felt her now-displayed beauty lips separate, just like those of her mouth. It was a highly embarrassing position. She felt sure that Ursula's gaze was fixed on her now prettily parted body lips.

Again there was a long silence.

Ursula picked up the report in front of her and began to read:

'In accordance with your instructions, after your departure for London, the undersigned waited outside Barnsley Hall. An hour later the young lady whom you had instructed me to keep under observation drove off in the direction of Frampton. I followed her unobserved. She went to the Angel Hotel, where I learnt she had booked a double room. Shortly afterwards she was joined by another lady, who I recognised from your photograph as the second lady to be watched.'

Terrified, Emma's breath was coming in gasps. She heard Celestia also catching her breath in horror. Ursula put down the report.

'You stupid sluts! Did you really think that I would go

off back to London knowing that you were probably in touch with each other again, without having you watched? You silly little creatures. Thinking you could be unfaithful to me without me knowing!'

She picked up the report again.

'... I was then able to take advantage of the young women ordering drinks to be sent up to their room to place a tiny radio microphone, or bug, near the door of their room. Reception varied, but the recordings on the enclosed tape, made when the young women were near the doorway, are particularly clear.'

Ursula leant forward and pressed the play button of a tape recorder. Emma was horrified to hear her own voice. It was quite clear.

'Oh yes, he's a splendid great brute of a man. I just wish he lived in England so that I could see more of him. In fact I was just about to telephone him to ask if we could meet again in London, when Ursula rang ...'

Ursula pressed the pause button.

'Well little Emma, I think that before long you'll be singing a very different tune,' said Ursula. Then her voice changed. 'You ungrateful little bitch! So you were planning to betray me were you? You'll soon be sorry my girl!'

Ursula pressed the play button again. Celestia was already trembling with fear. She gave a horrified gasp as she heard her own voice.

'Oh! You are lucky Emma. I'd love to have a really strong-willed lover who would take complete charge of me. It must be very exciting ...'

Ursula again pressed the pause button.

'Well little Celestia,' said Ursula in a grimly quiet voice. 'We'll see if you still have the same desire for the male sex by the end of the evening!'

Celestia looked down piteously at Ursula, sitting behind her desk.

'Please ... please ... I didn't mean ...' she cried.

'How dare you speak to me without permission!' screamed Ursula. 'And keep your head up! Look straight ahead! And you Emma.'

Emma was quaking with fear. Never in her worst nightmares had she ever supposed that Ursula would have a recording of her saying such incriminating remarks. But worse was to follow. Once again she heard her own voice.

'Well, we'll both certainly be for the high jump if she ever finds out about our fun and games in this hotel . . .'

'Yes,' said Ursula with an unpleasant little laugh. 'You certainly are now for the high jump, you unfaithful little sluts . . . Stand still! . . . No talking! . . . I don't want to hear any of your silly little excuses. Heads up! Look straight ahead!'

Once again there was a long silence. Emma just could not stand it any longer. Suddenly she broke position. She turned and ran towards the door. She just had to get away from the terrible punishment that she now realised awaited her. Forgetting that the Dragon had locked the door, she tried desperately to open it with her tied hands.

Neither Ursula, nor the Dragon, made any attempt to prevent her. They just watched her in silence until with a sob she gave up. She fell to the floor. They left her there for a full minute, cringing and crying in utter despair.

Then the Dragon came over and gave her a slap. Emma looked up. She saw Ursula silently beckoning her.

Mesmerised, Emma crawled back to the desk. She stood up alongside Celestia. She raised her head again. She thrust back her shoulder and again fixed her eyes on the wall behind Ursula.

Then, with a final sob of utter despair, she parted her legs, bent her knees and thrust her belly forward . . .

At last Ursula spoke again. She spoke very slowly and distinctly, as if relishing every word.

'As you apparently love each other so much, you revolting little animals, you can each punish each other for your wicked behaviour together. One of you will give the other several strokes of the cane and then it will be the turn of the other . . . I will tell the Dragon, as I know you call her behind her back, to put a little line with a marker on the skin just where I want the next stroke to go; across the bottom, thighs or belly, as I decide. And if I don't see a proper cane weal within half-an-inch of the line of the marker, then that stroke will not count. You'll then have to give your little girlfriend more strokes until I am satisfied that a proper weal has been placed where I want it . . . Moreover, I shall be standing behind the girl doing the beating with another cane – just to make certain that each of you properly beats the other. That's why there are two canes on the desk: one for the two of you and one for me!'

Ursula paused to let her words sink in to the minds of the two terrified girls.

'And how many strokes are each of you to have? Well! . . . For misbehaving behind my back you will both have twelve. But you, Emma, still have four strokes awaiting you from the punishment you ran away from in Norwich. And there will be an extra two for running away. So, little Emma, you're going to get eighteen strokes from Celestia, or more if I don't see a proper weal, and in the right place, after each stroke . . . And, of course, when it's your turn to beat Celestia, you'll get extra strokes from me if I don't consider that you are beating Celestia hard enough.'

Again she paused to let her words sink into the mind of each of the horrified girls.

'The Dragon will untie your hands and then we'll start with Emma beating Celestia . . . The Dragon will tie Celestia's hands to the bar that hangs from the ceiling in the corner of the room. Then you, Emma, will give Celestia six strokes of the cane – or as many strokes as it takes for six of them to be judged by me to be sufficiently hard . . . Then it will be Emma's turn to be hung from the bar, and Celestia will give her nine strokes. Nine proper strokes of course. Then it will be Emma's turn to give Celestia her remaining six strokes and then Celestia's to give Emma her remaining nine . . . Do you understand, both of you? . . . You'd better, or you'll both get an awful lot of extra strokes!'

Again there was a long pause before she continued.

'And there is to be no talking! But to make sure each of you is counting her strokes properly, I shall want to hear each of you bark, just like a dog, the number of times corresponding to the number of each stroke before it is applied by your little friend . . . Right, Fräulein, untie both girls' hands and tie Celestia's hands to the hanging bar!'

Moments later, the Dragon closed two handcuffs, hanging from the ends of the bar, round Celestia's little wrists. Then she went to the wall, unfastened a cord from a cleat and pulled it hard. As she did so, the bar was raised, pulling Celestia up onto the tips of her toes. Her bare soft little bottom, thighs and belly were now all prettily displayed for the cane.

As Emma looked on in horror to what was being done to her lovely friend, Ursula stood up. She was a tall woman and towered over the two young women in her power. Her eyes glittered as she picked up the two canes on her desk and silently handed one of them to Emma. She turned to the Dragon.

'Put the marker for the first stroke across the crease at the bottom of the slut's buttocks,' she ordered.

Celestia gave a little jump as she felt the marker pen being drawn across the softest and most tender portion of her bottom.

Emma looked at the cane in her hand with dismay. She had never beaten anyone in her life. The very idea shocked her. She was a passive masochist, not an active sadist like Ursula. The idea of having to inflict pain on her beloved little Celestia horrified her, just as Ursula had intended it would.

Her reverie was suddenly interrupted by Ursula snapping her fingers. It was the order for her to start punishing Celestia for having had the temerity to make love to her behind Ursula's back.

Emma heard Celestia give a dog-like bark – the signal for the first stroke. Emma had no idea what she should do. Nervously, and anxious not to hurt Celestia unnecessarily, she gave the girl's bottom what turned out to be no more than a gentle tap. There was no sign of a weal alongside the line drawn by the marker.

'You silly disobedient little slut,' screamed Ursula giving Emma a hard slap across her cheeks. 'When I tell you to beat Celestia, you damn well do so! Don't think that that one will count as one of Celestia's strokes. Now hold out your right hand!'

Ursula brought her cane down hard across the palm of Emma's hand. Emma gave a little scream and automatically tucked her hand under her left armpit in a desperate effort to seek relief from the searing pain.

'Now give that stroke to her again – and properly this time,' ordered Ursula. 'Like this!' with a sudden crash, she brought her own cane down hard across the top of her desk, making both young women shake with fear.

She snapped her fingers again. Celestia repeated her little bark. Emma brought the cane down again, this time just a little bit harder. Her fear of Ursula's cane was beginning to overcome her reluctance to hurt little Celestia.

Ursula stepped forward to examine Celestia's buttocks. The stroke had been on target, but there was no sign of a weal developing. She turned to the cringing Emma.

'So you're going to be disobedient, are you Emma?' she said with a sneer. 'Very well, we shall see! Fraülein, unbutton Emma's pyjama top and pull it back over her shoulders.'

Emma hated it as her breasts were exposed and her hands, still in the sleeves of her pyjama top, were pulled back behind her. Her eyes opened in horror as she saw Ursula raise her cane. Suddenly, Ursula brought it down hard across both her nipples, making Emma cry out with pain.

Desperately, Emma tried to wriggle her hands free so as to soothe the awful pain in her breasts. But the Dragon held her tight, and moreover, held her with her breasts still exposed to Ursula's cane.

'No! No! Don't beat me again!' Emma screamed. 'Please not there! Not there! I'll do it! I'll do it properly! I'll beat her hard! I promise! I will! I will!'

'Yes, I'm sure you will, after you have another stroke across your breasts, and an additional one for talking without permission!' said Ursula in a menacing tone. 'And after you've satisfactorily given Celestia her first stroke, then the next stroke is going to be across her little belly; low down across her little belly. I shall really enjoy watching you do that!'

The beatings continued, being drawn out by the inspection for accuracy of each stroke. The shock and pain of being thrashed on her breasts, almost overcame Emma's natural hesitation, and her desire not to hurt her darling Celestia. Indeed, after a long time she found, to her shame, that beating Celestia was rather exciting!

Soon, she started to beat Celestia quite hard, provoking screams of pain from the beautiful young woman, and also satisfactory weals on her buttocks, on the front and back of her thighs and across her belly, as Ursula varied the place to be given the next stroke.

The sight ot Emma's punishment across her breasts also had a marked effect on Celestia when it was her turn to beat Emma. Much to Ursula's delight, after only one unsatisfactory stroke, Celestia began to beat Emma quite hard, for fear of being thrashed herself on the breasts.

Emma got nine quite hard strokes from her beloved Celestia, strokes that left her sobbing with pain and humiliation, and which killed all the excitement that she had begun to experience whilst beating Celestia.

Then it was time for her to change places with Celestia again. Once again, despite the pain across her own buttocks and thighs and, worst of all, from a stroke across her tummy, she found it was rather exciting beating a beautiful girl. No wonder Ursula and her friends so enjoyed it! But her own enjoyment was tempered by the awful realisation that in a few minutes' time she herself would be beaten by Celestia again.

By the time the degrading beatings were over, both girls were in great discomfort and showing the marks of the cane on their bodies. However, they were also swearing to themselves that never, ever, would they touch another girl behind Ursula's back. Never! Ever!

'Bring me the belts, Fräulein,' suddenly ordered Ursula.

The Dragon went to a cupboard, and to Emma's shocked surprise brought out two chastity belts. They were just like the ones she had last seen in Ursula's harem before she was sent off to the Caid!

'Oh, no!' gasped Emma. 'Not that!'

'Yes,' said Ursula in a quiet menacing tone. 'You will both be wearing these in future – and I don't think you'll find you'll be able to have any more fun together . . . Perhaps it will be amusing to make certain, however.

The Dragon put the belts on both girls and adjusted them so that they were tight up between their legs. Then she locked the knee chains.

'Put the two sluts into bed!' ordered Ursula. 'And as they're so enamoured of each other, we'll leave them to lust for one another.'

Half an hour later, the two girls lay in bed in the bedroom, with the light patterned through the drawn curtains. Their arms were round each other as they kissed and consoled each other.

Their lips strayed down to their nipples and each girl found herself automatically, but ineffectually, trying to part her legs.

Each found herself becoming more and more aroused.

The door suddenly opened and in came Ursula, dressed in a tailored grey silk suit with a gold-coloured scarf round her neck on which was pinned a Cartier jaguar.

'Well, my little darlings, having fun?' she sneered. 'I have to keep an appointment, but I shall be thinking about you both . . . and when I return . . . well!'

The door shut behind her.

NEW BOOKS

Coming up from Nexus and Black Lace

The Palace of Eros by Delver Maddingley
May 1994 Price: £4.99 ISBN: 0 352 32921 1
In this, the fourth in the popular *Palace* series, the wily, randy Captain ventures into the world of erotic publishing. Once his licentious editorial team is assembled, their activities make the books seem tame by comparison.

Emma Enslaved by Hilary James
May 1994 Price: £4.99 ISBN: 0 352 32922 X
Emma's apprenticeship in servitude continues. Taken by her cruel but beautiful mistress to a North African harem, Emma discovers the sweet torment of being denied her own pleasure while forced to attend to the needs of her superiors.

Melinda and Esmeralda by Susanna Hughes
June 1994 Price: £4.99 ISBN: 0 352 32923 8
Just as she thinks she's found her life's happiness with her domineering lover Walter Hammerton, Melinda is sent to Spain to give pleasure to a new master. Far from home and victimised by her lord's cruel stepmother, the green-eyed blonde finds comfort in the arms of her beautiful fellow slave Esmeralda.

Lure of the Manor by Barbra Baron
June 1994 Price: £4.99 ISBN: 0 352 32924 6
At Chalmers Finishing School for Young Ladies, Miss Petty rules with an iron hand. All who step out of line face severe punishment – especially the pretty ones. From the manor house across the fields, Lord Brexford watches with interest, plotting to add his own brand of sexual depravity to the proceedings.

Outlaw Fantasy by Saskia Hope
May 1994 Price: £4.99 ISBN: 0 352 32920 3
Recovering from the sexually hypercharged events of *Outlaw Lover*, Fiona suffers a setback – the disappearance of a valuable sexual fantasy disc. The trouble is, the disc is so good that it will take some powerful persuasion to get it back.

Handmaiden of Palmyra by Fleur Reynolds
May 1994 Price: £4.99 ISBN: 0 352 32919 X
The author of the successful *Odalisque* brings us a third-century tale of lust and ambition. Samoya has been chosen to be the wife of the Palmyrene chief, Prince Alif: but the marriage seems endangered when she meets a man who awakens her innermost desires . . .

Black Lace Summer Blockbusters

River of Secrets by Saskia Hope & Georgia Angelis
June 1994 Price: £4.99 ISBN: 0 352 32925 4
Sexy young reporter Sydney Johnson is covering an archaeological expedition along the Amazon river. With several rugged men in the team, the trip through the jungle is steamy enough; but the action really hots up when a supernatural force begins to exert its libidinous influence.

Velvet Claws by Cleo Cordell
June 1994 Price: £4.99 ISBN: 0 352 32926 2
In the 19th century, it just wasn't done for delicate young ladies to strike out on exotic voyages of discovery – but that's precisely what Gwendoline does when she hears that anthropologist Jonathan Kimberton is going to Africa. Once the voyage is under way, the spirited adventuress begins discovering her own sexuality.

The Silken Cage by Sophie Danson
June 1994 Price: £4.99 ISBN: 0 352 32928 9
When university lecturer Maria Treharne inherits her aunt's Cornwall estate, she enters a strange new world. The mansion, steeped in mystical and erotic legend, has attracted the attention of others – notably the diabolically handsome Anthony Pendorran. But it's not just her house he's interested in . . .

THE BEST IN EROTIC READING – BY POST

The Nexus Library of Erotica – almost one hundred and fifty volumes – is available from many booksellers and newsagents. If you have any difficulty obtaining the books you require, you can order them by post. Photocopy the list below, or tear the list out of the book; then tick the titles you want and fill in the form at the end of the list. Titles with a month in the box will not be available until that month in 1994.

CONTEMPORARY EROTICA

AMAZONS	Erin Caine	£3.99	
COCKTAILS	Stanley Carten	£3.99	
CITY OF ONE-NIGHT STANDS	Stanley Carten	£4.50	
CONTOURS OF DARKNESS	Marco Vassi	£4.99	
THE GENTLE DEGENERATES	Marco Vassi	£4.99	
MIND BLOWER	Marco Vassi	£4.99	
THE SALINE SOLUTION	Marco Vassi	£4.99	
DARK FANTASIES	Nigel Anthony	£4.99	
THE DAYS AND NIGHTS OF MIGUMI	P.M.	£4.50	
THE LATIN LOVER	P.M.	£3.99	
THE DEVIL'S ADVOCATE	Anonymous	£4.50	
DIPLOMATIC SECRETS	Antoine Lelouche	£3.50	
DIPLOMATIC PLEASURES	Antoine Lelouche	£3.50	
DIPLOMATIC DIVERSIONS	Antoine Lelouche	£4.50	
ELAINE	Stephen Ferris	£4.99	Mar
EMMA ENSLAVED	Hilary James	£4.99	May
EMMA'S SECRET WORLD	Hilary James	£4.99	
ENGINE OF DESIRE	Alexis Arven	£3.99	
DIRTY WORK	Alexis Arven	£3.99	
THE FANTASIES OF JOSEPHINE SCOTT	Josephine Scott	£4.99	

FALLEN ANGELS	Kendall Grahame	£4.99	Jul
THE FANTASY HUNTERS	Celeste Arden	£3.99	
HEART OF DESIRE	Maria del Rey	£4.99	
HELEN – A MODERN ODALISQUE	James Stern	£4.99	
HOT HOLLYWOOD NIGHTS	Nigel Anthony	£4.50	
THE INSTITUTE	Maria del Rey	£4.99	
JENNIFER'S INSTRUCTION	Cyrian Amberlake	£4.99	Apr
LAURE-ANNE TOUJOURS	Laure-Anne	£4.99	
MELINDA AND ESMERALDA	Susanna Hughes	£4.99	Jun
MELINDA AND THE MASTER	Susanna Hughes	£4.99	
Ms DEEDES AT HOME	Carole Andrews	£4.50	
Ms DEEDES ON A MISSION	Carole Andrews	£4.99	
Ms DEEDES ON PARADISE ISLAND	Carole Andrews	£4.99	
OBSESSION	Maria del Rey	£4.99	
THE PALACE OF EROS	Delver Maddingley	£4.99	May
THE PALACE OF FANTASIES	Delver Maddingley	£4.99	
THE PALACE OF SWEETHEARTS	Delver Maddingley	£4.99	
THE PALACE OF HONEYMOONS	Delver Maddingley	£4.99	
THE PASSIVE VOICE	G. C. Scott	£4.99	
QUEENIE AND CO	Francesca Jones	£4.99	
QUEENIE AND CO IN JAPAN	Francesca Jones	£4.99	
QUEENIE AND CO IN ARGENTINA	Francesca Jones	£4.99	
SECRETS LIE ON PILLOWS	James Arbroath	£4.50	
STEPHANIE	Susanna Hughes	£4.50	
STEPHANIE'S CASTLE	Susanna Hughes	£4.50	
STEPHANIE'S DOMAIN	Susanna Hughes	£4.99	
STEPHANIE'S REVENGE	Susanna Hughes	£4.99	
STEPHANIE'S TRIAL	Susanna Hughes	£4.99	Feb
THE TEACHING OF FAITH	Elizabeth Bruce	£4.99	Jul
THE DOMINO TATTOO	Cyrian Amberlake	£4.50	
THE DOMINO QUEEN	Cyrian Amberlake	£4.99	

EROTIC SCIENCE FICTION

ADVENTURES IN THE PLEASUREZONE	Delaney Silver	£4.99	

RETURN TO THE PLEASUREZONE	Delaney Silver	£4.99	
EROGINA	Christopher Denham	£4.50	
HARD DRIVE	Stanley Garten	£4.99	
PLEASUREHOUSE 13	Agnetha Anders	£3.99	
LAST DAYS OF THE PLEASUREHOUSE	Agnetha Anders	£4.50	
TO PARADISE AND BACK	D. H. Master	£4.50	
WANTON	Andrea Arven	£4.99	Apr

ANCIENT & FANTASY SETTINGS

CHAMPIONS OF LOVE	Anonymous	£3.99	
CHAMPIONS OF DESIRE	Anonymous	£3.99	
CHAMPIONS OF PLEASURE	Anonymous	£3.50	
THE SLAVE OF LIDIR	Aran Ashe	£4.50	
DUNGEONS OF LIDIR	Aran Ashe	£4.99	
THE FOREST OF BONDAGE	Aran Ashe	£4.50	
KNIGHTS OF PLEASURE	Erin Caine	£4.50	
PLEASURE ISLAND	Aran Ashe	£4.99	
WITCH QUEEN OF VIXANIA	Morgana Baron	£4.99	Mar

EDWARDIAN, VICTORIAN & OLDER EROTICA

ADVENTURES OF A SCHOOLBOY	Anonymous	£3.99	
ANNIE	Evelyn Culber	£4.99	
THE AUTOBIOGRAPHY OF A FLEA	Anonymous	£2.99	
CASTLE AMOR	Erin Caine	£4.99	
CHOOSING LOVERS FOR JUSTINE	Aran Ashe	£4.99	
EVELINE	Anonymous	£2.99	
MORE EVELINE	Anonymous	£3.99	
FESTIVAL OF VENUS	Anonymous	£4.50	
GARDENS OF DESIRE	Roger Rougiere	£4.50	
OH, WICKED COUNTRY	Anonymous	£2.99	
THE LASCIVIOUS MONK	Anonymous	£4.50	
LURE OF THE MANOR	Barbra Baron	£4.99	Jun
A MAN WITH A MAID 1	Anonymous	£4.99	
A MAN WITH A MAID 2	Anonymous	£4.99	
A MAN WITH A MAID 3	Anonymous	£4.99	

MAUDIE	Anonymous	£2.99	
A NIGHT IN A MOORISH HAREM	Anonymous	£3.99	
PARISIAN FROLICS	Anonymous	£2.99	
PLEASURE BOUND	Anonymous	£3.99	
THE PLEASURES OF LOLOTTE	Andrea de Nercist	£3.99	
THE PRIMA DONNA	Anonymous	£3.99	
RANDIANA	Anonymous	£4.50	
REGINE	E.K.	£4.99	
THE ROMANCE OF LUST 1	Anonymous	£3.99	
THE ROMANCE OF LUST 2	Anonymous	£2.99	
ROSA FIELDING	Anonymous	£2.99	
SUBURBAN SOULS 1	Anonymous	£2.99	
SUBURBAN SOULS 2	Anonymous	£3.99	
TIME OF HER LIFE	Josephine Scott	£4.99	
THE TWO SISTERS	Anonymous	£3.99	
VIOLETTE	Anonymous	£4.99	

'THE JAZZ AGE'

ALTAR OF VENUS	Anonymous	£3.99	
THE SECRET GARDEN ROOM	Georgette de la Tour	£3.50	
BEHIND THE BEADED CURTAIN	Georgette de la Tour	£3.50	
BLUE ANGEL NIGHTS	Margaret von Falkensee	£4.99	
BLUE ANGEL SECRETS	Margaret von Falkensee	£4.99	
CAROUSEL	Anonymous	£4.50	
CONFESSIONS OF AN ENGLISH MAID	Anonymous	£3.99	
FLOSSIE	Anonymous	£2.50	
SABINE	Anonymous	£3.99	
PLAISIR D'AMOUR	Anne-Marie Villefranche	£4.50	
FOLIES D'AMOUR	Anne-Marie Villefranche	£2.99	
JOIE D'AMOUR	Anne-Marie Villefranche	£3.99	
MYSTERE D'AMOUR	Anne-Marie Villefranche	£3.99	
SECRETS D'AMOUR	Anne-Marie Villefranche	£3.50	
SOUVENIR D'AMOUR	Anne-Marie Villefranche	£3.99	

WORLD WAR 2

SPIES IN SILK	Piers Falconer	£4.50	
WAR IN HIGH HEELS	Piers Falconer	£4.99	

CONTEMPORARY FRENCH EROTICA (translated into English)

EXPLOITS OF A YOUNG DON JUAN	Anonymous	£2.99	
INDISCREET MEMOIRS	Alain Dorval	£2.99	
JOY	Joy Laurey	£2.99	
JOY IN LOVE	Joy Laurey	£2.75	
LILIANE	Paul Verguin	£3.50	
LUST IN PARIS	Antoine S.	£4.99	
NYMPHS IN PARIS	Galia S.	£2.99	
SENSUAL LIAISONS	Anonymous	£3.50	
SENSUAL SECRETS	Anonymous	£3.99	
THE NEW STORY OF Q	Anonymous	£4.50	
THE IMAGE	Jean de Berg	£3.99	
VIRGINIE	Nathalie Perreau	£4.50	
THE PAPER WOMAN	Francois Rey	£4.50	

SAMPLERS & COLLECTIONS

EROTICON 1	ed. J-P Spencer	£4.50	
EROTICON 2	ed. J-P Spencer	£4.50	
EROTICON 3	ed. J-P Spencer	£4.50	
EROTICON 4	ed. J-P Spencer	£4.99	
NEW EROTICA 1	ed. Esme Ombreux	£4.99	
NEW EROTICA 2	ed. Esme Ombreux	£4.99	Feb
THE FIESTA LETTERS	ed. Chris Lloyd	£4.50	
THE PLEASURES OF LOVING	ed. Maren Sell	£3.99	

NON-FICTION

HOW TO DRIVE YOUR MAN WILD IN BED	Graham Masterson	£4.50	
HOW TO DRIVE YOUR WOMAN WILD IN BED	Graham Masterson	£3.99	
HOW TO BE THE PERFECT LOVER	Graham Masterson	£2.99	
FEMALE SEXUAL AWARENESS	Barry & Emily McCarthy	£5.99	
LINZI DREW'S PLEASURE GUIDE	Linzi Drew	£4.99	
LETTERS TO LINZI	Linzi Drew	£4.99	

- -

Please send me the books I have ticked above.

Name ....

Address ....

....

.... Post code ....

Send to: **Cash Sales, Nexus Books, 332 Ladbroke Grove, London W10 5AH**

Please enclose a cheque or postal order, made payable to **Nexus Books**, to the value of the books you have ordered plus postage and packing costs as follows:

UK and BFPO – £1.00 for the first book, 50p for the second book, and 30p for each subsequent book to a maximum of £3.00;

Overseas (including Republic of Ireland) – £2.00 for the first book, £1.00 for the second book, and 50p for each subsequent book.

If you would prefer to pay by VISA or ACCESS/MASTERCARD, please write your card number here:

Please allow up to 28 days for delivery

— — — —   — — — —   — — — —   — — — —

Signature: ________________________________